HELEN ROW TOEWS

WITH LOVE FROM *Paris*

VINCI
BOOKS

By Helen Row Toews

Chateau de Belliveau

One Golden Summer
A Garden of Promises
Moonlight Over the Cinque Terre
When Love Blooms in Paris
With Love From Paris

Vinci Books

vinci-books.com

Published by Vinci Books Ltd in 2025

1

Copyright © Helen Row Toews

The author has asserted their moral right to be identified as the author of this work in accordance with the Copyright, Designs and Patents Act 1988. This work is a work of fiction. Names, characters, places and incidents are the product of the author's imagination or are used fictitiously. Any resemblance to actual persons, living or dead, places and incidents is entirely coincidental.

All rights reserved. No part of this publication may be copied, reproduced, distributed, stored in any retrieval system, or transmitted in any form or by any means, including photocopying, recording, or other electronic or mechanical methods, nor used as a source for any form of machine learning including AI datasets, without the prior written permission of the publisher.

The publisher and the author have made every effort to obtain permissions for any third party material used in this book and to comply with copyright law. Any queries in this respect should be brought to the attention of the publisher and any omissions will be corrected in future editions.

A CIP catalogue record for this book is available from the British Library.

Paperback ISBN: 9781036702892

Printed and bound in Great Britain by Clays Ltd, Elcograf S.p.A.

Chapter One

Tap-tap-tap.

With a small shriek of delight, Annette flew to her apartment door and threw it open, her heart racing. Gabrielle stood outside, leaning the extended handle of a small red suitcase against her hip, and shifting from one foot to the other.

"Ready to go?" Her eyebrows arched.

Annette's stomach dropped. She hated to disappoint her sister, but she was nowhere close to being ready. Grabbing Gabrielle's arm, she pulled her inside, the clattering of the suitcase echoing through the hallway. Today they would embark on their long-awaited journey to Canada. The trip was in celebration of Annette's four years of hard work towards her fine arts degree and she could hardly contain her excitement. Annette pushed the door closed behind them.

The small entry, that Gabrielle had kept scrupulously neat and tidy when this had been her apartment, was a testament to disorganization and clutter. She tripped on a jumble of Annette's boots, that were tossed in a heap beside the empty shoe rack, and pitched headlong toward a teetering trolley of art supplies. Just before impact, she righted herself by slamming the palm of her hand into the center of a dead fern.

She caught her breath and straightened. The brown fronds of the plant crumbled in her fingers, and she shook the remnants off distastefully as she glanced at Annette with a frown. An easel was set up in the kitchen, and tubes of paint, brushes and rags littered the table.

"Don't be upset. I know it's messy in here, and I should have packed yesterday, but I didn't have time." Ignoring the exaggerated sigh that issued from her sister's lips, Annette grasped Gabrielle's shoulders and kissed her cheeks, one after the other, four times in quick succession. "This might be a good time to remember," she suggested mischievously as she led the way through the salon, "that you love me."

She stepped aside as her sister entered the bedroom where an enormous, suitcase lay open nearly buried under piles of clothes. Gabrielle's sharp intake of breath was unmistakeable, and her eyes widened in horror.

"It's not as bad as it looks," Annette hastened to say.

"It's not…how?"

"I'm almost done," she said defensively, tucking a strand of curly chestnut hair behind one ear. "What time did you say our flight leaves?" She tucked the protruding leg of a favourite pair of trousers further into the bag.

"How can you *not* know this?" Gabrielle threw her hands in the air with exasperation. "We need to be on route to Charles de Gaulle airport in one hour. And at the rate you're moving…" she explained and waved at the cyclone of clothes spread over the coverlet, "we may need divine intervention to achieve it."

Annette giggled remorsefully and bent to grab a pair of lilac high heels from the closet behind her. She held them in the air, admiring the lavish satin bows over the toes and the long ribbons that would secure the fragile shoes to her ankles. The colour matched a dress she'd recently purchased, and she was looking forward to wearing the ensemble. Exams had concluded in May, and she'd treated herself to the outfit with a little of the money her father had sent as a graduation gift. It was an extravagance. Yet holding the shoes up in the light of the small bedroom window, she admired them without regret.

"You can't take those!" Gabrielle gasped, pointing at the shoes as though they were coiled rattlesnakes. "Put them down and step away from the closet. We're going to a ranch. Not New York City for a luxury stay at the Ritz." Gabrielle gestured at the gaping suitcase already full of brightly coloured clothes. "And this bag is too big. I didn't pay for checked luggage. Trade it for your carry-on, and pack less. They have washing machines in Canada, you know." Sarcasm lent an edge to her tone.

"Relax," Annette soothed. "I can downsize…maybe." With a sinking heart she surveyed the mound of clothes already overflowing from her bag and glanced at the closet where others she had planned to take, still hung. Despite all that she had removed, the wardrobe was still stuffed to overflowing. How could anyone be expected to make do with such a cramped space? Boxes filled with shoes, purses, and scarves were stacked underneath the full hangers and she stifled a groan of disappointment to think that Gabrielle would no doubt prevent her from taking any of her outfits' co-ordinating accessories that littered her dressing table.

She didn't want to annoy her sister, but packing was difficult. She had painstakingly curated so many outfits and loved each of them. After all, for the past several months she had eagerly anticipated this trip. Still holding the shoes, she flipped through a heap of garments on the bed and found the co-ordinating dress before folding it with care and laying it on top of the to-go pile. She added wistfully, "I have to take a few nice clothes, don't I? What if we go out for dinner somewhere? Or to a party?"

"Parties!" Gabrielle spluttered. Closing her eyes, she took a few deep breaths and appeared to be counting, then responded in an even tone. "If, by the remotest chance, we go out to dinner, we'll wear our very best jeans with a nice blouse." She tossed her signature braid of glossy black hair over her shoulder. "Honestly, you have no idea what it's like in Canada. It's not a resort, it's a working ranch." She sighed and shook her head. "We talked about this already. Andrew's mom owns a gorgeous piece of the rolling foothills near Canada's Rocky Mountains. But you're not going to sit inside the house staring at the scenery through a window. Or drink cocktails on the veranda while I gallop past on horseback. I want you to experience this week *with* me. It will be an adventure. That's the whole point in you going." Her voice rose in annoyance. Lifting a pastel-pink crop top from the piles of clothes already in the case, she examined it with deep disapproval.

Annette turned away to rummage through hangers in her closet, struggling to remain unperturbed. She chose another dress and whipped around to fling it on the heap. "But it's still a holiday, right? I want to be prepared." She folded her arms, knowing it was a losing battle as Gabrielle took another deep breath.

"Please listen to me, Annette. No one will be wearing dresses. You need to take a warm jacket, sweaters, jeans, boots, t-shirts, long-sleeved shirts, and maybe a couple of prettier blouses. It's June in Canada. Sophie said it might be cool, especially at night. And we'll be outside a lot." Despite the warmth of this beautiful morning in Paris, Gabrielle was a living example of what she was trying so hard to convey. She plucked at the sleeve of her light blue, hooded jacket with a white turtleneck peeking out the top, and leaned across the bed to catch her sister's eye.

"See," she said meaningfully indicating to her outfit. "These are the sorts of things I've packed. No party dresses or ball gowns in sight."

Annette sniffed. "Ugh, I suppose you'd be happy if I wore head-to-toe flannel. Or a shapeless, plaid sack that drapes to my ankles with a nice pair of rain boots underneath?" She lifted her hands in a pleading gesture. "Fashion is part of who I am." She looked down at what she was wearing for the flight. It had taken hours to pick her outfit: a form-fitting cream, off the shoulder long-sleeved t-shirt that exposed her bare midriff before her fashionably high-waisted, baggy blue jeans began. The ensemble was finished with a pair of short, chunky black leather boots. It was comfortable, but stylish and she knew it perfectly set off her shining halo of nearly waist-length hair. She twisted one of the gold hoop earrings she wore, and hesitated. Gabrielle would know what was best. She squinted at the heap of clothes she'd accumulated on the bed and began to rethink her choices.

"Fashion isn't going to impress a herd of cattle or amaze a pack of coyotes," Gabrielle continued to explain. "Be reasonable. I've been to Canada a few times now and it's not a beach holiday."

Although it hurt her to do so, Annette flipped the case over, dumping the contents onto her bed, and set it aside. "Fine. I believe you. Well then, help me to decide please.

But the dress and heels are going." Firmly, she set the lilac-coloured ensemble into a corner of the smaller bag, feeling her sister's displeasure but avoiding her gaze. Some things were worth fighting for. She straightened and waited expectantly.

Half an hour later, with the much smaller case rolling behind her, Annette locked the door, and tucked the keys into a zippered pocket of her purse. She slung it over her shoulder, and followed her sister out of the sturdy cream-coloured building in the Marais and onto the street below. The apartment had been Gabrielle's home when she'd attended university in Paris. Once she and Andrew married, it had passed to Annette. However, the small rooms were too perfect and orderly for her taste. She liked clutter and didn't allow a little dust to rule her life. Art and fashion were far more important.

Annette continued to refer to it as her *chambres parmi les étoiles*, or her rooms among the stars, as Gabrielle had done, due to its lofty position on the fifth floor. And she had lived happily in the apartment for the past four years as she studied art at the famous Beaux-Arts de Paris in Paris. The two women fell into step as they strode down the street toward the metro.

"You'll thank me for this when we get there," Gabrielle said with satisfaction. "And you'll never wear that purple dress, but if it makes you happy to drag it across two countries and an ocean—"

"It does," Annette interrupted resolutely. Just knowing it was tucked in her bag had cheered her immensely.

They continued the trek in silence until seating themselves on the train, at which point Annette's thoughts brightened a bit more. Gabrielle was right, it would be an adventure. She reached forward taking her sister's hand.

Squeezing it she said, "I'm sorry to be so much trouble. I should have asked for your advice yesterday. Packing on the morning of the trip was foolish."

Gabrielle squeezed back and smiled. "We're going to have a wonderful time. And maybe while we're there, we can help Andrew's mother. It's only been a year since her husband died. Running the ranch alone has been hard on her."

"Sophie, right? I remember her from your wedding."

"Yes, she was born in Bordeaux and grew up in the Dordogne. But fell in love with Mason, Andrew's father, when they were quite young." Gabrielle's face took on a faraway look. "They'd been married forty-three years when he died, and were still very much in love. I can't imagine what it feels like to lose someone like that..." Her voice trailed away. She stared out the window as the train burst from a tunnel into the bright morning sunshine. She twisted the diamonds on her left hand.

"You and Andrew shut the store and stayed with her for close to a month after he passed, yes? Do you think she'd come back to Paris? Perhaps she could sell the ranch now that her husband's gone, and leave those struggles behind."

"No." Gabrielle was emphatic. "The ranch has been her home for all those years. Besides, her youngest son Jayke lives in Canada. He moved to Vancouver two years ago, but he's home often. Andrew asked her if she wanted to sell and return to France. She refused."

"Well, I'm sure having us visit will be exciting for her and I'm willing to help in any way I can. Just not sure what an art student, fresh off the streets of Paris, and wearing a lovely mauve dress and heels could do. Maybe, I could try to rope a few steers. Although, it would probably help if I knew what those are." Annette watched her sister closely as she tried to lighten the mood.

Gabrielle laughed. "I love you, but you're crazy, you know that?"

In no time at all, they were disembarking at the airport and running through the usual stressful muddle to get through security and find their way to the correct gate. They plunked into two vacant seats, some distance from the loading area. Since the space was filled with throngs of people, most of them looking anxious and drawn. Annette gazed around her.

An older lady sat nearby, primly holding a blue plastic pet carrier on her knee, and staring with a fixed, slightly frazzled expression at the gate as though she was trying to will the airline attendants to allow her on board the plane an hour ahead of schedule. Annette knew why too. A cat yowled from within the confines of the cage, sounding as if it was being slowly strangled to death. It drew the stares of all those around her. Studiously, the woman ignored the din, pushing back in her seat to sit a little straighter.

Meanwhile, two young fathers bounced whimpering babies on opposite sides of the waiting area. One held a squirming toddler on his shoulder as he paced the aisle with the fractious child. While the other, his face red and perspiration glistening on his forehead, tried to offer his wailing baby a bottle of milk, to no avail. The child only batted the comforting drink away and renewed his howls of displeasure. Each person studiously ignored the restless crowd surrounding them and for good reason. Looking at the faces of her fellow passengers, Annette knew they were all thinking the same thing. "Please, oh please don't let them be sitting next to me."

She chuckled and turned her attention to Gabrielle who

was busy texting. "Sending a few last words of love to Andrew? Or telling him how to run the store in your absence?"

"That would never happen. Besides, I've already hidden notes around the house for him to find," Gabrielle said loftily. "If you must know, I'm sending a text to Sophie to inform her of our arrival time. Of course, it's only three in the morning over there. So, she won't get the message until we're flying over the Atlantic, but at least she'll be aware that all is well."

"Will she be picking us up?"

"Yes." Gabrielle looked dreamily out the massive airport windows, her wide green eyes getting a faraway look in their depths. "It's beautiful there. Quite unlike anything you've seen before. And the people that live and work on the ranch are so nice." She clasped her hands together. "I have a few favourite spots to show you, too. Hidden places that are only accessible by horseback."

Annette coughed. Hesitantly, she voiced a concern she'd had since this trip was first proposed. Brushing lint from the black bomber jacket she'd thrown on as they left the apartment, she mentioned casually, "You know I can't ride a horse, right?"

Gabrielle patted her hand. "Of course. But don't worry, I'll teach you."

"But what if I don't want to be taught?"

"You don't..." Gabrielle gaped at her, then smiled consolingly. "That's only your nerves talking. I promise you'll be fine once I saddle Lassie for you. She's elderly, doesn't like to move past a walk, and is quite safe for beginners."

"Is Lassie a big dog, or a horse?" Annette asked dryly, raising her eyebrow. "And, if you say horse, is she also toothless? I have no desire to be chomped on by those gigantic, horsy teeth." She shivered just thinking about it and clutched her rose-coloured Prada purse to her chest with fuchsia-tipped fingernails.

Her sister laughed out loud. "No. Not a dog, silly. And 'horsy teeth,' really? Do you think horses bite people for the sheer fun of it?"

"I don't know. Maybe," Annette answered doubtfully. "I don't want to take any chances. Is there a possibility I *could* just sit on the veranda and watch? Uh, I—I'm a little concerned about those coyotes you mentioned, too."

"Don't be ridiculous," Gabrielle began and then held up her hand as a boarding announcement was made for their flight. Automatically, people began leaping up and hurrying to form a queue. As though stuffing themselves into a cramped seat, before anyone else, was going to get them to their destination faster.

"We'll discuss it on the plane," Gabrielle said, standing and stretching. "Though first let's make one last trip to the toilet before we board."

Dutifully, Annette nodded. Together, dragging their luggage behind them, they hurried away.

Annette had been peering out the plane window for the last half hour, straining to see something below, to no avail. Heavy clouds obscured the land, and she wondered if it would be raining when they landed. As if reading her mind, the captain of the plane cleared his throat and interrupted the movie she was only half-watching, to make an announcement.

Well, that's too bad, she thought as he concluded. Apparently it *was* raining and only twelve degrees Celsius in Calgary. Although she hated to admit it, her sister had been right. She drew the edges of her faux leather bomber jacket together and zipped it as they descended through the heavy white mist and bumped onto the tarmac.

It was a large plane and their seats had been situated toward the back. So, it felt as if an eternity had passed before they were free of the mob and striding out the other side of passport control.

Gabrielle beamed at her as they turned the last corner and burst through double doors into a milling throng.

"See," she said with quiet triumph. She gestured toward the heavy-lidded, yawning people who loitered by the conveyer belt that would eventually bring them their checked luggage. "This is what we avoided." They walked past the crowd, dragging their smaller bags, and made their way toward the exit. "Isn't it wonderful? We're free to leave as we please."

"Yeah. Great," Annette mumbled, thinking of all the extra clothes she could have brought—especially an extra sweater. She shivered.

"That's odd." Gabrielle drew her phone from her purse and turned it on. "I'm sure Sophie said she'd meet us at door number ten, but I don't see her anywhere." They waited while her device flickered to life. Annette noticed an attractive man wearing a battered black cowboy hat standing near door number ten with a small cardboard sign in his hand.

The name *Tremblay* had been scrawled on the surface with a black marker. Annette elbowed her sister, who was craning her neck to see over the crowd.

"I don't think your mother-in-law is coming," she whispered. "That guy over there is holding a card with your name on it."

"What?" Gabrielle was only half listening. She raised herself onto her tiptoes and alternated between punching her phone and tipping her head one way and then the other in an effort to locate Sophie.

"That man in the big hat is staring at us. Now he's waving the paper with your name on it," she hissed again. "Do you recognize him?" Taking Gabrielle by the hand, she turned her sister to face the man. By this time, he was bearing down on them with a determined step and a face like a thundercloud.

"No," Gabrielle squeaked. But it was too late to say more as the man stopped in front of them and spoke.

"Gabrielle Tremblay?" he asked brusquely.

"*Oui*." Gabrielle answered in French, clearly taken aback.

"Sophie asked me to come get you," he said, touching the front of his hat in some semblance of a polite greeting which wasn't the slightest bit welcoming. He glowered at them both from beneath dark eyebrows. "Is that all of your luggage, or must we wait for more?" He scowled over the heads of the crowd to where the conveyer belt remained unmoving. "I'd like to get back home to see what's happening."

"No. We 'ave everything with us," Gabrielle switched back to English, but narrowed her eyes suspiciously as she peered at the man. "Who are you, may I ask? And where is Sophie? Is she alright? What do you mean you want to see what is 'appening back 'ome?"

The man turned his velvety brown eyes on Gabrielle and his face relaxed for a moment. "Uh, sorry," he said. "I should have explained everything immediately. Sophie sends her apologies, but something pretty serious happened on her ranch this morning. She couldn't get away. She was upset by it, but she's fine. My name is Jeff Douglas. I own the ranch adjoining your mother-in-law." He held out his hand and she took it, if dubiously. Their hands shook in greeting.

Annette studied him as he spoke to her sister. He was about six feet tall and slim, but powerfully built. At least, that was what she could tell from the breadth of his shoulders underneath the pale blue jean shirt he wore. The sleeves were rolled up as though he'd been working, and the metal snap buttons undone at the throat, exposing a dusting of hair on his chest. She assumed the hair on his head was the same colour, but she couldn't tell with it hidden beneath the large hat.

His face was handsome, if one liked that sort of rugged, outdoorsy look, however she didn't. His chiseled jawline and upper lip were covered in a couple days growth of beard. A leather belt with a large silver buckle sat at his waist holding rumpled jeans tightly to his narrow hips. The jeans looked as though they'd seen hard labour, with a hole ripped across the knee and several dark stains on his thighs. She assumed he'd wiped his hands on his clothes to rid them of some particularly unpleasant substance and shuddered. As if only noticing her for the first time, Jeff turned to look at her.

She was unprepared for the way his dark brown eyes swept over her from head to toe in a cool assessing way, appearing unimpressed. His face hardened once more, but he held out his hand anyway and grasped hers in a crushing grip.

"And you must be the sister," he noted. "Nice to meet you." But even as he said the words, he was already turning away. Annette felt oddly indignant at his dismissal. "I'll explain more once we're in my truck. Can I take your bags for you?" His eyes flicked from one woman to the other.

"No, thank you, and my name is not 'Sister.' It's Annette," she ground out the syllables. Really, five seconds after meeting this man she found him insufferable.

"Okay, Annette," he shrugged. "Whatever you say. Now, if you and Gabrielle could walk this way I'll take you to my truck and we can get out of here."

A comic sketch of the phrase, *walk this way*, in which the people walking behind the speaker adopted the mannerisms of the person they followed, caused her to giggle. She could imagine herself striding similar to him with her chest puffed out, taking giant steps, and exuding an overbearing air of command. He glared at her over his shoulder. Sighing, she realized he must have heard her laugh and taken umbrage.

Jetlag, she thought, shaking her head with surprise. It was causing her to become giddy and getting her in trouble.

Crossing a busy road in front of the airport, they entered a huge concrete parking garage, and she began to wish she'd taken him up on his offer. He was walking so fast that she struggled to keep pace. She glanced at her sister and knew Gabrielle was puffing too. Her blue jacket had been removed and slung over one arm. At least she'd worn sensible white trainers and wide-leg jeans which allowed her to move easier.

Perhaps her stylish chunky boots hadn't been such a great idea. Her left heel was already starting to throb. Ahead, Jeff used his key fob remote to unlock the doors of an enormous, four-door, black truck. Looking around them, Annette realized that almost every vehicle in the parking area was a similar looking truck. How strange. She'd never seen so many of them in one place before.

"I got a text from Sophie," Gabrielle whispered, falling

into step with Annette as she caught up. "She's very sorry she couldn't be here, but assures us we're in safe hands with Jeff. I was a little concerned until I heard from her."

Gabrielle flicked her long black braid over her shoulder, a trademark move, and hurried ahead when Jeff opened the back door of the vehicle and beckoned to them. He grabbed her bag and set it on the seat, pushing it to the far side. After thanking him, she straightened her purse on its long strap, stepped back, and smiled encouragingly at Annette.

Annette withheld comment on this latest revelation. She didn't get a good feeling about the man at all, and wasn't convinced his hands were all that safe. Nonetheless, she waited while he tossed her bag to join Gabrielle's on the seat and added her own thanks.

"Please make yourself comfortable," he said stiffly, as he held open the door for her to scramble inside the monstrous vehicle. She felt his hand on her elbow and felt like shaking it off. Instead, she allowed him to steady her since her rather clumsy boots caught on the chrome step.

"Thank you," she said with reluctance, and noticed him lift an eyebrow as he closed the door behind her.

She settled herself and searched for the seatbelt amongst the rubble of a hammer, a length of coiled rope, an old black and red checkered blanket that looked and smelled like it had been used to bed down a cow, and an odd-looking leather contraption that must be used to lead animals. Her mind was reeling with questions. What did this visit hold in store for her? Why was their hostess not meeting them? And who was this strange brooding man that had taken charge of their immediate destiny?

"Like I said earlier, Sophie asked me to pick you up," he explained, rattling a set of keys as he started the engine. A throaty roar echoed in the concrete parking garage. "Since she couldn't leave the ranch after what happened this morning." He reversed smoothly and they were on their way.

"I appreciate you coming to get us," Gabrielle said gravely. "And I'm so sorry Sophie is 'aving trouble. If we 'ad known..." She broke off with a concerned shake of her head. "Well, we most certainly would not 'ave come. Can you tell us what's 'appened?"

"It's been difficult for her," he said, gripping the wheel until his knuckles showed white. "But she's determined to run the ranch alone. Jayke could come home and help, but she won't hear of it. I don't think she's told him half of what's gone wrong. She doesn't want him to feel obligated." Clearly, he didn't agree with this reasoning.

"You mean there's more than what 'appened today?" Gabrielle turned to look at him, and then at Annette, her face registering shock.

He nodded, but said nothing.

It was only after he'd paid for parking and entered the stream of traffic on the busy highway, that he tilted his hat backward on his head, ran the back of his hand across his brow, and started to explain.

"I'm sure you're wondering what's going on," he began. "And I'll try to keep it simple since, according to Sophie, Annette has never been to Canada, or to a ranch before." He caught her gaze in the rear-view mirror, and she looked swiftly away.

"As you know, losing Malcom was really hard on her." He darted a glance at Gabrielle. "But she's a determined woman and was doing well, until about a month ago. It just seemed like everything went wrong. Machinery broke down, cattle unaccountably disappeared, and two of her most valued employees quit. She confided in me yesterday that she hadn't said anything about it for fear of worrying you and Andrew, or causing you to cancel your plans to come for a visit..." He paused to navigate a lane change.

"I'm so sorry to 'ear this," Gabrielle closed her eyes and took a deep breath. "It's true we did not know. Of course, we are aware it 'asn't been easy for her since Andrew's father died. But she's insisted she is okay. We 'ad no idea she was struggling."

Annette wondered if this was why Jeff appeared so unfriendly. Perhaps he thought their presence would add more stress on Sophie. It might be true, she thought ruefully, but how could they have possibly known what was happening on another continent. She stared out the window at the traffic, thinking how life could change in an instant, and wondering if she and Gabrielle could be of any help to their host. It might be best if they left as soon as possible, so as not to become a burden.

"Anyway..." he cleared his throat. "I'll leave it to Sophie to fill you in on the particulars, but the worst thing to happen, so far, occurred this morning. One of the ranch hands came to work early. He found a heifer dead and three others very sick. They had been brought in from pasture yesterday, very healthy, and put in a corral ready to be transported to a buyer in northern Alberta today. Those four animals were some of her best breeding stock and worth a lot of money, making their deaths a serious loss. No one could understand what had gone wrong, so the veterinarian was called. He came immediately and said it looked as though the cows had consumed some sort of toxic substance."

Gabrielle gasped. "Oh no...poor Sophie."

"I assume a heifer is some sort of cow?" Annette

remarked, but no one appeared to have heard her. She raised her voice. "Will the others live?"

Jeff shrugged. "We couldn't figure out how it happened, because the animals were fine the day before. They hadn't been given anything to eat, but some good hay. It wasn't until someone started the pump to fill a trough for the horses, that a strange odor was detected." He sighed heavily. "The water was turned off immediately. Fortunately, all other animals are out in pastures anyway, except of course, those four. Sophie's worried the well is somehow contaminated. She hauled the dead cow to the veterinary clinic for an autopsy and is having the water tested."

"If that is true, then it could easily 'ave killed a person?" Gabrielle gasped.

"Yes," he answered simply. "But it didn't, so that's some good news. But until the water has been cleared, no one can touch it." Jeff shrugged. "It could have been worse. Sophie called Public Health and they're sending someone out to test the water quality right away." He stopped for a traffic light and turned to look at Gabrielle. "She's a good lady. I just don't know why everything's been going wrong for her."

"There is no way we can 'elp I suppose?" Gabrielle asked, her brow furrowed with concern.

Jeff's voice softened. "No, there's nothing you can do, but it's nice of you to offer. She's had quite a day so far. She'll also have to call the buyer to explain that their deal she was counting on is off. She can't even be sure the other three cattle will live."

"Is Sophie in trouble financially?" Gabrielle asked quietly.

"That's for her to tell you," he said. "She confided a little in me, because our families have been close for years.

But I certainly don't claim to know every detail. Nor have I asked."

A nasty suspicion was forming in Annette's mind. Leaning forward to strain against the seatbelt, she rested an anxious hand on the console. Without pausing to phrase it in gentler words she blurted what she was thinking.

"We're not going to be staying with you, are we?"

She watched his reflection in the mirror and saw his lips tighten before he answered.

"Sorry for your luck," he said with a hard edge to his voice. "I know Sophie feels bad about the situation, but nothing else can be done." His narrowed eyes flicked up to hold her appalled stare.

"Yes. Until this gets sorted out, you'll be staying with me."

Chapter Two

What was it about people that rubbed you the wrong way upon sight? Annette slumped in her seat, coming to terms with the startling news that she and Gabrielle would be spending quality time with this…uh, person behind the wheel.

Of course, this situation they were in wasn't about *her* feelings or discomfort, she reminded herself, sitting up straight. Sophie was coping with some serious problems. It was understandable, but not pleasant to think they would have to stay with Jeff. She felt herself seethe with dislike for the man. Although, none of it was his fault, she grudgingly admitted. However, her feelings weren't entirely unwarranted. He'd been short and unfriendly, in fact bordering on rude since the moment he'd laid eyes on them.

Well, maybe not toward Gabrielle. But no one could be angry with Gabrielle. She was beautiful with a disposition to match. As the two occupants of the front seat continued to discuss the grim state of affairs on the ranch, Annette gazed admiringly at her sister from the seclusion of the back of the cab. Gabrielle's eyes were so brown they were almost black, her thick sweep of dark lashes fanned a porcelain complexion, and the natural ruby-red of her full lips was striking. All these attributes conspired to turn men's heads and always had since they were young.

Annette wasn't jealous. She was proud of her lovely sister. But sometimes it was hard to have a beautiful sister. She herself was plain and uninteresting by comparison. At least she didn't have to wear glasses any longer, since the laser eye surgery. Though it really didn't make much of a difference. Her sense of fashion, long curly hair, and artistic talents were the only assets she possessed. She thought of all her lovely clothes lying on the bed back home in Paris. What a shame they were left there without her. Never mind, she would comfort herself with knowledge of the pretty lilac outfit tucked away in her bag. At least it had made the trip.

She turned her thoughts to the rigid back of the man seated in front of her. What had she done to deserve his annoyance? It had been evident in his every word and gesture since the moment they met. Perhaps he was naturally unpleasant. She would avoid him…but that was going to be harder than it sounded, considering they were staying at his house.

Annette groaned inwardly. *Ugh!* This was not good. Not good at all.

The powerful beast of a truck ate up the kilometers with a low growl of its diesel engine. Before long they were out of the city and speeding toward the mountains on a busy highway. Ahead of them, a hazy blue ridge of mountains rose in the distance, just under a bank of cloud. The Rockies promised tranquility and beauty, Gabrielle had spoken so lovingly of them both. Annette edged as far to the center of the seat as she could, where she could get a better view, and wished she'd been able to bring her paints. The landscape was already inspiring her. She was glad to be finished with her studies. Despite that four years at Beaux-Arts de Paris had left her wanting to put her own artistic stamp on the world.

Jeff slowed, signalled right, and they turned onto a road covered in coarse, grey rock. Clouds of choking dust billowed behind them, but a storm swirled overhead. A few drops of rain began to hit the windscreen, promising to settle the dust.

Annette took in the rolling green hills that appeared to have no end. Occasionally she saw cattle grazing, but mostly nothing except vast open spaces bordered by the occasional barb-wire fence. Each field stretched like an adjoining, perfectly fitted carpet that disappeared over the hills.

The truck roared past fields of lush, emerald-green crops and tall fronds of sea-foam grass that rippled in the breeze like waves across the Mediterranean. She assumed it would be cut for feed, but wasn't entirely sure. She'd grown up in the city of Toulouse, in the southwest of France, and the only time she spent in the country was in passing through it on her way to somewhere else. The scenery was lovely though, and her heart lightened just from the sheer pleasure of looking at it.

The road carried along, for perhaps a half hour before they turned onto a narrower gravel track that led over a tall rise out of sight. Over the entrance a huge slab of weathered wood was suspended by chains from two stout logs that rose high in the air. On the wooden sign were carved the words, *Douglas Ranch*.

It was still a long, winding drive until they mounted a hill and looked across a sweeping valley to the buildings nestled against another rise. Seemingly, not far away, the fitful peaks of the Rocky Mountains disappeared into the looming clouds.

A massive log home drew the eye to where it backed into a stand of dark fir trees. It was two-storied and broad, with high windows that jutted to a peak in the center. Two verandas on the upper level, one on either side of the center peak, projected out from glass doors. She could see chairs for the occupants of those rooms to enjoy a fantastic view on warm summer nights. The lower veranda, on the bottom floor, ran the whole length of the structure.

A neatly trimmed expanse of lawn rolled gently down a rise at the front of the home, and bordering it was a stout, wooden-plank fence. Flowers bloomed in profusion from long boxes that hung along the fence. Small shrubs and what appeared to be perennials flourished just under the deck at the front.

On the right hand side behind the house, corrals could be seen built with metal poles. Each area was fitted with a brick-coloured shed to house animals during the harsh winters Gabrielle had told her about. Then, like a beacon, an enormous red barn rose in the background. And all of it was set against the ridge of towering, snow-capped peaks.

"Your home is beautiful, Jeff," Gabrielle noted. She twisted in her seat to see her sister's reaction. "Now you know why I wanted to bring you 'ere. Sophie's ranch is just as spectacular. Imagine living in this place."

"It's gorgeous and I am imagining it. I'd love to live here," Annette breathed, then suddenly realized what she'd said. "Uh, I mean…" she hastily corrected herself, "not specifically living here…with you. I meant this area…not this exact place." She could feel her face growing hot and fell back against the seat feeling stupid.

"I knew what you meant," Jeff said without even a trace

of humour. "My grandfather always called it his 'little patch of heaven' which sums it up about right. Although the buildings have changed quite a bit since his father first arrived here in the early 1900's, the land remains the same. It will always be part of who I am," he explained.

Maybe the man wasn't such a cold rock after all, she thought curiously, considering his last statement. Annette slid sideways to lean on the two suitcases beside her for a better view out the other window.

It didn't matter that grey clouds hung overhead. Somehow they only added to the magical ambiance of the scene. In any case, they had parted enough for her to see into the distance. Although the mountains looked close, due to their size, she was aware of the acres and acres of huge rolling hills between the ranch house and them. It was idyllic. Exhaling with rapture, she leaned forward and touched Gabrielle's arm.

"Thank you for bringing me to Canada," she breathed. "And thank you Jeff, for your…uh, generous 'ospitality." She stumbled over the correct English phrase to use in the end. Only realizing that the awkward moment made her words sound sarcastic rather than politely grateful, as she'd meant them.

Jeff stiffened. "You're…welcome," he responded in kind.

Annette's stomach curled. *Great*. She'd offended him again.

He stopped the truck in front of the house. In one fluid movement he jumped out and opened her door before striding around the other side to do the same for Gabrielle. He then busied himself with retrieving their luggage from the back seat.

Annette was glad he hadn't tried to help her climb

down. She would have felt worse than she did already, but it was too late to explain her error. Instead, she bypassed the step, and slid from her seat to the gravel driveway.

Rain was beginning in earnest now. A crack of thunder split the air, causing her to jump. Zipping up her jacket she followed the others up a flight of steps to underneath the roof of the deck. Jeff was already at the heavy wooden door with a suitcase in each hand. He tucked one bag under his arm, turned the door handle, and kicked it open wide.

"Why did you say it like that?" Gabrielle whispered in French. She frowned at her sister, as they followed their host inside.

Annette grimaced and shook her head, then quickly plastered a smile on her face as Jeff turned to look at them.

"I'll show you to your bedrooms right away," he declared, with a face devoid of emotion. "I'm sure it's been a long day for you both and you might want to wash your face or something." Still gripping their bags, he whirled away and set off across the large room toward a staircase in the far corner.

Gabrielle followed immediately, while Annette lingered to gape in awe at the living room. She'd only ever seen homes like this in photographs, or in movies, but never thought she'd stand in one. It looked as though everything in the room was made from monstrous, fawn-coloured logs, apart from one wall. Stones were inlaid to create a dramatic fireplace with a broad hearth and a good supply of kindling lying in wait.

Windows stretched up to the cathedral ceiling, following the triangular shape of the center peak and letting in natural light despite the darkness of the storm outside. Moving further into the room, she realized that the same sort of windows was mirrored on the other side of the home, offering a dazzling view of the mountains.

"*Oh la la,*" she marvelled. "*C'est magnifique.*"

"Coming?" her sister called, and Annette made her legs move in the direction of her voice, still trying to take in the surroundings. Of course, not quite everything was made of logs. She brushed past several plush leather sofas in a lovely caramel colour, a contemporary glass and metal coffee table that almost looked out of place, and an area rug in shades of burnt orange, browns, and cream that lent a cozy warmth to the room.

No deer heads adorned the walls, for which she was grateful. However, a complicated mass of antlers formed a strange light fixture that hung low overhead.

"Annette!"

With an exasperated sound, she dashed to the staircase, also made of beautifully polished poles, and took them two at a time to the next floor.

Gabrielle stood alone waiting for her. She spoke French, as they'd agreed to use English only when with non-French speakers. "Jeff has taken our bags into these two rooms," she said, pointing. "He said they're both the same, and I told him I'd take this one." She leaned in close and whispered again. "I'm hoping we won't have to bother him by staying long, so I wouldn't unpack." With this sage advice, Gabrielle shot her sister a smile and disappeared into the room she'd chosen.

Jeff emerged from the other bedroom with his brows furrowed. "I put your bag on a chair. I have a few chores to take care of. My housekeeper will prepare the evening meal. Her name is Mrs. Lewis," he said with great formality. "When you're ready feel free to go downstairs and make yourselves comfortable. Dinner will be at six." He pulled his hat, still glistening with raindrops, farther down on his head, and turning on his heel walked to the head of the stairs.

"I do appreciate all you're doing for us," she called faintly. He paused for the briefest of moments, then touched the brim of his hat in answer, and clomped downstairs.

Annette moved, rather robotically, to the room she'd been assigned. So much had happened since the morning. She yawned and her eyes felt heavy. She wondered if it would curb or prolong the problems of jetlag if she laid down for a nap.

Then she stepped into the room and snapped awake. If she had thought the downstairs was beautiful, this space was absolutely fantastic. Her room was built into the corner end of the house which meant she had windows on two walls—but what windows! A queen-sized bed sat against a whole wall of them, all looking out on the white peaked Rockies in the distance. Heavy brocade drapes of mossy green, sprinkled with pink roses, were pulled to either side. The material co-ordinated perfectly with the bedspread and pillow shams. A beautiful night table made from the fat knotted trunk of a tree had been varnished until it was glossy. On top of it sat an ornate lamp in the shape of an old-fashioned urn, also in a pretty shade of rose.

An arched door, tucked on the other side of the room must lead to a bathroom. She'd make use of that soon, but first to explore.

The other wall was the one she'd seen from the road with double glass doors leading to a sheltered sundeck outside, but the design wasn't rectangular and basic. They were gracefully rounded at the top and set into the heavy logs making her feel as though they led out of a Hobbit hole into some fantastic tale of magical proportions. She walked to them, drawn by the loveliness of the design, and stepped outside.

About twenty horses grazed in a pasture nearby and as she watched, they lifted their heads as if on cue to peer at something. Following their line of vision, she saw Jeff, wearing a long raincoat and rubber boots, walk toward the animals carrying a pail and some sort of harness. He set the pail to one side, looping the harness over one arm, and reached over the wooden rails to pat them as they trotted over to greet him. Then, he unlatched the gate and slid inside. He lifted the halter and fastened it over the head of one white horse. Deftly he manoeuvred the beast by itself out the gate before closing it behind him.

As the horse joined him, even from this distance she could see that it wasn't young. Its head hung low against the driving rain. The animal moved slowly beside him as Jeff picked up the bucket and headed off toward the barn. Tugging her purse from where it hung at her side, she dug around for her cell phone and turned it on. Annette lifted it, adjusted the settings a little, and took several pictures.

The pair disappeared inside the barn and Annette felt a tug at her heart. The man was kind to animals. It was obvious, even to her, that he had taken the old horse out of the lashing rain, giving it something extra to eat where it would be warm and dry.

She turned away, not wanting to feel anything for her unwilling host, and looked up. The room was in the eaves and high above her head the ceiling rose to a peak showing a skylight.

Her jaw dropped in astonishment. She would be able to lie in bed and count the stars tonight if it stopped raining. Flopping onto a mossy green, velvet chair, like the one where Jeff had set her bag, she hooked a footstool with one foot and pulled it in front of her. She sank into the luxurious depths, propped her feet up, and contemplated her room.

"I don't think I ever want to leave," she muttered, hugging herself with glee. If it wasn't for their unpleasant host, it would be perfect. But then she thought of Sophie and the reason they were here with Jeff. No. It wasn't ideal, she chided herself.

She looked at the phone in her hand. How unusual that she hadn't checked for messages since arriving. Except there had been too much to see and think about for that, she supposed. Besides, all of her friends knew she was on holiday. Her relationship with Philippe had ended five months ago, so there was no one special in her life that would care she was gone for the next week. She dropped the phone back in her small, quilted circle purse, letting it slide to the floor as she folded her hands over her stomach and simply gazed about her.

A light tap came at the door.

"Come in," she called, jumping to her feet, and hurrying to open the door. It must be Gabrielle, wandering over to check on her. Well, that was good. She hadn't had a chance to speak privately with her sister since landing.

But it wasn't her. Instead, a solid-looking woman, her longish blonde hair greying at the roots, and scraped into a ponytail, stood in the doorway with hands on hips. She wore a bright purple tracksuit that was, perhaps, a size too small. The lady appeared to be somewhere in her fifties, Annette gauged, with hazel eyes, an upturned nose, and a face lined from hard work in a harsh climate.

"Bun-jure," she said haltingly, and her mouth relaxed into a sheepish grin. "Sorry, my dear. I know that was a terrible attempt to greet you in your own language, but you have to give me marks for trying. I took French classes all through high school, but nothing really sank in." She tapped her forehead and rolled her eyes with a laugh. Annette liked her instantly.

"It is nice to meet you. You must be Mrs. Lewis?"

The lady nodded vigorously. "I am. I've just come up to tell you and your sister that supper will be ready in half an hour. Oh, and to check if you needed anything."

Annette shook her head. "I've never seen such a pretty bedroom," she said. "I 'aven't looked at the bath, but I'm sure it 'as everything I'd ever need. Thank you."

"You're most welcome." Mrs. Lewis backed away and turned toward Gabrielle's room, lifting a hand to knock.

"I can tell Gabrielle if you like," Annette offered, stepping into the hall. "I'd like to see 'er room anyway."

The plump little lady grinned. "Mercy," she called, and headed off downstairs.

Now that Annette had thought about food, she could smell the most tantalizing aroma and sniffed appreciatively. The last meal she'd eaten was on the plane, and it hadn't been great.

"*Oui?*" Gabrielle responded to the tap on her door. "Isn't it lovely?" she went on rapturously, as Annette opened the door and stepped inside. And it was, but not quite as beautiful as her own, she thought privately. The décor was similar, except the colour scheme was turquoise and cream. The room had the rounded doors leading outside, but no windows over the bed and no skylight.

"The rooms are wonderful," Annette agreed. "I feel quite spoiled. Is it this nice at Sophie's house?"

"No. Not really. It's a nice home, of course, and the setting is fantastic, but hers is much older. This house is something outstanding, don't you think?" Gabrielle's smiling face suddenly fell. "I am so worried about Sophie. I wonder if Jeff has heard from her yet."

"We'll know soon enough. Mrs. Lewis, the housekeeper, was just at my door to say dinner would be ready soon." She sidled close to her sister. Even though they were alone, she whispered. "I feel strange about staying with the neighbour. Especially since he isn't all that friendly. And it doesn't seem like there's anything we can do to help Sophie. Do you think we should try to get a flight back home tomorrow?"

Gabrielle raised a hand to her forehead as if she had a headache and walked to the glass doors to look outside. "I understand how you feel and I'm sorry. This was supposed to be a celebration of your achievements, a wonderful time for you and me to share. But I can't leave until I know what's happening with my mother-in-law, and offer my help." She glanced at her watch. "It's five here, so well after midnight in Paris…and too late to call Andrew. I sent him a message to say we'd arrived, but that's all he knows." She spread her hands in a helpless gesture. "There may be nothing we can do, but I can't leave either. If Andrew were here he would stand by her and do all he could…" her voice trembled. "I love Sophie like my own mother."

"Oh Gabby," Annette rushed across the room and flung her arms around her sweet sister, reverting back to the childhood name she'd called her. "I'm so selfish! Naturally, you want to stay and help if you can. We'll both do whatever possible to sort this out. Please forgive me."

They stood together for a few moments before Gabrielle stepped back and dabbed at her eyes with a crumpled tissue she pulled from her pocket.

"It's okay. I feel strange too, and I'm not entirely comfortable staying with her neighbour. But he has been kind, and you have to admit," she gave Annette a watery smile, "it's sort of like being at a resort."

Annette giggled in an effort to lighten the mood. Linking her arm through her sister's own, she tugged her gently to the door. "Let's go downstairs and see what Mrs. Lewis has made to eat. It smells divine and she's a sweetheart." She stopped and pulled her sister around to face her. "And don't give me another thought. I'm fine really. I'm with you in this, okay?" She gazed at her sister with love.

Gabrielle nodded and together they walked downstairs to find the kitchen.

The smell of roasting meat drew them like moths to a flame. Once reaching the main floor, they turned left. Altogether avoiding the living room and continuing down a short hallway till the sounds of clanging pans announced they had arrived at their destination.

The kitchen was rustic yet thoroughly modern in design. Beside them and set in front of another wall of windows, was a long dining table that could easily seat fifteen people. Curving away from it was a horseshoe-shaped bar with frosted glass lamps dangling from long metal hangers. Behind the bar, the kitchen opened up to a rock wall on one side that housed two large gas ranges and a professional-looking, indoor grill. Wooden doors with heavy black metal handles covered cupboards, drawers, and what looked like a walk-in pantry. And overtop an island workspace hung a metal rack holding antique kitchen implements, some of them resembling instruments of torture.

Mrs. Lewis had covered her purple track suit with a voluminous white apron that bore the words, *'Never trust a skinny chef,'* across the front. She bustled out from behind the bar to greet them.

"You must be Sophie's daughter-in-law, Gabrielle," she said warmly and nodded approvingly as Gabrielle spoke.

"*Oui*. I am glad to meet you Madame Lewis. The dinner smells wonderful. Thank you."

"Please, both of you call me Sandra. My husband's mother was the real Mrs. Lewis. She was a lovely woman, but a terrible cook." Sandra rolled expressive eyes and laughed. "Now, why don't you two sit here at the bar and talk with me while I finish making the meal?"

Needing no further encouragement, they hopped onto stools. Annette sniffed appreciatively. "What are you cooking?" she asked. "And could I 'ave the recipe?"

"My goodness yes," Sandra grinned at them over a pot of steaming potatoes. "But it's pretty simple. When you work on a ranch where they have all the cattle Jeff does, you get good at roasting beef." She plunked the pot down and flung open a drawer to scrabble inside. After a moment, she withdrew an electric hand mixer, fitted it with metal beaters, and plugged it into the wall.

"Excuse me a minute," she announced. "It's going to get loud in here." They stared, fascinated as she added butter, chives, and sour cream to the pot. She picked up the mixer, flipped the switch on high, and brandished it in the air as though auditioning for a part in the next Chainsaw Massacre movie, before thrusting it into the steaming heap of cut vegetable.

"My children often tell me I'm too dramatic," she proclaimed, yelling at them over her shoulder. "But if a person can't have a little fun, life would be boring. Don't you agree?"

Annette looked at Gabrielle and the sisters grinned. It was true. Sandra scooped the potatoes into a bowl and added a sprinkle of cheese to the top before popping it into an oven. She wiped her hands on her apron and faced them.

"Would you like a drink? Water, juice, tea, or maybe a glass of wine? We have most anything you could want."

They both asked for a glass of water. Sandra bustled across the kitchen to grab two glasses from an overhead cupboard and held them one at a time under the water dispenser of a massive refrigerator. Ice rattled, hitting the bottom before water splashed inside.

"There you are," she said brightly, setting them down with a clunk on the bar. "Did you have a good flight? Must have surprised you to have Jeff waiting at the airport?" She raised eyebrows at them as she hurried away to fling open another cabinet door and reach for plates. These were piled onto the counter with a handful of cutlery tumbled on top. Then she was off again flitting about to snatch a pair of heavy red oven mitts from another drawer and pull them on.

"The flight was fine," Annette answered. "But we did *not* expect to be met by…Jeff." His name was forced from her lips. She knew she should feel grateful for what he was doing, but her instant dislike of the man made it difficult.

Sandra cast her a sideways glance, but said nothing. She opened the second oven and stepped back from the heat before diving in for the dish. The meat was a sizzling, golden brown, its exterior glistening with savory juices as the mouth-watering aroma wafted through the air in waves. Annette's stomach growled.

"And you've never been to Canada before?" Sandra asked, straining the juices into a saucepan, and covering the roast with aluminum foil before setting it aside.

Mesmerized by this whirling dervish of a woman, Annette sat spellbound until she realized she could at least help out by setting the table. Whisking off the stool, she hurried around the bar.

"No, I 'ave never been outside of Europe," she answered. "It is beautiful here."

"Why thank you, Annette," Sandra said, as Annette scooped up the dishes and carried them to the table. "Just throw them down at the far end. Well," she added with a wink, "perhaps 'throw' was a poor choice of words. It might be best if you set them gently." She turned back to her work. "And I'm so glad you liked your first glimpse of the Rockies. I'm sure you two will find plenty of interesting things to see and do while you're here."

As Annette busied herself, she wondered who each place setting was for. There were six in total, but who would be occupying the chairs was none of her business. So, she set each blue plate onto the cheerful yellow mats stacked at the center of the long oval table, and kept her curiosity to herself.

Gabrielle helped by finding heavy glass tumblers and bringing them over. "I 'ave a variety of activities planned for my sister," she announced, loud enough for Sandra to hear over the busy sounds of stirring that now emanated from the kitchen, "but I'm not sure what will 'appen with Sophie's ranch. We don't want to be in the way."

Sandra turned to them with her mouth open, as though about to speak, with a metal whisk raised and dripping in the air. Any further remarks were interrupted by the sound of a door crashing shut at the front of the house. Then voices could be heard, and footsteps approached. All three women turned to the double swinging doors, much like what might be featured at the entrance of a saloon in an old western movie, to see who was coming inside.

The doors flew open, and two women marched

through. One was Sophie, but the other was a dark-haired woman dressed completely in denim and wearing a ball cap. Gabrielle rushed to throw her arms around Sophie. She was tall like her son, Andrew, with short hair that was far greyer than Annette remembered.

"My dear girl!" Sophie gushed, folding Gabrielle into a loving embrace. "It's *so* good to see you." She kissed Gabrielle's cheeks three times, before sliding an arm around her daughter-in-law's waist. The older woman led the way to where Annette was standing, wringing her hands—unsure of herself. Clearly it was a terrible time for them to visit, and part of her felt as though they ought to get back on a plane and return to France. She clasped her hands together, knowing her smile was wobbly.

But, as the two women approached, she relaxed a little. Sophie looked so genuinely happy to see them both that it warmed Annette's heart. At least for the moment she wouldn't allow herself to worry.

Sophie met her gaze with a broad grin, slipped her arm free of Gabrielle with a final squeeze, and stretched both hands out to Annette. What a striking woman. Without wearing a bit of makeup, Sophie was beautiful. Her icy blue eyes, the same as her son Andrew's, held Annette's gaze with a look of genuine welcome. Lines at their corners and near her mouth spoke of laughter and of the smile always on her lips. Today, of course, there was a tiredness in her expression, and she moved slowly across the floor. Annette's heart went out to this hard-working woman who had been struggling to keep her family ranch running smoothly after the death of her husband.

Because Annette always noticed what people wore, she took in the simple pair of jeans over cowboy boots, the long brown jacket, stained and worn from long years of use, and pulled in at a narrow waist with a drawstring. It was zipped up to Sophie's neck as though offering a thin veneer of protection from the worries that plagued this beautiful lady. Annette was swept into her arms and given the very same effusive welcome as Gabrielle.

"I am so glad you came to see me," Sophie said, still with a trace of French accent. "I am only sorry I could not be there to greet you at the airport." She shrugged and a look of sorrow crossed her lovely features.

"*Merci beaucoup*," Annette said. "Thank you for asking me to visit. I'm sorry we came at such an inopportune time."

"Nonsense," the lady said, turning to capture Gabrielle with her free hand and pull all three of them together for a hug. "No one could have predicted the future. I'm pleased you're both here." Letting them go, she ran a hand through her closely cropped hair and shook her head. "It was a difficult day, but enough of that for now."

Stepping back, Sophie closed her eyes and took a deep breath. She looked pale and tired, but her eyes sparkled as she looked across the kitchen at Sandra who had gone back to her meal preparations with renewed zeal. "I see my dear friend has been busy cooking us a wonderful meal. No doubt Jeff has told you both that you'll be staying with him until our water problem is fixed?" A cloud crossed her face.

"Yes," Gabrielle said. "It's very kind of him, but I'm worried about you. Is everything alright?"

A crack of thunder split the air, and lightning flashed outside causing the lights to flicker and her words to appear almost ominous. Simultaneously, the rain outside turned into hard pebbles of hail that clattered against the many windows of the home. The sound became almost deafening.

Sophie hurried to the window and squinted at the sky.

"It was supposed to rain heavily today, but hail is unexpected. This will make everything just a little more difficult," she added cryptically. Then, with a forced lifting of her eyebrows and a smile, she beckoned to them. "Come," she shouted over the din, "let's sit. I want to introduce you to Rosa. She started working for me a few months ago and I don't know what I'd do without her. Rosa manages the books and works alongside me at the ranch. She has been invaluable over the last few months."

At this, the tall, dark-haired woman stepped forward with her hand outstretched. She didn't look exactly happy to see them, in fact her face resembled the thunderclouds outside, but Annette put that down to the concern they were all feeling. Rosa's lips were pursed with disapproval, or so it appeared, and her grey eyes were cold as flint, but she was a pretty woman with bobbed hair and a nice figure. When she wasn't scowling, she was probably quite attractive. She wore the ubiquitous jeans and matching jacket that Gabrielle had once laughingly referred to as the Canadian tuxedo. Beneath the jean jacket was a pale blue t-shirt. At least her colour palate was consistent, although monochrome.

"Rosa, this is my daughter-in-law Gabrielle and her sister Annette. They flew in from Paris this morning."

Rosa's lips stretched across her teeth, but it couldn't really be called a smile. It was a bit foreign to shake so many hands, but Annette knew customs in Canada were different than those in France, and she murmured a polite greeting as they shook.

"I'm pleased to meet you," said Rosa. "We hope to get you back to Sophie's house as soon as possible. It's unfortunate you're forced to stay with Jeff." She moved to the opposite side of the table and sat, pushing the plate out of her way as she folded her hands on the table. Gabrielle joined her.

Annette took the chair Sophie pulled out for her, seating herself beside the older woman who dropped into a chair. "The rooms are lovely," she said, "and from what I can tell, Sandra is a wonderful cook, so we will not be suffering. But of course, I 'ope the problems are soon fixed." She looked at Sophie with lifted brows, eager for good news.

"I'm waiting for a call from our veterinarian," Sophie shrugged out of her coat and hung it on the back of her chair. "Until then, I know nothing. The animal that died was taken to the vet clinic for an autopsy. I must learn the results as soon as possible and then take whatever action is necessary."

"I'm so sorry." Gabrielle shook her head.

"Yes, my dear, I know," Sophie forced an unsteady smile. "But these things happen when you raise animals. Knowledge is power. Once we know what happened to them we can proceed." Taking a phone out of her pocket, she placed it on the table in front of her and tapped it to make sure there were no messages.

"You really think something seeped into the water?" Gabrielle's forehead was creased with worry. "Perhaps there was a noxious plant in the feed?"

"*Ne t'inquiète pas, mon lapin.*" Sophie slipped into her native French as she hastened to reassure her daughter-in-law. After all these years her accent had nearly disappeared, but her ability to speak the language remained. "Please don't worry, my dear" she translated. "To have one animal die might mean a natural cause, or something like you suggest, but when the other three are also very sick…? No. Something drastic would have happened to cause this. One must be pragmatic and look for an external reason." She shrugged. "But please, let's not talk of that now. Soon you girls will come to stay with me."

"Are you sure we couldn't stay there now?" Annette asked hopefully. "Perhaps we could help with something."

"No, no, there is no water," Sophie shook her head. "It's best you stay with Jeffrey. He'll take good care of you and can bring you to visit me during the day. Perhaps 'e will even lend you a truck, so you may come and go as you please. Everything will be back to normal soon, I promise. Then I shall 'ave you to myself." She swung around and flashed them a bright smile. "There are many things planned for us to do."

"Parties?" Annette asked without thinking. Her thoughts had immediately flashed to her pretty purple dress, but she could have kicked herself when all eyes turned to her in surprise.

"Were you hoping for a cotillion where you could wear a ball gown and satin slippers to be introduced to all the eligible males in the district?" a male voice asked dryly from the doorway.

Annette jumped. She threw a hand up to her throat to calm her racing heart and felt her cheeks flush. It was so close to the truth that she felt like a fool. Where had *he* come from? And why, of all moments, had he chosen to walk in at that one. The man was unbearable.

"Jeff," Sophie spoke his name in a reproachful tone. "She's never been to Canada before and doesn't understand how a ranch operates." Turning to Annette, she caught her hand and squeezed. "Don't pay any attention to him, my dear. I'd like both of you to tell me about your graduation and how Andrew is doing with the store."

Annette's face was hot with embarrassment. She hadn't meant to blurt that word. Clearly the foolishness of it had shocked the whole group into silence. It was all because she and Gabby had argued about the lack of social events on this trip that the word, parties, had jumped to her lips.

Jeff strode to the table and, for the first time, Annette saw him without a hat. His hair was darker than his eyes, almost black, and pushed straight back off his forehead while the back curled over his ears and collar. He pulled out the chair on Sophie's other side, sat, and was blocked from her view.

Instead, Annette's attention was caught by the sudden flurry of activity across the table. Rosa had whipped off her hat and tossed it to one side. Then she pulled the ponytail free from its elastic and was fluffing her hair with both hands, her cheeks suffused with colour.

Granted, not as flushed as Annette, but why was Rosa embarrassed? Annette narrowed her eyes. Oh, it wasn't embarrassment. She watched as the young woman darted a look at Jeff and realized Rosa was attracted to their host. Interesting. She wondered if the sentiment was shared by Jeff, then her ears picked up on what he was saying.

"Dr. Roberts was just here."

"He was? Then where is he?" Sophie craned her neck to look out the window and into the driving rain.

"He couldn't stay because he wants to go check on the three heifers in the barn. He's hoping they've improved since he treated them this morning."

"Okay…" Sophie took a deep breath. "And what did he learn from the autopsy?" Sophie's hands clenched together on her lap. Annette couldn't see her face, but she could feel the tension as the lady braced herself for the worst.

Jeff reached out and covered her hands with his large ones. "He said they were poisoned, and that it was only extreme thirst that drove them to drink the water, because it was about fifty percent pesticide."

Sophie tore her hands away and covered her face with a groan, her back heaving.

Jeff placed a hand on her shoulder. "There's more."

"More…?" Her voice was strangled.

"He thinks someone poured jugs and jugs of the stuff into your well. They deliberately poisoned those animals… and it could have just as easily been one of you that died. Of course, you would have smelled the chemicals, but the intention was there, nonetheless. This was no accident, my dear friend. I'm doubting that all the other problems you've had lately were simply bad luck. I believe someone is out to destroy you."

Chapter Three

Dinner was a grim affair.

"I do apologize Sandra," Sophie called in a quavering voice, "but I'm just not hungry." To Jeff she said, "I—I have to go." She half rose from her chair, but he gently pulled her back into her seat.

"I know you want to get home in order to speak with Roberts and check on your animals, but they're in good hands and I doubt if you've eaten all day," he said. "Am I right?"

She shrugged.

"Okay, then eat something and I'll drive you over there myself. I don't feel good about you going on your own anyway."

He was solicitous, bordering on super nice, and Annette could almost see why Rosa was so enamoured. She turned her gaze to the young woman who was digging into a pile of mashed potatoes like she was shovelling snow. None of this news appeared to have affected *her* appetite in the least.

"That's right," Rosa agreed, her words slightly garbled

as she swallowed and lifted another heavily laden forkful to her mouth. "You have to take care of yourself. Jeff and I will drive you over later." Gravy dripped down Rosa's chin and her eyes flashed to Jeff as she hastily wiped it with her napkin.

Blinking in surprise, Annette turned away. Sophie slumped at the table, white-faced and trembling, but she didn't argue. Gabrielle put some food on her plate and Sophie pushed it from side to side, picking up a small mouthful here and there.

Everyone must feel the same way. They wanted to help, but there was nothing any of them could say or do to alleviate her worries. The authorities would need to be involved now. The situation had become much more serious than had been anticipated and Annette wished fervently, yet again, that they hadn't come. Their presence could only make matters worse, as Sophie would feel an obligation to them, and Jeff would be forced to keep them as his guests. *Great.*

She looked down at her own food. It was difficult for any of them to do justice to the fabulous meal Sandra had prepared. Well, except for Rosa it appeared. The woman busily helped herself to seconds of the delectable meal. She indulged in a heavy-handed application of the rich and flavourful gravy, pouring it liberally over the potatoes, slices of juicy roast beef, and crispy Yorkshire puddings on her loaded plate. Annette gazed around the table, noting that the rest of them weren't able to gum down more than a few mouthfuls. It was a terrible state of affairs.

Scraping her chair away from the table, Sophie stood to her feet and dragged on her coat. Rain still pelted down outside, and the gloom of the evening only added to the greyness everyone felt. Annette knew without being told that she and Gabrielle could not go to Sophie's ranch now. If the poisoning had been a deliberate attempt to scare the lady, or to threaten the continued operation of Sophie's Triple T Ranch, then it had worked.

"I must go," Sophie muttered.

"Of course," Jeff said, already helping her on with her coat. "And I'll drive, but once we make sure everything is okay, you'll come back here for the night. Agreed?" He bent to look inquiringly into her face as though she were a small child. "And Rosa too," he added with a quick smile for the other woman.

Sophie shook her head. "I can't leave the ranch unattended. We don't know who did this, Jeff. What if they strike again? What other damage might they do?" She straightened her back, a picture of resolution. "I won't leave my home."

"You don't have water," he stated reasonably. She opened her mouth to object, and he lifted a hand. "And," he continued, "you, alone, will not be able to stop whoever is doing this to you and your ranch. Look what took place last night while you were there. No. You need help and twenty-four hour surveillance. I've already hired a security company to stay there for a few nights."

"You did what?" she took a step back.

"I went over your head, and I apologize, but you know Malcom wouldn't have wanted you there alone, and neither do any of us, here. Right?" Jeff crossed his arms across his chest and looked around the table.

Annette scrunched her paper napkin into a ball and set it onto the table. "We're all concerned about you Sophie. I agree with Jeff."

"Yes," said Gabrielle. "Please let him help you Sophie." She rose to her feet and went to put her arms around her mother-in-law. "Andrew would want you to stay safe, too. Please?"

Rosa got to her feet as well. "It's the best thing to do," she said, reaching for her jean jacket. "Thanks for a marvelous supper, Sandra. I don't suppose there was dessert?" She looked expectantly at the housekeeper who stood wringing her hands at the other end of the table.

But Sandra didn't answer her. "Sophie, ma'am," she said, "For what it's worth, I think you'd best do what Jeff says too. We'll all sleep a whole heap better if you're under this roof where you're out of harm's way. And I've made a delicious chocolate cake that we'll have in the living room when you get back. I'll even start the fire, so we can cozy up after this storm."

Sophie smiled wanly. "I suppose you're right." She laid a hand on Jeff's arm. "I know you're doing what you think is best, and I appreciate it. I just don't like the thought that I've been scared away from my own home."

"That makes sense," said Rosa, ramming the ball cap back onto her head. She made her way around the table and held the swinging doors open for the three of them to leave. "But you're not scared. You're taking precautions and that's just being smart."

They disappeared through the opening and the doors swung sadly to and fro behind them. Annette and Gabrielle stared at one another. This was unbelievable.

After a moment, their focus shifted to the table and mechanically, they moved to it and began to clear away the dishes and food.

"Thank you," Sandra said, as they carried everything into the kitchen. Her bubbly nature appeared deflated. "If you girls could scrape off the plates and place them into the dishwasher, I'll put away the food and we can all go sit down. I don't think any of us feel too ambitious. And you must be suffering jetlag."

Speaking for both of them, Gabrielle answered, "I think our concern for Sophie would make it impossible for us to sleep yet. We'll wait with you until they come back and have a slice of that cake you mentioned. Besides, I want to know how the other animals are doing."

Working together, they soon tidied the kitchen, but silence reigned. Each of them was occupied with her own thoughts. Annette longed to get her sister alone for a chat, but it didn't feel right to leave Sandra alone. The idea was frightening that close by there were people so sadistic and vengeful.

Annette thought back to when Andrew and Gabrielle had met. Her sister had been stalked and attacked by a man who had been thrown in prison for his crimes, but it had been Andrew who had saved her. Annette wished her brother-in-law was here now. Yet, he didn't even know what was happening with his mother and the ranch. Would Gabby tell him? She didn't think so. What could he do all the way from Paris except worry himself sick thinking about it.

They retired to the spacious living room. Annette and Gabrielle seated themselves at either end of the long caramel-coloured sofa and, almost in perfect unison, tucked their feet under them.

Sandra busied herself starting a fire in the enormous stone fireplace. It was June, and the grass and trees on the rolling hills outside were lush and green with new growth. Though somehow a fire was a comforting presence, and it would take the chill out of the air. A tiny flame flickered to life and soon spread to the kindling Sandra had artfully arranged. In moments, a crackling fire sprang up and the faint hint of wood smoke wafted through the room.

"I should be getting home." Sandra straightened with a grunt and brushed bits of bark from her knees. "My husband texted me a while ago, but I just can't leave until I know that Sophie and Jeff are safe...and Rosa," she added as an afterthought.

"*Je comprends*," Annette sighed and then, realizing what she'd said, corrected herself. "I mean, I understand. Jeff mentioned that other incidents 'ad taken place at the Triple T Ranch. Perhaps you could tell us about them?"

"I knew what you said in French," Sandra said with lifted eyebrows. She grinned. "What a surprise. Guess my French education wasn't entirely wasted."

She sobered and lifted a hand to rub her forehead as if in pain. Looking at them with bleak eyes and a sigh, she explained. "You see, Sophie is my friend. We met shortly after she moved here to be married. Anyway, the problems started just over a month ago. First off, cattle started to go missing. There was no sign of the bodies, so they hadn't died, but about fifteen head still can't be accounted for. According to Jeff they were some of her best breeding stock." Sandra walked to one of the easy chairs and sank into it with a huff of air. She stared out the huge windows and into the gathering gloom of a rainy evening for a few moments before continuing with her tale.

"Then Sophie's Jeep was stolen while she was in town one day. The police found it down a dirt track about twenty kilometers from here. It had been driven into a tree and was demolished, but the whole incident was put down to a random act of crime. There were no fingerprints and no suspects." She leaned forward, resting her chin on her hands.

"After that it got less random. The air seeder was sabotaged. I don't pretend to understand farming or machinery." She made a grimace, suggesting she didn't *want* to understand the inner workings of it either. "But I was told that the line to the monitor box was cut. The monitor controls the quantity of seeds that are sown and probably other things as well." She waved disinterested arms in the air. "At any rate, that took significant time to fix because everyone was busy seeding their fields and repair shops were busy. It set her back a week. She reported it to the authorities, but it wasn't taken very seriously. So, she got it fixed, but then the tractor broke down. The engine was completely blown." Sandra sat back again and clasped her hands until the knuckles turned white.

Annette knew, without looking at her sister, that Gabrielle was on the verge of tears. The shock of all that was happening to her mother-in-law, combined with jetlag, was taking a toll.

"It was a huge blow, and the financial burden was massive," Sandra continued in a low voice. "The mechanic who was called out to the ranch, found a discarded iodine bottle in the grass nearby. Someone had deliberately poured iodine into the fuel tank...blatant vandalism. The police were called again. But they had no leads, no one had seen suspicious vehicles around the place, and there were no fingerprints anywhere. Sophie was left with another bill and the tractor was out of commission for three weeks. Her fields were only planted last week which is a good month behind schedule. Potentially there will be problems with feed for the cattle this winter."

She looked across at them and shook her head. "Maybe I shouldn't have told you so much," she said. "But you're her family and I think you should know. She tries to carry the entire burden herself, but…" Sandra jumped to her feet and began to pace. "But I don't know how she can keep going at this rate. Most recently, in fact only a couple of days before you arrived, the two men she had employed to help her with running the ranch, quit. Very mysterious indeed since they'd been with her since Malcom died and seemed to enjoy their work. But they disappeared without giving notice."

"I wish she would have…t-told us," Gabrielle moaned, her voice breaking. "Andrew should be here. He would have closed the sh-shop and come."

"That's what Sophie doesn't want," Sandra supplied, a hint of irritation in her words. "She is so determined to run the ranch the way Malcom did, without the help of her sons, that she's become blind to the fact that she could lose it."

Annette slid across the sofa and put an arm around her sister just as the huge wooden outer door slammed back on its hinges with a gust of icy air. Sophie, Jeff, and Rosa had returned.

The three women leaped to their feet and rushed to the door to hear if there was any news, but Sophie shook her head.

"All three cows are recovering, thank goodness," she quavered, allowing Gabrielle to help remove her wet coat and walk her over to the sofa with an arm around her shoulders. "Jeff took them fresh water from here, and everything looks normal, and quite peaceful—considering it's not." She sat down, her features drawn and haggard, and buried her face in her hands. Gabrielle sat beside her, and Annette took a seat close by.

Rosa flung herself into one of the chairs and pushed damp strands of hair from her face. She looked tired and wan too. "Maybe you should consider one of those offers you got to buy the ranch," she said, her voice serious. "It would be a lot less stress for you. Who knows where this craziness could end?"

Jeff cast her a furious glance. "She'll do no such thing," he barked. "The RCMP will find whoever's responsible and it will be over." He caught Annette's eye. "Sorry," he said quietly in explanation. "RCMP stands for the Royal Canadian Mounted Police." She nodded her thanks.

"Will they find them?" Sophie asked feebly. "They 'aven't 'ad much luck so far." She patted Gabrielle's knee and looked around at each concerned face. "I suppose you girls both know what's been 'appening by now," she looked meaningfully at Sandra who held herself erect.

"Yes. I told them," Sandra answered without regret. "It's high time your family steps in to help you, that's what. But I didn't know you received an offer to buy you out." Her stare narrowed in on Jeff. "That sounds suspicious, don't you think, Jeff? Maybe they're behind all this trouble. Trying to run you out through fear and intimidation. Who are these people?" she shot back at her friend.

"Old man Danbury paid her a visit about a week ago," Jeff ground out between clenched teeth. "But I can't see him, or his insipid son, stooping to such dirty tactics. Besides, the police already talked to them both and didn't see any reason to take it further."

"But do we really know the secret intentions of the heart?" Annette asked softly.

"She's right," Sandra announced. "I say anything's possible. We don't know what they're capable of."

Sophie straightened. "In any case, I'm not beaten yet," she said. "But we shouldn't point fingers until there is evidence. Someone is trying to run me out of my own home and scare me into leaving the land Malcom's grandfather settled." She slapped her knees and rose to her feet. "I don't intend to let that happen. Now, I think it's time for some of that cake you mentioned earlier, Sandra. I know I could do with a strong dose of chocolate."

Annette eyed her sister's mother-in-law. Sophie looked as if she was putting on a brave face for her friends and family, but Annette wasn't at all convinced the woman could keep going on. It was obvious the Triple T Ranch was in danger and if the guilty party or parties weren't captured soon, the financial problems were liable to run the ranch into ruin. She didn't know much about ranch life, but anyone could see that if there wasn't any feed for cattle, or money to pay for day-to-day operations, equipment and hired help, it would fail.

Annette's heart went out to this brave lady who persevered despite the odds. She accepted her slice of cake and lost herself in the flames of the fire, quietly following the effort to introduce a much lighter topic of conversation into the room. She looked up only once to find the dark eyes of their host boring into hers and wished yet again that they had never come.

Chapter Four

The first light of day, streaming through the windows that surrounded her, woke Annette early the next morning. Why hadn't she shut the curtains last night? She rolled over with a groan and pulled the blankets over her head. Not even the splendour of the Rockies, bathed in golden sunshine, could induce her to get out of bed.

Before they had retired for the night, Jeff insisted they use two of his most trusted horses to go for a ride today. She believed this concession was an effort to play the part of a magnanimous host. But she wasn't buying it.

It wasn't like she even *wanted* to ride. She'd felt irritation, despite the glares she had sent her sister, when Gabrielle happily told everyone that Annette had never ridden before and would like to try. Now she was trapped, and facing a lesson from the master of the house himself.

Fabulous.

Sure, she liked horses well enough. She'd petted them through a fence on several occasions. It was the getting-on-their-back part that was worrying her and their teeth.

She flipped the comforter off her face and looked at the clock on the bedside table. Six o'clock was too early to get up. "Ugh! That's jetlag for you," she grumbled. Her toes curled into the soft rug beside the bed, and she stretched before padding across the hardwood floor to the bathroom.

In the spacious room, Annette found a fluffy white robe hanging behind the door and a deep, Roman-style tub stocked with delicately scented soaps and shampoos. It looked like a great place to pass some time until everyone was up for the day. She ran it full and added several generous capfuls of a thick, pink bubble bath to the hot water. Sighing with pleasure, she sank into the frothy depths. The room took on the aromatic scent of roses. She lay her head back on a small pink pillow affixed to the tub for just such a purpose, and allowed her body to relax.

Some time later, she was startled to hear an incessant banging on her door and shook herself awake. She'd fallen asleep. Shivering from the cold water, she called, "Come in." She heard the door open and knew it had to be Gabrielle. Who else would enter her room? She lunged to her feet, reaching for a towel from the stack arranged in a tower cabinet next to the tub. Quickly, she fashioned it into a turban on her head, grabbed another, and began to rub. She'd been hoping for a private word with her sister before the riding lesson. So, this was perfect.

She paused, hearing footsteps approach.

"I'll be right there, Gabby," she called, resuming her attempts to bring warmth back to her chilled flesh. But a light tap came at the closed bathroom door and a man cleared his throat.

"Ahh!" she screeched. "*Arrêt! N'entrez pas!*"

"I don't know what that means," came Jeff's derisive reply. "But I assume you think I'm going to barge through the door in some schoolboy attempt to see you naked. I can assure you nothing could interest me less. I only wanted to tell you everyone is downstairs eating breakfast and I have the horses waiting in the barn. Your sister asked me to tell you to wear something appropriate. Apparently she doesn't think you would listen to her, so she sent me."

He didn't wait for a response. His footsteps receded and the bedroom door closed. Annette breathed a sigh of relief mixed with chagrin. What made him such an unpleasant man? Why was he invading her privacy? She wrapped the warm robe around herself and belted it tightly, upset with herself for also wondering why he'd made such a production of his lack of interest in her possible nudity.

Clearing the condensation down the center of a full-length bathroom mirror, she peered at her reflection. Squinting hazel eyes stared back at her. Stepping closer, she examined herself critically. Yes, she wished she was taller, and more slender, as being only 5'2" made her rather petite and dumpy. She wasn't overweight, not exactly, but always fought with the same ten pounds.

She turned her head to one side, eyeing her hourglass figure, yet knowing she was nothing special to look at. Makeup at least helped to make an upturned, freckled nose, even teeth, and a heart-shaped, plain face, presentable. She turned away and bent over to remove the towel from her head, then looked back at the woman in the steamy mirror with a little smile tugging at the corners of her mouth.

Oh, but her hair was special. It tumbled in long, glossy waves to her waist. They were wet waves and rather straggly, but when her hair dried it would be glorious. She scrunched a handful to accentuate the curl and opened the door, exiting the room in a cloud of steam.

And she had style, she thought with a lifting of her chin.

What's more, she knew she was a talented artist. She had prospects waiting for her back home. A prestigious gallery had expressed interest in her art and had spoken of holding an exhibition of her work.

Who cared what this cowboy thought of her anyway? She liked who she was. Maybe she would never command the male attention her sister always had. So what? She had other things going for her.

However, time wasn't one of them. Pulling herself together, she hurried to her suitcase. What could she wear that would be considered 'appropriate?' After some contemplation she decided on loose-fitting, high-waisted jeans in a darker denim than she'd worn yesterday, a soft mossy-green turtleneck in a light cotton blend, her belt, brown boots that she'd somehow crammed into her case, and the yellow, lined, wind-breaker jacket Gabrielle had insisted she bring.

Tossing the outfit onto the bed, she carefully combed out her hair and flipped it over her shoulders to dry naturally. It cascaded over her shoulders in ringlets that looked more auburn than brown these days. She dressed and took a few moments to apply a shimmer of eyeshadow, some mascara, and a swipe of fresh peach lip gloss. Done.

Even though the day before had been difficult, she had a song in her heart today. She would make her best attempt to ride a horse, even if Jeff was part of the teaching. Also, she'd do what she could along with Gabby to help Sophie recover from the latest setback to her ranch. After all, she cared about Andrew and his family, which now included her beloved sister and…maybe down the road, a niece or nephew. One never knew.

Folding the jacket over her arm, she gave her curls another fluff-up and tied them back with an elastic. If she didn't, she knew her hair would get in the way. She took one last look in the mirror before hurrying downstairs to the kitchen. Something smelled delicious. It had gotten late when Sandra was persuaded to head home last night, but clearly she was back again to prepare some other delicacies.

The group was already gathered around the table when she rounded the corner, and a chorus of greetings met her ears.

"Sit down, dear, and help yourself," Sandra instructed as she bustled to the table with a heaping plate of round cakes. Just like yesterday the housekeeper had her hair scraped into a ponytail, and she wore a similar track suit. Although this time it was in a shade of lime green.

"Good morning," Annette called, sitting beside Gabrielle. She avoided Jeff's gaze. Unfortunately, he was seated across from her looking every centimetre the typical cowboy in a black button-up that was a little frayed around the collar. Like Gabrielle had tried to warn her, Annette guessed it didn't make sense to wear good clothes when working on a ranch.

A glass of orange juice sat in front of her, and she grasped it, taking a sip while she contemplated what to eat first. The steaming plate of cakes resembled crepes, but they were thick and fluffy. The others appeared to be piling them on their plates and pouring something from a jug overtop.

"Maple syrup," Gabrielle whispered in her ear. "Try some, it's delicious."

Annette stabbed two cakes with her fork, then added a few slices of crispy bacon and a heaping spoonful of scrambled eggs before settling back and eyeing the jug of brown syrup. Finally, she grabbed it by the handle and tipped it over her plate, drenching the entire contents in the sweet goo.

"Oh!" she wailed, as her bacon floated to the other side of the enormous plate in a sea of stickiness. "*Je suis désolée.*"

"Well," Jeff remarked with raised eyebrows and a smirk as his eyes fastened on her swimming food, "if that means, 'I like having a little breakfast with my syrup' then I get it. No interpretation necessary."

Annette glowered at him, but at the same time, a giggle rose to her lips. The man was teasing her. Did he actually have a sense of humour?

Everyone else laughed, even Sophie, whose spirits appeared to have revived since the day before.

"I was, in fact, apologizing," Annette admitted loftily, stifling the giggle with a cough. "I certainly did not mean to pour so much."

"*Pas de problème,*" Sophie said, wiping her mouth on a napkin. "It's refreshing to hear a little French. Thank you." She looked around the table. "In France, we grow up with *crêpes*, never pancakes, as they are called here. It's a different concept, but very good." She nodded at Annette, "Try it."

Annette sliced into the cake and took a dripping mouthful. It was tasty and she quickly took another bite.

"Today," Sophie said, directing her remarks to Rosa and Jeff, "I'll return to the ranch. There's work to be done that I cannot ignore, regardless of these attacks. The RCMP are coming at eleven for my statement and to look around. I must determine the best way to restore the well. I'll hire someone with a vacuum truck to suck the contaminated water out as much as possible. That way nothing else will be polluted." Her eyes were an even more startling shade of light blue today, thanks to the plaid shirt in shades of sapphire that she wore. However, dark circles around them gave away her worry and sleepless nights.

"I'll drive you two over," Jeff said. "Then you can bring your vehicle back here tonight."

She raised a hand of protest, but he overrode her argument. "I simply won't allow you to stay there without water, and alone in the house at night. I've paid the security company to keep someone on duty at the Triple T. When it's safe to return to the ranch, I won't try to stop you." His brow furrowed with concern. "I'm only following through on what I know Malcom would want."

Sophie ran both hands through her silver hair. "I know you are, and I thank you. Okay, I guess we'll both come back here for the night." She glanced at her watch. "We'd better go. If you don't mind?" she asked, looking at Rosa who hadn't said a word. "The two new employees I hired are coming at nine."

In response, Jeff pushed back his chair and got to his feet. Then he placed a big hand in the middle of the table and leaned over it to stare into Annette's startled eyes. "Save some for me," he whispered loudly, jerking a thumb at the syrup jug. "And maybe have a glass of milk to wash it down. We don't want you all hyperactive as you ride Black Beauty into the sunset."

He chuckled as he straightened and ushered Sophie and Rosa out the swinging doors. Annette's face burned with colour. She looked at Gabrielle in exasperation.

"What an awful man!" she fumed, so only her sister could hear.

"I think he likes you," Gabby whispered with a wink.

Chapter Five

After helping to tidy the kitchen from breakfast, despite Sandra's objections that it was her job to do it, Annette and Gabrielle walked outside. The storm of the previous night had passed, leaving behind a landscape drowned in vibrant shades of green.

For a few moments they lingered on the veranda, breathing in the fresh mountain air that swirled across the hills and valleys as it made its way to them from the blue peaks in the distance. A sense of peace and renewal filled the air. Annette leaned on the rail. Puddles of water dotted the driveway, reflecting the early morning sunlight in a dazzling display, while droplets of rain still clung to the grass like scattered diamonds.

They basked in the quiet tranquility.

"Do you hear that?" Annette turned to question her sister.

Gabrielle frowned, straining to listen. "No," she confirmed finally. "Hear what exactly?"

"Nothing. That's the point. It's so peaceful here. There

aren't any cars, horns, or sirens," she said in wonder. "No people. I don't think I've ever been anywhere so quiet." Annette hadn't thought she would like it, but she did. Growing up in a city of almost five hundred thousand, and then spending four years attending college in Paris, didn't offer much opportunity for solitude. She lifted her face to the warmth of the sun and reveled in this unusual feeling of serenity.

The crunch of tires on gravel caught their attention. It was Jeff, returning in his enormous black truck. He spun past them, continuing along the driveway, past a low building that looked like a small house, until he parked in front of the hip-roofed barn. He jumped out and beckoned to them.

"Have you met him on other trips to Canada with Andrew?" Annette asked in a low voice as they descended the stairs and began to walk toward where their host slid open the big double doors of the building.

"No, although I've heard Andrew and Sophie talk about him as a friend and neighbour. Actually, I think Andrew went to school with him, but Jeff is a couple of years older." She looked at Annette with a puzzled expression on her face. "You don't like him, do you?"

Annette angled her head and thought for a moment. "There's just something about him that irritates me," she said. "His arrogance, for a start."

"That's strange. I don't find him that way at all. He's been more than kind to Sophie—and to us. How many neighbours would take in foreign visitors? Or give them riding lessons?"

"I didn't ask for lessons," Annette said bitterly. "If it wasn't for you and your big mouth…"

"*Shhh!* He'll hear you." Gabrielle plastered a grin on her

face and increased her pace. Jeff stood waiting for them in the doorway, a length of rope coiled in his hand.

Annette had to admit he looked the part of the enigmatic rancher she'd seen in movies. He wore a black cowboy hat, jeans that fit snugly across his narrow hips, and a faded canvas jacket that looked as though it had seen a few years of hard labour.

"Tomorrow's lesson will involve saddling and bridling," he said, in an authoritative tone. "But today we'll focus on getting you used to mounting a horse and riding in a corral."

He led the way inside where Annette's eyes took a few seconds to adjust to the dim lighting. When she could focus again, she saw a wall of empty pens that looked like solid wooden boxes down either side. The sisters followed Jeff until he stopped in front of a pen that was partway down the aisle. He rested a hand on the handle.

"This is the horse I'll use to teach you how to ride. Her name is Pearl," he explained. Even in the gloom, Annette could see his eyes softening with love for the animal. He reached between the bars of the gate and rubbed the mare's broad white face. "We bought her when she was only a yearling, my father trained her, and she belonged to my little sister for—well—until she didn't need the horse anymore. Pearl has been part of our family for seventeen years." He lifted the latch and swung the gate open. Annette and Gabrielle stepped forward to peer inside the stall.

A dapple-grey mare stood just inside the opening, watching them with dark inquisitive eyes. In the shafts of light that angled through the small window of the stall, Annette thought the horse's coat reminded her of a snowy winter's day. Parts of it were white turning to grey and all were flecked with areas of a darker colour. She was beautiful. Pearl's mane and tail were a gleaming silver. Her feet were black and neatly shaped.

Jeff grasped a small plastic pail and scooped something from its depths. "Cup your hands and hold them out," he instructed Annette.

She did as he told her, and he trickled a small measure of grain into her palms. Pearl seemed instinctively to know what was happening. She nickered low in her throat and stepped eagerly toward them.

"Now, extend your two hands to her. As she eats the oats, flatten your hands so she can get the treat. I don't want you to get nibbled."

As he spoke, Annette had been tentatively reaching out, but at his final words she snapped her hands back, spilling some of the oats into the sawdust at their feet.

"*Quoi!*" she demanded in French before she could correct herself. "*Je ne veux pas être mordue!*"

Jeff gave a long exasperated sigh. "You're going to have to stop that," he said, raising his eyebrows. "I don't have a clue what you're saying."

"She's afraid of being bitten," Gabrielle explained, grasping her sister's hands, and cupping them for Jeff to fill again. After he did so, she bent to look into Annette's face. "Just stay like this until Pearl has had a mouthful of oats and then flatten your palms, so she can get the rest. She won't bite you. I promise."

With trepidation Annette looked from her sister to Jeff. It was the closest she'd ever been to an animal of this size and her knees quivered. Nevertheless, she stepped within reach of the mare and lifted her arms.

Pearl blew through her nostrils, her ears flicking back and forth as she stretched her neck to reach the oats. "I don't know which of you is more suspicious," Jeff said to

Annette followed with a snort of derision. "You or the horse."

Finally, Pearl's twitching nose reached her hands, and a little shudder ran through Annette's body. But the nose was soft and gentle, and Pearl was very much a lady. Carefully she nuzzled at the oats with wet lips until she had enough to chew, then lifted her head away, and stared at Annette with her dark eyes; her strong teeth grinding methodically.

Why...it was a wonderful experience. Annette took a step closer, flattening her palms as she'd been told. Pearl swallowed and came back for the remainder of the oats. The velvety nose nuzzled Annette again, and a little thrill went up her spine. The mare was sweet.

"Can I pet her?" she asked Jeff, who nodded with a half-smile on his face. He unwound the length of rope he'd coiled around his arm, and clipped it to the bright pink halter Pearl wore. Then he led the mare out of the box. Hesitantly, Annette stepped back. Only when Pearl came to a standstill did she move forward again, with far less fear.

She ran a hand down the horse's neck, taking note of the silky hair, the warmth, and the scent that accompanied horses. It was pleasing and friendly. Eagerly Annette looked at the people beside her.

"I like Pearl," she said with surprise. She wasn't so sure about riding the animal, but this much contact was working out well. Pearl stood very still as Annette continued to stroke her. From somewhere inside the barn, another horse whinnied and Annette jumped.

"That's just Panda," Jeff said. He handed Annette the end of the rope, which she accepted without thinking, and turned to Gabrielle. "He's the gelding I brought in for you to ride. I'll show you where he is, and the tack room. Feel free to take him for a ride anytime you wish." The two of them strode down the alleyway, talking.

Annette looked at the rope dangling from her fingertips like it was a cobra, and then at Pearl. Why would they leave her alone with this huge beast? Petting her was one thing, but being left in charge was quite another. What if Pearl became scared and ran? Or charged out the door and across the yard to find the others? *Don't be silly. You'd let go, of course.* But what was she to do in the meantime? Again, she looked at the cord in horror and backed away, craning her neck to see where her sister had gone.

Unbelievably, Pearl followed her. Startled, Annette dropped the rope. Was the horse chasing her? Yet Pearl had stopped a reasonable distance away, and was flicking her ears back and forth, appearing bored. She realized the horse was just well-trained. The lead rope lay on the ground between them. Picking it up, she coiled the slack in her hand and walked toward the open doorway. The horse plodded willingly behind.

Wow. This is simple.

Together, they ambled into the bright sunshine, Pearl making an effort to avoid puddles as Annette walked slowly. Together they made a big loop around the gravelled area and strolled back into the barn. The mare was so close that her nose brushed Annette's elbow.

By this time, Gabrielle and Jeff were waiting for her. She felt a bit giddy with her success, and grinned at their astonished faces. A big black horse, with large white splotches over his body and a wide strip of white down his face, fidgeted behind them. His colouring explained why his name was Panda.

"Well, look at you going for a little tour all on your

own," Jeff's deep voice sounded impressed. "You handled that like a professional."

Annette flushed with pleasure. She'd finally done something right.

He spoke to Gabrielle. "You said you wanted to go for a ride. So, if you're comfortable with it, why don't you saddle Panda and take him out for some exercise? Out the back way is a long pasture and a beautiful view. Meanwhile, I'll give Annette a lesson."

If he hadn't just praised her, she'd almost feel threatened by his words. *Give her a lesson. Great.*

"I'd like that." Gabrielle accepted Panda's lead. After sending her sister an encouraging smile, she led the horse back down the darkened alley. Annette watched her go wistfully. She would much rather have Gabby teach her. Nonetheless, she realized it *was* Jeff's horse and they *were* his guests, unfortunate as that was. She reminded herself to accept his help graciously and be as pleasant as possible.

"Now then, bring her this way," Jeff said, rubbing his hands together with invisible soap. He set off for Pearl's box stall. "We'll tie her just outside the door where I have everything waiting. Then, I'll show you how to bridle and saddle her. It'll help you remember how to do it for tomorrow."

The man looked positively gleeful. Her earlier feelings of triumph vanished. Why was it so important to Gabrielle that she ride? Wasn't it enough that she liked the animal? Did she have to tour the countryside on its back? She'd never expressed any interest in learning. Irritation mixed with her unease.

Obediently, she trailed after Jeff with Pearl stepping daintily beside her. Turning, he motioned for the lead rope and Annette handed it over with an unmistakeable eagerness. Jeff narrowed his eyes, searching her face. "You're nervous, hey?"

She nodded.

"I understand," he said, tying the rope to a metal ring embedded in the wall of the enclosure. "It's always hard to push yourself out of your comfort zone. Learning anything new is difficult. Especially if you are afraid." He leaned back against Pearl and crossed his arms.

Clearly, he could read her expressions. She would have to work on that. Avoiding his eyes, she stared at a saddle that was slung over a wooden rack along with a leather contraption she could only guess was a bridle.

"If you don't want to do this, you don't have to...but think about it for a minute." He shrugged and pushed himself upright, moving to rub at a thick layer of dust on the brown saddle. "I should have noticed it was so dirty." He spoke reproachfully to himself, as though he were alone. "Everything you see here was Jessica's. Her horse, her saddle, her bridle. She was the last one to use it and that's been..." His voice was raw and pained, laden with memories. "It's been eight years since she sat in it, I guess. No wonder it's covered in dust." Pulling a rag from within the depths of his coat pocket, he began to clean the leather.

"Jessica, she is your sister?" Annette asked before thinking again. It was none of her business, but she could hear something in his tone that made her curious.

"Was," he said shortly. "She and my father were killed when she was only fifteen." He bent his head over the saddle and scrubbed at a smudge of resistant grime.

Annette's heart melted. "*Oh la la.* I am so sorry, Jeff. Forgive me for asking."

He straightened his shoulders and turned to face her, unashamed of a tear that trickled down his cheek.

"Thanks," he said. "Sorry to burden you with the knowledge. I hadn't considered how much it might affect me to get out her things." He brushed the wetness away with his sleeve and took a deep steadying breath.

Annette reacted. Stepping closer, she reached out to lay a comforting hand on his arm. It brought her into close proximity with the man. When their eyes met, and locked together, she was unprepared for the rush of emotion that flooded her being. Being right next to him, she saw his irises change from brown to black in an instant, and her breath caught. Was she picking up on his hurt? No—it was more than that. Hastily, her face flushing, she moved away, babbling the first thing that came to mind.

"*Je suis vraiment désolée.*" With an aghast expression, she cupped her hands over her mouth. "Oh! I did it again! I always say something in French, and you don't understand it." Her voice was muffled. Dropping her hands away, she wrung them together. "This news you tell me is terrible. I am so sorry that 'appened to you," she repeated, beginning to feel foolish.

"It's fine. Actually, your concern is touching," he noted, the trace of a smile lifting one corner of his mouth. He sniffed. "So, do you want to learn how to ride, or not? It's no problem either way." He pulled a thick, red saddle pad from under the saddle and looked at her expectantly.

"I will," she answered emphatically, surprising herself. "As long as you don't mind me using Jessica's things."

"Good. And no, I don't mind at all. I'm sure Jessica would want them to be put to use." With slow, deliberate movements he placed the pad on Pearl's back, explaining every move he made.

"This goes on first to cushion the horse's back and protect the saddle from dirt and sweat." He reached for the saddle and swung the straps on the far side, over the seat. "I did that, so when I place it on the horse's back, the stirrup and the cinch don't bang into the animal on the other side and startle it." He threw the saddle onto Pearl. Her ears flicked, but otherwise she didn't move a muscle.

"The saddle should sit just behind the horse's shoulder and over the withers," he rested a hand in each place to demonstrate. Walking around to the other side, he lowered the straps and then, ducking under Pearl's neck, he returned to reach under her stomach for them. Moving to one side so Annette could see, he beckoned her closer.

"Watch how I fasten the cinch together and tighten it," he said, pushing the stirrup from this side, out of his way. "If all goes well today, you can do this yourself tomorrow. Of course, I'll be here to supervise."

"Don't you have better things to do?" she asked. Then, seeing him frown, and his nimble fingers stop as they slipped the leather straps into place, she hastened to explain. "I mean, you must be busy on a ranch this size. I feel as though I'm taking you away from your work."

He swivelled to face her, crossing his arms across his chest in what she was beginning to realize was a classic move.

"Are you saying you'd rather I wasn't here? Perhaps you'd like your sister to teach you instead?"

This was exactly what she'd like. Still, she hadn't meant for him to know it and her mouth dropped open in surprise before she caught herself. He was only trying to show her kindness. "No." She shook her head. "I just feel guilty that you're spending so much time with me. You certainly didn't plan on having house guests, and now you're stuck with us."

Jeff went back to tightening the straps. "I don't mind. Sophie didn't ask me to host you and Gabrielle here—I offered." He pulled the stirrup into place and turned to Annette. "Now, we'll spend about an hour outside and then you can be rid of me." He finished and reached for the bridle, giving her further instructions on how to slip it over the horse's head and gently slide the bit into its mouth.

"Done," he said, handing her the reins. "Lead Pearl out of here."

Her heart clenched with anxiety, but this time she hoped he couldn't tell. Taking the supple straps from his outstretched hand, she wheeled around and headed for the open door, thankful he couldn't see her face.

She blinked. The sun was rising high in the sky and the freshness of this green world after the heavy rain was blinding after the dim light of the barn. She took a few steps sideways to see if Jeff was following and set her foot into a puddle of muddy water. Gasping, she shook her foot, trying to banish the apprehension from her thoughts, but worried about her good leather boots, and wondering how she was supposed to stop Pearl. He could have at least told her that much before he sent her off.

"Over here," Jeff called.

Annette lifted her wet foot and wiped it down the back of her jeans. She hoped it would get rid of the water and remembered her dismissive remark to Gabrielle back in Paris concerning rain boots. It was hard for her to admit, but they might have been a good idea. Hoping Pearl would follow her like last time, she made a loop and saw Jeff unfastening a gate to the left of the barn.

He swung it wide, and she walked into a round paddock with the mare trailing her. Underfoot was sand that appeared to have been smoothed by some machine, because it was completely flat. Jeff pulled the gate closed behind him and slid the bolt shut before walking to where she stood with

Pearl, shading her eyes against the powerful sun. He was a handsome man, she had to admit. He reminded her of Andrew; strong and capable, someone who was a bulwark in the middle of a storm, with old-fashioned ideas of chivalry and courtesy to the point of putting himself out to help others.

Her most recent boyfriend, Philippe, was the complete opposite. They'd met in her third year of university. He'd been charming at first; taking her places, sharing long intimate discussions over dinners, and showing what she had thought was a genuine interest in her work and passions. But it was all a charade. After two months he began to show who he truly was and why he was attracted to her.

His attentiveness ceased abruptly, only to be replaced with arrogance, indifference, an excessive need for admiration, and a grandiose sense of his own importance. Annette had heard her friends talking about people they thought to be narcissists, but she was unprepared to believe that Philippe was one. But he was. Before she had broken up with him, he inadvertently revealed that he planned to exploit their relationship for all the money he could.

She dragged her thoughts back to the present. Jeff had gone to Pearl and rechecked the girth, tightening it a little. Removing his hat, he ran a hand through his curly black hair and shoved the hat down low over his eyes.

"So," he began, attempting a smile that looked more like a grimace. "Lesson number one is how to mount a horse."

"That makes sense." She was a bit flippant, but honestly, did he take her for a fool? Of course, she had to get on Pearl before she could learn to ride. She moved to stand beside him.

His eyebrows drew together, but he merely continued as

if she hadn't spoken. "First, gather the reins in your left hand, like so, and take hold of the saddle horn." He demonstrated. "Then, put your left foot into the stirrup, balance your weight, bounce lightly on the ground with your right foot, like this, and swing your right leg over the horse as you pull up with your arms." In one fluid motion he was astride Pearl, his long legs hanging well below the stirrups.

Seeing she'd noticed this issue, he remarked on it. "We'll adjust the stirrups to your leg length once you're up here." He swung himself back down to the ground and indicated that she take the reins. "Your turn."

Well, this was the moment she'd been dreading. Her stomach did flips, but she was determined he wouldn't see the fear in her face. She moved slowly, pausing to stroke Pearl's neck and pull a twig from her mane. Then she took the reins and held them in her hand just like Jeff had shown her. She closed her eyes, willing herself to be calm. She knew dogs could sense fear in humans, could horses do that too?

Jeff held the stirrup for her and helped to guide her foot inside. Then, she hopped, made a wild grab for the horn, and threw herself into the air. For a moment she was airborne, a wild tangle of flailing arms and legs, and then she toppled backward into Jeff's arms.

He caught her, with a loud *OOF*, and they both tumbled to the ground in a heap. Annette was too stunned to move. For a moment she lay sprawled on top of him, looking into the sky feeling breathless and thoroughly ridiculous. His muffled voice made itself heard from beneath her.

"Get. Off."

Immediately, she rolled onto her stomach in the sand and hid her burning face from view. She heard him scramble to his feet and dust himself off. Oh, if only the earth could open up at this very moment and swallow her whole.

"We have a saying in Canada. Perhaps you have something similar in France," he said dryly. Out of the corner of her eye she saw him stoop to pick up his hat and slap it against his thigh to remove the sand. "Here it is: 'If you fall off your horse, get right back on.' Of course, that doesn't strictly apply here, since you were never actually *on* the animal. Still, I think it was close enough to count."

Annette groaned. Coming up onto all fours, her head hanging in shame, she heard a strange noise. It sounded like someone choking. She leaped to her feet, trying to remember how to clear an obstruction from a person's throat and wondering what he'd swallowed to cause it.

But he wasn't choking. He was laughing. Bent over double, hat held to his stomach, he belly laughed. For one crazy moment she stared at him. Even surprising herself, she joined in. Throwing her head back she roared. Really, it was too bizarre not to have a giggle. She could imagine what the scene would have looked like to a casual observer. Her body had thrashed through the air like some wild woman, knocked this man to the ground, and then they lay motionless, two people caught up in the wet sand.

At length Jeff rammed his hat back on his head, wiped his eyes, and went to collect the fallen reins. Pearl was so well-trained that she still stood like a post, rooted to the spot as though this sort of thing was an everyday occurrence. Annette brushed herself off, tucked a strand of flyaway hair behind one ear, and prepared for another try.

"Glad to see you're not giving up," Jeff observed. Merriment still danced in his eyes, and she realized how infinitely more attractive he was with a genuine smile on his face.

"We French women do not give up easily," she said stoutly. Reaching for the reins, she placed her foot into the stirrup again, but this time she made sure she was balanced before liftoff. She got a firm grip on the saddle horn, bounced on her right foot, and swung herself up.

"Lift your leg higher," he cautioned. "Otherwise, you'll kick her rump on the way through and that wouldn't be a good idea."

At the last moment, Annette had the presence of mind to raise her leg. To her surprise, she settled into the saddle like it had been made for her. Amazing. She looked around at the world from her elevated position, feeling as though she'd really accomplished something. Pearl's long neck stretched in front of her with her ears perked and attentive. She could feel the horse breathing and the warmth of its body. So far it was lovely. Maybe Gabrielle was right, and she would enjoy riding.

Jeff looked up at her with a grin. "You did it." He patted her leg as he walked around to the other side and helped slide her foot into the other stirrup. "Now. Put all your weight in the stirrups and stand up," he directed. "I want to see if they need adjustments."

She did as asked and he looked at her, assessing. "Nope, it's perfect just as it is. Your legs are the same length as Jessica's were." A cloud crossed his face, but he shook it away with a smile for Annette. "Now the lesson begins." He waggled a finger at her. "Pearl was taught to neck rein. This means that with gentle pressure from the reins, laid against her neck on the opposite side from where you want to go, she will turn. To stop, you will pull gently on the reins and sit farther back in your seat. Got it? Or should I prepare myself for another ambush?"

She giggled. "I'll do my best to stay up here." Then, as

he moved away, she added, "But I'm not making any promises."

"Oh, that I believe! What's the word you're always using to apologize? Dess-u-lay?"

"*Oui.*" She giggled all the more. "That's not correct, but…it's close enough to count."

"*Touche,*" he quipped, his eyes, filled with laughter, gleamed up at her. "Okay," he said, clearing his throat. "First we will get you used to the horse's rhythm by walking around the corral."

Annette listened carefully to Jeff's instructions as they circled the pen and strove to implement everything he told her. Consequently, they spent the next forty minutes in an enjoyable camaraderie. Steadily, the sun rose in the sky and the day grew warm. Birds flitted back and forth, chirping at one another in a line of pine trees that screened the corral from the driveway and house. In the distance, cattle were bawling. While she wasn't what you'd call relaxed, she did feel a strange sense of peace flood her soul as she took a moment to gaze out at the hazy blue mountains in the distance. Today, she was glad she'd come to this beautiful place.

At the end of their time together she was rising up and down in her stirrups as Pearl trotted, and struggling to grip the horse's sides with her legs.

"You look great," Gabrielle shouted. She'd climbed the pole fence and sat astride the top rail. Annette glanced at her sister and smiled. With one hand on the reins and the other on the saddle horn, she didn't have anything available to wave.

"That's enough for today," Jeff called. He walked to the gate and waited for Annette to join him.

As she drew to a halt beside him, he grabbed the horse

by the bridle and held Pearl. Looking up at Annette with mock fear, he said, "I find myself a little concerned as we reach the final lesson of the day—getting off." A smile tugged at the corners of his mouth. "The key is to maintain your hold on both the reins and the saddle horn as you swing your right leg over and step down to the ground. Try to avoid flinging yourself into space, or flattening your instructor." He tipped his hat back on his head, giving him a boyish look, and his white teeth flashed her a grin. "Shall we give it a go anyway?"

Annette answered with a peal of laughter. Glancing up, she was amused to see Gabrielle's jaw drop and her eyes widen.

"*Oui Monsieur*," she called. She climbed off Pearl without further incident, but her legs felt stiff and bowed out of shape. She stretched, then bunched the end of the reins in her hand and followed him.

"Muscles you didn't know you had, will ache tomorrow," Jeff promised, unfastening the gate. He pushed it open for them to pass through. "But you did well for your first time out." He cast her a sideways glance. "Well, after you got on, that is."

She aimed a playful swat at him with the end of the leather straps. Annette was amazed at herself for suddenly feeling so familiar with this enigmatic man who only an hour ago she had barely tolerated. Jeff went on ahead.

From the side of her mouth, Gabrielle hissed in French, "What is going on with you two? I leave you hating each other with an unbridled passion, and come back to best friends." She lifted her hands in a gesture of disbelief.

"I don't know. It's weird. I think we bonded when I was laying on top of him," Annette noted blithely.

"What!" Gabrielle came to a full, flabbergasted stop.

But Annette just chuckled and led Pearl through the wide opening into the barn. She heard her sister's frustrated footsteps behind her. Jeff was waiting for her with brushes in his hands. For the moment she wouldn't have to answer any questions until Gabby and she were alone.

"Do you want me to unsaddle her?" Jeff asked. He set the brushes on a shelf beside Pearl's stall and reached for the reins.

"No. I'll do it," Annette said, chin in the air. "This day is all about learning new things, so why stop now?"

"Good answer," he said in a satisfied tone. He showed her how to gently remove the bridle and slip on Pearl's halter. Then he tied the mare to the steel ring on the wall.

Annette ignored her sister's raised eyebrows and moved closer to see how the straps were fastened around Pearl's belly. Jeff demonstrated, and then stepped back to allow her room to work.

"I don't think I'm doing it right," she said uncertainly, struggling to tug the tightened straps loose. Pearl swung around, almost knocking Annette off her feet. Jeff pushed her away.

"She's getting restless," he said.

Annette shot him a pleading look. "I think you will have to 'elp me."

"The strap is snug," he agreed. Stepping in, Jeff's practised fingers loosened the binding while she watched, so that she'd know for next time. However, she was unprepared for the sudden awareness of him that flooded her senses as Jeff's arm moved against hers to release the knot. As if also becoming conscious of her touch, he swivelled his head, staring into her eyes. They were mere centimetres apart. His eyes dropped to her mouth and her breath caught in her throat.

"There…" he said with a slight catch in his voice. He coughed and stepped back, breaking the spell. "I've started it, now you finish it."

Annette shook herself. "*Oui. Bien sûr.*" Right at this moment, she wished her long hair hung free, so that it might hide her flushed face. But no, it was tied at the nape of her neck. She couldn't use it to screen her from Jeff's scrutiny or her sister whose eyebrows had lifted even higher.

Her fingers faltered as she unthreaded the straps and finally tugged them apart. The metal ring on the end of the cinch dropped to the cement floor with a clang. She jumped.

"Do I pull the saddle off?"

"I'll do it," he said briskly. "And I'll take it to the tack room while you brush Pearl down. I'm sure Gabrielle can show you how." He dragged the saddle and bright red pad from Pearl's back and disappeared. The horse gave an audible sigh of relief and shook herself.

Gabrielle was beside her sister in a flash to snatch up the two brushes Jeff had brought. She handed one to Annette. "This is called a curry comb," she said loudly, maintaining English. It seemed only polite to speak this way when Jeff was with them. Then in a whisper, she added fiercely, "You are going to explain all this to me the second we are alone. *Comprendre?*"

Annette nodded mutely. It was funny to see her sister so intrigued, but she couldn't quite muster up a smile. Jeff's proximity had flustered her. She was grateful she didn't have to explain what had happened over the last hour, quite yet, because she didn't understand it herself.

"Brush Pearl with short firm strokes, avoiding too much pressure on bony areas. I'll follow behind with the soft brush to remove dirt and hair." Gabrielle issued orders like a drill sergeant, but Annette didn't mind. Her sister had been riding many times over the last four years and knew what she was talking about.

"Did you have a nice ride on Panda?" Annette asked, raising a cloud of dust from Pearl's beautiful grey coat. It shimmered in the beams of light that slanted through windows built into the eaves of the building.

"Yes. The pasture behind the barn is lovely. We'll go there together. Maybe in a couple of days you'll feel confident enough."

"You really think we will 'ave to be 'ere that long?"

"Yes," Jeff answered sharply. He appeared from behind Pearl with Panda clomping beside him. "Untie her and follow me. We'll put them in with the other horses." He waved a hand at Pearl and marched out the doors.

Annette closed her eyes and took a deep breath.

Zut! Honestly, the man always appeared at the wrong moment. Now she'd offended him again. At least his displeasure was something familiar to her. What she didn't want to repeat were the intimate moments of the last hour. Those were unlike anything she'd experienced before. The situation was unnerving.

Chapter Six

Jeff left them once the horses were put away. He wasn't unpleasant, but rather abruptly claimed he had work to do elsewhere, and would see them later. Annette noticed he avoided further eye contact with her.

She wasn't unhappy to hear he was leaving them on their own. Although it did mean she had to describe the past two hours to her sister. They made their way to the veranda and sat on a swinging bench covered with red cushions, rocking back and forth as they gazed across the verdant green of the landscape. The swing creaked gently, echoing the melody of their conversation.

After sharing with Gabrielle the tale of her flying leap, and the consequences of that hasty action, both women shared a laugh.

"I think he's attracted to you," Gabrielle noted, tapping her fingers on the arm rest. "I saw that look the two of you shared in the barn and…"

"Please don't say any more," Annette interrupted.

"We're barely tolerating one another, trust me. I don't need you reading more into what there is."

Gabrielle shrugged expressively, and made no further comment. They fell into a comfortable silence punctuated only by the happy chirping of birds and the hum of a fat bumble bee as it buzzed about the hanging baskets of brightly coloured petunias that swayed in a slight breeze. In front of them, the jagged, purple peaks of the Rocky Mountains sliced the clear blue sky like shards of opaque glass.

"I could sit here and stare at this scene all day," Annette said presently. "But not today because I'm falling asleep. Do you want to walk with me?" She stood to her feet and stretched her arms above her head.

"I thought you'd never ask." Gabrielle yawned. "I feel the same way. For me, jetlag is always worse the next day."

They found a rocky path that led around the house to a huge garden. Although it was early in the growing season, and most of the produce was immature, Annette could make out a row of lettuce and another of green onions that were flourishing. When she was a child, growing up in Toulouse, her family had always had a garden. Of course, it was much smaller than this, but seeing it brought back memories of home. She wondered who worked the plot, since there wasn't a weed in sight.

They spent the rest of the morning wandering around the yard, looking at flower beds, talking, and enjoying one another. While they were bending over an area of perennials, trying to decide what they were called, Sandra tapped on one of the massive floor-to-ceiling windows and beckoned them inside. She pointed to a side door and met them as they were kicking off their shoes.

"I'm not sure if you've worked up an appetite out there this morning, but lunch is ready," she announced. A light dusting of flour graced the rolled-up sleeves of her lime green top. An apron covered everything else, apart from her legs from the knee down and a pair of sparkly red tennis shoes.

"Are those *paillettes*?" Annette asked in surprise, squinting at Sandra's footwear as the woman swung around and marched in front of them. How had she not noticed these before? They were positively garish.

"Pie-ettes?" Sandra repeated. She stopped and looked around the room with a puzzled expression on her face. "Did they get in through the open door? For heaven's sake, keep your eye on them and I'll get the fly swatter." She turned to rush away.

"Wait!" Gabrielle called with a laugh. "*Paillettes* aren't alive. It's the French word for sequins. I think Annette is asking about your shoes."

"Oh," Sandra rested a hand over her heart. "Well, that's a relief. I mean, I'd never heard of such a creature as a pie-ette, but I was prepared to do battle with them." She giggled, lifted a foot, and tilted it back and forth to catch the noon-day sun that streamed through the huge windows of the dining room. They got the full effect of the sequins.

"I ordered them from Amazon," she exclaimed with pride. "I also have them in blue, pink, and silver. Sadly, the gold pair are on backorder. Beautiful, aren't they?" She looked expectantly at the young women standing before her, waiting for words of praise.

Both of them nodded quickly. "They're very…uh, glittery," Annette observed. She stared at the shoes again, partly in disbelief at seeing this travesty of a fashion statement, and partly in admiration. This woman didn't care what was being worn on the streets of New York, London, or Paris. She was content in her gaudy green track suit and sparkly red running shoes. But who was to say she was wrong? You couldn't argue with happiness. And clearly these bright things made Sandra happy. Annette pondered this revelation as she took a seat across from her sister at the table.

They finished a light lunch, consisting of a delicious soup that Sandra called Pepperpot Chowder. Just as they went into raptures about her fluffy biscuits with butter, Jeff clomped through the swinging doors.

"Hey, Sandra," he called to the woman, "sorry about my boots." He had the grace to look behind him for a possible mess. "Could you make me something quick to bolt down? I just got a call from Matt. There's a couple of calves lame in the far pasture. Looks like foot rot. I have to go treat them and then get down to the Triple T. Sophie sent me a text just as I was walking through the door."

"Of course." Sandra whirled about the kitchen.

"Sophie wrote you. Is something wrong?" Gabrielle queried, half rising from her chair.

Jeff flashed her a look. "Not sure, but I doubt it." He lifted the battered black hat off his head and ran a sleeve over his brow. "She suggested I bring you two along. If you want to go?" He didn't look overly pleased at the prospect though.

Annette was content to stay where she sat. Her body was really dragging, and she felt her eyelids getting heavy, yet again. The warm sun and the delicious meal were conspiring along with jetlag to put her to sleep. She looked at her sister, knowing Gabby well enough to realize she'd wanted to be at the Triple T Ranch ever since arriving the day before. Gabrielle was part of the Tremblay family, it was her husband's boyhood home and she had been there many times before.

"Of course," she said. "Let's go."

Sandra hurried from the kitchen, her shoes squeaking as she rounded the counter with a bundle of thick sandwiches she was busy stuffing into a paper bag, and two tall flasks that must have contained hot drinks. Extending them she said, "I made enough to share with whoever is at the Triple T. They're only peanut butter and honey, but I didn't have much notice."

"That's perfect." Jeff accepted the items gratefully. "They'll appreciate it. Thanks Sandra."

"You're welcome." She whirled around, grabbed a travel mug off the counter and handed it to Annette. "Would you mind carrying it to the truck for him, dear?" She glanced to the wall where a large clock hung inside of an ancient looking wagon wheel. "I'll have dinner ready to pop into the oven with instructions, but I'll leave before that. Hubby got a little peevish last night when I got home so late. Although," Sandra sighed, "he's worried about Sophie just like the rest of us. He thinks maybe she should sell the ranch and take life easy."

"She won't," said Gabrielle's quiet voice. Grabbing her dishes, she walked into the kitchen to set them by the sink. "Sophie believes in the legacy of the family farm. She'll kill 'erself working to keep the ranch afloat before she'd sell. If all of these problems are really caused by someone trying to scare her off, then they don't know 'er very well."

"That's true," said Jeff. He looked meaningfully at Annette. "Coming?"

She roused herself. "*Oui*." Quickly she ran her dishes to the sink and followed Jeff and Gabrielle from the room.

She was expecting to clamber into the same, enormous

black truck from the day before, but a much smaller and older truck sat in the driveway waiting for them. It was grey in colour and somewhat rusty.

"Will you drive, Gabrielle?" Jeff asked. "Then I can eat this bit of lunch before we get there."

"Of course," Gabrielle held out her hand and he dropped the keys in her palm.

Great. Now Annette would be forced to sit beside the man whether she liked it or not. And she didn't like it at all. She wrenched at the passenger door, and it opened with a screech of protest. Scrambling inside with his mug tilting precariously, she slid across a hole in the pleather where a chunk of the foam filling was missing. Making herself as small as possible, she sat primly in the center of the one bench seat, hugging her knees tightly together. A large can of nails rattled at her feet and a thick layer of dust covered everything. She felt a sneeze coming on.

Jeff eased himself in beside her, sticking the bag of sandwiches on the floor under his feet. He wedged the two thermoses between them as he balanced his sandwich on a knee before hauling the door shut. Gabrielle put the keys in the ignition and the vehicle roared to life.

"Drive until I tell you where to turn," Jeff mumbled, using his sandwich to gesture. Then he fell upon the bread with gusto.

Annette forced herself to imagine the paint colours she'd use if she were to capture this scene, rather than looking at the jeans-clad legs that were so close to hers. A tingle of awareness shivered up her spine. As long as he kept to his own side of the truck, it would be alright.

They rumbled down the drive on their way back to the main road, and their tires crunched onto thick gravel as they turned left at Jeff's instruction. The road was not dusty today, due to the rain of the night before. He rolled down his window, and the pure scent of mountain air was invigorating. It ruffled through her thick ponytail of hair.

"Do you see that entrance on the left?" Jeff asked. He brushed crumbs from his lap and motioned for his drink. "Thanks. Okay, slow down a little because that's the one we want." Gabrielle signalled, although the road was deserted, turned, and stopped in front of the fence. Jeff handed Annette his coffee mug again and hopped out to open the gate. To her, it didn't appear to be anything more than a few sticks and some barbed wire.

Waving her through, Jeff dragged the gate shut behind them and jumped back inside. Reaching for his coffee, he took a slurp and said, "Alright, just aim for the far corner of this field. Drive slow. It's rough out here."

He wasn't joking. They'd only travelled a short distance when the front right tire dropped into a hole and bounced out again. The vehicle lurched, and so did Annette. Her body slammed into Jeff with such force that it almost knocked the wind out of her.

"You okay?" he probed gruffly, but made no attempt to help her straighten herself. "And don't bother saying it, because I already know what you're going to tell me—dess-oh-lay. Correct?"

She nodded, jamming her feet against the floor, and vowing to be prepared if it happened again. They lumbered on across the pasture. Most of the grass had been grazed low to the ground, but in some areas the tall, pale green fronds shivered in the breeze. They passed huge rocks occasionally. Otherwise, the land rolled on and on, like a great, green sea stretching into the distance until reaching the base of the mountains.

"Likely a badger made that hole," he added conversationally. As they reached the summit of a hill, he pointed ahead and leaned forward to speak exclusively to Gabrielle. "See that bluff of trees down there?"

"Yes."

"I want you to drive straight for it." Jeff settled back in the seat and tipped the rest of the drink down his throat.

They bumped along in silence. It was getting hot in the cab of the truck with the sun's heat bearing down on the roof. Gabrielle rolled her window down and rested her elbow on it. The sounds of the prairie came alive—the haunting cry of a hawk high overhead, the chirping of small birds flitting past, and eventually shrill, high-pitched whistling sounds.

"What's that noise?" Annette asked.

"A noise?" He reared up, cocked his head to listen, and then looked at her questioningly. "Was it a knocking sound from up front, in the engine? Or that grinding sound when she put on the brakes? Or maybe it's the chugging sound from underneath the carriage? I mean, the muffler does have a few holes in it I guess, but that's to be expected with the kind of—"

"No," she interrupted sharply. "I'm not talking about your wretched truck. *Écouter!*"

Jeff muttered indistinctly, "Wretched? My truck is wretched? It's a perfectly good vehicle I'll have you kn—"

Gabrielle cut in. "You mean the whistles?" When Annette nodded, she laughed and went on. "Sorry Jeff, but my sister wouldn't be referring to vehicle sounds. Those are gophers," she explained. "At least that's what Andrew calls them. See all those mounds of earth?"

"*Oui.*"

"Just watch and you'll see the small, tan-coloured animals that made them."

Annette did, and presently saw one of the gophers standing on top of his burrow to sniff the air. He flicked a little tail with a black tip and stared at them with wide, almond-shaped eyes. "Oh!" she said excitedly. "Isn't he cute?"

"No." Jeff growled with a glare. "He is not cute at all. Gophers are the reason we fell in a badger hole. Badgers dig gophers out and leave a huge mess behind that a cow or horse could step into and break their leg." He fell into a stony silence.

"Then, isn't it the badgers at fault, rather than the gophers?" she ventured.

But Jeff didn't respond. His phone suddenly beeped, and he unfastened his shirt pocket to retrieve it.

"Yes…" he barked. There was a long pause, in which another man could be heard shouting over bawling cattle. "You've caught them? Great. We're almost there." He put his phone away.

The truck bounced along the last stretch of open land before the bluff of trees and now that they were closer, Annette saw a herd of white cattle huddled together near a corral. Two all-terrain vehicles were parked nearby.

As they pulled up along the fringes of the cattle, Gabrielle stopped, and Jeff slid out. He leaned into the bed of the truck and lifted out a green, rather beaten up, metal box only to disappear when he plunged into the stamping herd of animals. The herd had to be over one hundred cattle here. Inquisitive creatures that they were, the cows soon surrounded them. They pushed into one another with their huge heads, sniffed the truck, and a few even licked it with unbelievably long tongues. Annette was glad Jeff had left them in the safety of the vehicle.

"This gives you a real taste of ranch life, don't you

think?" Gabrielle draped herself over the wheel after having rolled the windows up most of the way to keep the interior of the cab from being inundated with cows. She turned off the engine and looked at Annette's sour expression with amusement.

"Apart from the smell, yes. It's interesting. I've always enjoyed learning how people live in other countries." She raised her phone to snap a few pictures. "There are so many beautiful scenes to paint. How I wish I could."

"You brought a sketchpad, didn't you? Why don't you take some time tomorrow and draw a little. Pencil drawings have always been a favourite of yours, right? So do it."

"That's true," Annette reflected on the words of an instructor at the school of art where she'd just spent the last four years. He was an older man who wore shabby suits with greying hair that most often stood straight up from his head. Monsieur Moreau had squinted through heavy glasses at them on this particular day, after someone had made a disparaging statement concerning sketches. He had slammed a hand on his desk before proclaiming, "Artists have been using graphite pencils to draw with for centuries. Never discount the importance of sketching, for through it, the raw essence of your vision begins."

Gabrielle was right. Somehow, she'd managed to slide a sketch book into her bag, along with a small selection of pencils. She would make a point to draw each day, so she could carry the images of this place back to Paris with her. But for now, she would capture as many images as she could with her phone.

"I'm moving," Gabrielle announced and pushed the truck door open into the milling throng of white beasts. "Jeff will want to drive now."

"Are you crazy?" Annette flung herself at her sister to

stop her, but it was too late. Gabrielle was shimmying through the cattle, who shied away from this strange new person, and soon was climbing in the other side of the cab.

"Why did you do that? And how? All you had to do was ask me to slide over. Why don't you sit in the middle? Please?" she asked in a wheedling tone.

"Sure, I don't mind," Gabrielle responded with an evil smile. "We'll hop out with the cows, and you wait there with them while I get back in. Then you follow."

Annette glared at her. It would have been so simple before her sister got out, and then she wouldn't have been stuck sitting next to Jeff again. But no, it was obvious her sister was playing a bit at matchmaker.

She had just opened her mouth to complain again, when the cattle at the front of the truck parted and fell over themselves to move out of the way like the waves of the Red Sea. Through the opening came Jeff, still carrying his green box, but with a smudge of dirt on his cheek and grass stains on his knees. He flung the container into the back where it landed with a clatter, and climbed behind the wheel.

Flashing them a toothy grin, he started the engine and said, "That went better than expected. Matt had the calves all ready for me." He reversed the truck slowly away from the herd and then they bumped back the way they'd come.

"What did you say was wrong with them?" Gabrielle asked. Annette gritted her teeth and braced herself against the floor. The bumping and jerking of the truck were worse since Jeff drove faster than Gabrielle.

"The calves have something called foot rot," he began. Pushing his hat off his forehead, he draped an elbow out the window, and took a deep breath before continuing with his explanation. He expelled it in a gust of air as Annette spoke.

"*Ça a l'air horrible,*" she muttered darkly.

"Hang on," Jeff yelled suddenly, as he cranked the wheel to the left, dodging a gopher hill that had appeared in the long grass. Annette fell against him despite her best efforts not to, and in turn, Gabrielle fell against her. It took some time to pull themselves upright again. For a moment Annette clutched Jeff's arm for support. His muscles felt as hard as cast iron.

"Sorry about that," he said. "Now, could you repeat your statement—in English?"

"I said, that sounds horrible," repeated Annette. "Does the animal's foot actually rot away?"

"It is horrible," he agreed. "Bacteria can easily enter a cut or abrasion if the animal steps on a stick or a sharp rock. It doesn't take much. The infectious, decaying disease goes to work on destroying the tissues of the foot. We check the animals every day to watch for all sorts of problems, but this is a major one."

"And what did you 'ave in your green medical kit that would cure those animals?" Gabrielle interjected.

"Penicillin," he replied without missing a beat.

The discussion was closed. As a comfortable silence fell inside the cab, Annette looked around with interest. They had looked upon the Rockies on the way in. Only now, facing the other direction, she could see the outbuildings of another massive farm set well back from the road on the opposite side. When Jeff stopped back at the fence line, she could see a discrete sign, nailed to two poles at the entrance, *Danbury Farms.*

"Can you drive it through for me?" Jeff asked, craning his head to look at her. She nodded mutely. However brief, those few seconds where his big brown eyes had captured hers had left her a bit tongue-tied.

"Thanks," he said. "Not everyone is cut out to drive such wretchedness." With a squeal he shoved open the door, got out, and strode in front of the truck to unfasten the gate and haul it out of her way. Flushing with embarrassment, Annette slid behind the wheel, put it in gear, and rolled through. As she passed him, he tipped his hat and grinned at her.

Annette giggled and Gabrielle raised questioning eyebrows. Thankfully, he had a sense of humour. She hadn't meant to call his truck names, but she'd heard someone use that particular word in an American movie once and it had stuck in her head.

"Is that the Danbury you mentioned before? The one who made Sophie an offer?" Gabrielle queried when Jeff got back in and resumed driving.

"Yep. He's not well-liked, but I think he's honest enough. Jim and his son have a pretty big ranch and they're always looking to buy more land."

"Is it not reasonable to think that they might 'ave something to do with the troubles at Sophie's?" Gabrielle flipped her long black braid over her shoulder and sighed. "I realize I'm an outsider. I don't know the people around 'ere like you do, but someone is at the bottom of this. And if this man is buying up land, it makes sense he'd want 'ers. It's next door. So, why not 'im?"

"He'd have a lot to gain if she were scared off or ended up in financial trouble and was forced to sell," added Annette. "She might even sell cheap."

Jeff ran a hand back and forth across his chin, the day's growth of black beard making a scratchy noise. "I agree," he conceded. "And those two are shifty, there's no doubt about it. But would they stoop to such depths? Old Sam Danbury, Jim's dad, was good friends with Malcom's folks.

And mine too for that matter. He was hard as nails, but he was a good man. I just can't imagine his son would go so far wrong."

Gabrielle slumped in her seat and lifted a hand to push a strand of hair from her face. "But it's possible," she said quietly.

Chapter Seven

A few kilometres later, after passing the massive sign leading to Jeff's home in the foothills, they crested a hill overlooking a valley. Below, a large yellow house and various red outbuildings huddled at the end of the curving lane that followed the side of the gorge until reaching the far end.

"That's it!" Gabrielle cried in excitement. She reached out to clutch Annette's hand. "We're almost there. Isn't it pretty?"

It was indeed pretty. Annette shaded her eyes, wishing she'd brought her sunglasses. They motored down the hill and turned to the right. Huge trees, tall, silent sentinels lined the road, their lofty branches bowing low and creating an arbour overhead. Immediately, Annette thought of the countryside in France where enormous plane trees had been planted beside ancient roads.

When she was a child, her father had told her that in the 19th century, Napoleon had ordered plane trees to be planted on both sides of the road in order to keep his marching armies in the shade, rather than in the blistering sun. She wasn't at all sure if the story was true, but she'd always remembered it.

"This is lovely," she whispered, squeezing her sister's hand in response. Far below them, on the right, was a stony creek bed where a trickle of water still ran. She imagined the great snows of winter in this land, and how such places must rush with icy water in the spring. They climbed a knoll and at last saw the ranch spreading out before them.

An old white farmhouse peeked out from behind a bank of maple trees that appeared to have been planted around the entire property. Beyond the house, an enormous hip-roofed barn stood solidly, a testament to the fine craftsmanship of a bygone era. Surrounding the barn, as though it were the hub of a wheel, smaller sheds and corrals extended out like the spokes. In winter, it would be a warm place to shelter the animals. Facing this, but set well apart, was a long silver building covered in tin.

Several vehicles and a huge truck with equipment on the back and a sticker on the door reading, 'Water Well Digging and Servicing,' were parked in front of the house. Jeff pulled up and stopped, but no one could be seen. In a flash, Gabrielle was gone. She ran across the yard to leap across flower beds and hurtle over a low picket fence that separated the lawn from the driveway. In a single bound she had thrown herself onto the long white veranda and was banging on the front door.

Annette stepped to the ground, watching her sister, and aware that Jeff had come to stand beside her. It was picturesque. The home, actually the whole yard, looked like a glossy picture taken straight from a high-class architecture magazine. However, no one answered Gabrielle's knock, and she returned to them looking dejected.

"Sophie has to be 'ere somewhere, doesn't she? You said

she texted you?" Without waiting for an answer, Gabrielle set off toward the barn and Jeff strode after her. Annette lagged behind, almost afraid to hear the reason Sophie had asked Jeff to come over. Had something else happened? Not another tragedy?

A long metal gate creaked open on Annette's left and a group of people marched into view, every one of them wearing rubber boots. It was a good thing too, because they were caked in mud up to their ankles.

She spotted Rosa first, since the woman gave a little screech of happiness and rushed to Jeff. She leaned against his arm to whisper something in his ear. Annette sniffed. The woman was more than obvious about her intentions, but she wondered what Jeff thought of it all. She peered at him as Rosa tucked her arm into his with a big grin on her face. Only she couldn't detect anything, but slight embarrassment on the man's part. He listened intently to what she had to say, and nodded, but then stepped forward to shake hands with the three men who accompanied Sophie.

Gabrielle hurried to greet her mother-in-law. By the time Annette reached them, Sophie was assuring everyone that things were fine, and the three cows were improving. She wished the men a good day and thanked them for their time.

"We'll be back Tuesday," one of the men said as he climbed into the larger vehicle.

"I appreciate it," Sophie called. He slammed the door shut. With a wave, the two heavy vehicles turned around and pulled out of the yard.

Sophie took Gabrielle's hands and smiled into her face. "I am so glad you are 'ere, at last. I am so sorry for this mess that 'as ruined your visit."

"Not at all," soothed Gabrielle. "Jeff 'as been so kind to

us. I went for a ride this morning, he gave Annette her first lesson, we enjoyed a wonderful lunch, and then we went with him while he treated two calves with foot rot."

"Yes," inserted Annette. "It's been most educational." She didn't miss Rosa's narrowed eyes as she spoke, or the way Jeff flashed her a questioning look. Hastening to explain, she said, "I wasn't being sarcastic. It's truly been a very interesting day."

A smile of relief washed over Sophie's face. "Oh, that's wonderful. I'm so grateful to have such good people to 'elp me." She raised a weary hand to her forehead and rubbed at the frown lines embedded there. "It will cost several thousand dollars to have the well cleaned out and then the water must be analysed before it can be trusted." She sighed, then made a visible effort to smile at the tall man beside her. "Somehow I will repay you for your kindness, my dear." Reaching up, she laid a hand on Jeff's cheek. "You 'ave been like a son to me."

Annette was amazed to see Jeff turn red and stumble over his next words. "You know I'm happy to help you, Sophie. You were always there for Mom and me after the accident."

"That's what family is for," she murmured. Clapping her hands together, she became brisk. "So now we come to the next order of business. I'm sure you're wondering why I asked you here."

"Excuse me for interrupting," Rosa interjected, "but I have some work to attend to in the house. I'll see you later." She spoke to the group, yet looked only at Jeff. He smiled at her—was it lovingly? Annette couldn't tell, but either way it didn't matter to her.

"Of course, my dear," Sophie said, patting the other

woman on the arm. "I'll be in later." And with that, Rosa sashayed to the house.

Annette had never actually thought about anyone strutting in a provocative way before, but it certainly fit the way in which Rosa swivelled her hips as she crossed the driveway and climbed up the steps of the house. Then, as she reached the veranda, she cast a look over her shoulder, again to Jeff. A very coquettish glance, full of meaning. Annette quickly looked at him. He was indeed watching the attractive young woman, but was there the merest suggestion of unease on his face? Again, Annette couldn't tell. Perhaps they were secret lovers and this evocative behavior discomfited him. It intrigued her, purely from an interested bystander point of view.

Sophie tucked her arm through Jeff's, and they began walking toward a low building next to the house. "It's my old truck," she said. "It wouldn't start this afternoon when I tried to take it out to check on the cattle next to Dead Horse Creek. Malcom was the mechanic, not me." She sighed. "Could you look at it please? I asked Marcus, one of the new people I hired, but he was lost. Mechanics aren't his thing, apparently."

"Of course," Jeff assured her. "Also, Sandra made you all some sandwiches and coffee. They're in my truck." He took off his hat and dragged an arm across his forehead. "If you'll forgive me for saying so, basic mechanics is a necessary skill when working on a ranch."

"I know," she sighed. "He wasn't entirely honest with me about that when I hired him. But he seems good with the animals, so that's something. Anyway, I hate to bother you with it since I know you're busy with your own work, but…"

"Say no more," Jeff patted her hand where it rested on

his arm. "I'll see what I can do. Why don't you take the girls and sit for a few minutes? Are the keys in it?"

She nodded. "Thank you, Jeff." He broke away and strode the rest of the distance to the garage where he disappeared inside through a side door. After a moment, the large overhead access slid open. Sophie ran a hand through her hair that was already standing on end.

"It's been quite a few days," she said quietly, as though only she could hear. Then, rousing herself, she turned and tucked an arm through each of the girls' arms before leading the way to the porch steps. She reverted back to her native French now that they were alone. "We haven't had time for a proper visit," she said. "Tell me about your graduation Annette. And Gabrielle, how is Andrew doing with the wine shop?"

"We will tell all. But I must be honest, because I love you..." There was a note of reproval in Gabrielle's tone. "I think you need to tell your sons what is happening here."

The smile faded from Sophie's face, but Gabrielle continued. "They love you and will be very upset when they find out you didn't share your troubles with them."

"They have their own lives, and you are part of Andrew's..." Sophie faltered. "I don't want to put any of you in a position where you must take care of me—or the ranch."

They mounted the steps, three abreast, and Sophie pointed to a cushioned patio swing and chairs all done in blue and white stripes. Multi-coloured flowers overflowed from huge ceramic pots and hung from wicker baskets overhead. Just looking at the space was relaxing. They sank into the chairs and resumed the conversation, although Sophie looked pained to do so. With head bowed, she wrung her hands together in silence.

"It's not about obligation," Gabrielle said softly, "It's about love. We care about the ranch, but we love you. Can you imagine how they'd feel if something happened to you? And if knowing what you were going through means that they decide to come here and help, then that's what they should do." She leaned forward, her braid swinging over her shoulder, and placed a hand over Sophie's clasped ones. Her eyes were pleading. "Also, I happen to know Jayke used to love tinkering with engines." A smile lifted the corners of her generous mouth. "What's he doing in Vancouver, anyway?"

Sophie looked up, but avoided her daughter-in-law's eyes. Instead, she gazed over the whitewashed railings of the veranda with a sheepish look on her face. "He's a mechanic…"

Annette laughed aloud. "You're kidding!" Then she subsided with a cough when she saw that Sophie was dead serious. "Sorry. It just seems a little ironic when..." She fell silent and began fingering the flowers next to her chair, studying the velvety, purple pansies with great interest. This was a family situation, and she should stay out of it.

"Annette is right," Gabrielle said emphatically. "Has Jayke told you he isn't interested in taking over the ranch one day?"

It was a long minute before Sophie answered, and then it was with obvious reluctance. "Not exactly. But I don't want him to feel obligated either."

"Have you ever asked him? Or talked about it?" She flipped her braid out of the way and sat back.

"Not that I can remember," Sophie said in a low voice. "I suppose, if anything, I encouraged him to leave. To seek his happiness wherever he might wish." She shrugged. "Perhaps that was wrong, I don't know. I just wanted him to have choices."

"It's not wrong." Gabrielle joined Sophie in staring out across the landscape toward the rough edges of the Rocky Mountains, hazy in the distance. "You are a wonderful mother and I know you have the best interests of your sons at heart—it's just—you're not looking at this from all sides. I'm not telling you what to do. I'm just encouraging you to talk with them candidly. It's not my place to do so, and you have my word that I won't. But you need to tell them."

"Malcom didn't have that choice," Sophie blurted suddenly. She looked at Gabrielle with beseeching eyes. "I've never told this to anyone, and I beg you not to tell the boys. Their father wanted to be an architect. He had no desire to run the farm once he was grown, but—but he wasn't given that opportunity. It was expected that he take over the ranch and keep it in the family," she lifted a shoulder and let it fall. "Above all, Malcom wanted to please his father. So, he did what was expected of him." She blinked rapidly, but a tear escaped and ran down her cheek.

"We had a good life here, Malcom and I, but he should have been allowed to follow his dreams. It was wrong of his family to force a life decision on him, and I won't allow that to happen to my boys," she said fiercely. "Malcom agreed with me. That's why neither of us talked to them about the ranch, or asked them if they wanted to stay here and take over. Then," she drew a deep breath and flicked away another tear, "Malcom died. Jayke was already making plans to live in Vancouver. Meanwhile, you and Andrew were starting a new life in Paris. I couldn't lay my burdens on you."

Sophie got to her feet and stepped to the railing. Leaning on it she sniffed and dabbed at her eyes. "You're right, though," she said unsteadily. "I do need to tell them what's been going on. Thank you my dear." Turning slowly, she moved to Gabrielle who jumped to her feet. The two women embraced for a long moment punctuated by deep sobbing breaths on both sides.

Discretely, Annette got to her feet and tiptoed to the other side of the veranda. She leaned over the rails and took a deep cleansing breath. They hadn't even been here for two full days and already so much had happened. She heard the rumble of an engine and looked up to see the bumper of a truck nose its way out of the garage where they'd left Jeff. Beyond it, peering around the corner of the riding arena, a tall figure stood in the shade, watching them. Odd. Annette squinted, wishing she had her old glasses at hand, but the figure melted into the shadows and vanished. It must have been one of the new ranch hands.

A cloud of blue smoke accompanied the roar and so did the cab of a bright yellow truck. It wasn't new, but it certainly made a statement. Annette loved statements and she was impressed. Sophie travelled in style.

She watched in fascination as Jeff stopped and hopped out to ensure that the garage doors were closed before he drove the large vehicle up the driveway. As he passed, he tipped his hat to her and grinned. She found herself grinning back, her heart suddenly happy.

Maybe, just maybe she was glad she'd come to Canada.

Chapter Eight

True to her word, Sandra had left a casserole in the refrigerator for them to put in the oven upon their return. While Jeff went out to attend to other obligations, Annette and Gabrielle put together the meal. Instructions had been scrawled on an orange note that was stuck to the counter, but most of the words were obliterated by numerous messy drips of something brown and gooey. As Annette held the page up to squint at it, the unknown substance trickled down the page. She quickly laid it flat again.

"I think it says to set the dish on a cookie sheet and preheat the oven to three hundred fifty degrees before we cut a slit in the top of the pastry and bake it for one hour. But I can't be sure," she said, hovering over the page at every angle. "It might be telling us to strap the dish to the back of a cooked sheep and turn often at a three hundred fifty degree angle over an outdoor spit."

Gabrielle laughed. "You're crazy. I think we'll go with the first set of guidelines, just to be safe."

Working together, they assembled the makings of a

salad and set the table. With the casserole in the oven a delicious aroma soon flooded the kitchen. They debated the contents of the unknown meal, since Sandra hadn't mentioned what ingredients were used. It was doubtful they could have read it if she had, but it smelled divine. Annette's mouth was watering by the time Sophie and the ever-silent Rosa, arrived. Rosa contrived to sit opposite them at the table, with an empty chair beside her. Annette and Gabrielle were next to one another, and Sophie sat stoic at the head.

Dinner that night was a dismal affair. Sophie remained lost in thought, which was understandable given all that had happened, and especially after Gabrielle had spoken to her. Jeff only appeared at the last moment. They sat silently at the table waiting for him as he crashed around at the back entry, taking off his things and washing his hands. When he appeared, he ran wet fingers through his hair, pushing it off his face which caused his bearded jaw to look even more chiselled and handsome than it already was.

Annette forced herself to look away, aware that Rosa's eyes were riveted on her this time, rather than on Jeff. *The woman has nothing to fear*, she thought with distaste. She had no interest in this rough and tumble man from Canada's outback. She was attracted to men of refinement with good taste—who understood wine pairings and dressed according to the current trends.

"Sorry if I kept you all waiting," he called, dragging out the chair beside Rosa and flinging himself into it. "You should have started without me."

"It's not the same without the man of the house," Rosa responded with saccharine sweetness. She looked up coyly and fluttered her lashes.

Annette's stomach tightened with revulsion. *Note to self:*

never, ever, under any circumstance, do you act like a simpering ninny for a man.

Steam from the hot casserole dish rose into the air like a pillar of smoke, releasing a delectable scent.

"Chicken pot pie," Sophie announced dreamily. "Sandra makes it better than anyone I know."

Annette and Gabrielle exchanged looks. Oh, that's what it was. Of course.

"May I serve you?" Annette asked Sophie first. Picking up the large spoon she brandished it in the air. "I am armed, but not dangerous." Her attempt at levity fell a bit flat, but Sophie managed an exhausted smile and handed Annette her plate.

"Please," she said.

Annette busied herself filling everyone's dishes while the rest of them passed around salad and the homemade dressing Sandra had prepared. A stack of sliced, freshly baked bread was also part of the feast.

Annette ladled out Jeff's meal last. Afterward, she couldn't think how it happened because it didn't with anyone else. Yet as she handed him the plate, for a brief moment, his fingers covered hers before sliding away. Involuntarily, her body shivered. Her eyes snapped up to hold his in a shocked glance that went on for far too long. Then she shook herself and sat down with a bump, feeling flustered.

"I 'eard from Weaver today," Sophie suddenly announced. Jeff dropped his fork to his plate with a clatter.

"Isn't that the oil tycoon from up north who was buying the poisoned cows?" he asked in astonishment. "What does he want?" Jeff reached for his glass and took a deep drink.

"Yes, that's 'im." Sophie offered nothing more. She stared at her plate, making no move to eat the tantalizing food. Perhaps this was why she looked so preoccupied tonight. A pregnant silence ensued in which Jeff waited patiently for more information and Annette felt something was wrong.

Rosa cleared her throat with a tiny cough. "I know it's not my decision," she said, dabbing her mouth delicately with a napkin. "But I care about Sophie, and the Triple T, and I think she should consider what he proposed."

"What did he say?" Jeff disregarded this last statement and stared at Sophie with growing concern. Raising his voice, he scraped his chair around to face her. "Does he want to buy other cattle?"

Sophie sighed again and ran a hand through her cropped hair. "Weaver said 'e 'as been thinking about the troubles I've been 'aving and wants to follow through with the sale of the remaining three animals."

Jeff frowned. "Okay, well that's not so bad. It's kind of weird, but decent of him actually." His brows knit together in a frown. "That's not all though, is it?" he probed.

"No, that's not all." Sophie twisted a napkin between her hands, pouring all the stress she was feeling into the cloth. "Yesterday, when I was trying to explain why the animals weren't on their way to 'im, I told Weaver more than I should 'ave about the problems I've been 'aving." She lifted an anguished face and stared at Jeff. "He not only offered to still take the sick cows…" she paused and took a long slow breath. "He offered to take the ranch off my 'ands—again." Her eyes fell to the table. "A month ago, when 'e came to look at the cattle I 'ad for sale, 'e offered the same thing."

"I see," Jeff said slowly. "Well, I can't say I haven't thought it might be the best thing for you to do. But I don't think it's what you want. Is it?"

Annette sucked in her breath. Gabrielle tensed beside

her. The atmosphere at the table was strained and watchful as all eyes turned to Sophie. The older lady shrugged.

"I don't know what I want," she finally admitted. "Weaver seems like an 'onest fellow and 'e made me an offer that would be 'ard to refuse. It's well above what the place is worth." She wrapped the napkin around her clenched fist in agitation and then ripped it off and wrapped it around the other hand. "If I wasn't 'aving financial issues, I wouldn't even consider it, but…" She lifted her hands in resignation. "Losing Malcom really changed things, and I'm just not as sure I can run the place alone." She glanced up at Jeff and Rosa. "Even with the support of friends."

Sophie looked quickly at Gabrielle. "Don't worry," she said with emphasis, "I'll call the boys before I make a final decision, but I won't let them give up the lives they've built for themselves to come running 'ome for me." Her voice grew stronger as she spoke. "I'll sell the place before I do that."

Everyone sank into a grim reverie after Sophie's final statement. What could be said? The chicken pot pie didn't receive the attention it should have, the salad wilted into a dejected heap, and the bread dried to a husk before their very eyes. It was a sad end to the day.

Of course, Rosa appeared to have no trouble cleaning her plate, but Annette had already decided that the woman didn't care about Sophie as much as she professed. She made a mental note to ask Gabrielle about Rosa as soon as they were alone.

This opportunity came sooner than expected. After everyone pushed their dinners around their plates for the required amount of time, they made their various excuses, got up, and left.

Sophie complained of a headache and retired to her room. Jeff went back outside, and Rosa lounged on a sofa in the living room in front of the television. Annette and Gabrielle cleared the table.

Once the dishes were stacked in the dishwasher and the food was put away, they both decided to call it an early night. They slipped past Rosa and noiselessly climbed the stairs to their rooms.

"Do you want to come in and chat for a few minutes?" Gabrielle asked when they reached her door.

Nodding, Annette followed her sister inside and flopped down on the bed with a groan. "What a day!" she said, coming up on one elbow to gaze out the wide expanse of window beside her. The sunset was radiant. Colours transformed before her eyes from soft pinks and oranges to deep amethyst and fuchsia. The mountains were bathed in a warm glow, their peaks outlined in gold against the sky.

She felt a sense of envy for the people who lived here. This was an everyday sight for them. They didn't deal with the exhaust fumes of a busy street, or the incessant clamour of humanity passing by their front doors. They would never feel the need to shut the world out while they tried desperately to create something beautiful on a canvas as the sound of a siren's wailing cry drove past their window.

Her heart almost ached from the beauty of this country. She studied the distant summits. They were an ever-present strength; steady and strong. She felt compelled to tell Sophie to draw power from them, to not give in to the forces seeking to drive her from her home nestled in the embrace of the majestic Rockies. She wanted to say that it was worth fighting for. But it was not her decision to make, nor to influence. Soon she would return to the familiarity of her apartment in Paris. She would leave this alternate world and all of its troubles behind, moving on to the next chapter of her life.

She sagged back on the bed and stared at the ceiling. Poor Sophie.

"It's been a whirlwind since we arrived," Gabrielle agreed. She sat on the bed and scooted herself backward until she was propped against the pillows. Drawing her knees up to her chest she said, "I have no idea who this Rosa is or why she seems to carry such weight with Sophie."

Annette flipped onto her stomach and held her chin in her hands. "I can't believe you just said that," she admitted with a look toward the door as though the subject of their discussion was lurking just outside. "I've been meaning to ask you that very thing."

Gabrielle shrugged expressively. "As you know, Andrew and I stayed with Sophie after Malcom died. Rosa wasn't here then. But a month or so later, we started hearing her name."

"In what context? I mean, is she a secretary? A personal assistant? A freeloading friend? What?"

Gabrielle made a face. "I'd have to guess she's more of a freeloading friend, but that's not likely to be Sophie's description. When Andrew spoke to his mother, she credited Rosa for bringing her through a very difficult time. I think she's with Sophie as an office manager and bookkeeper, but Sophie has a number of horses too. Apparently Rosa trains them for barrel racing."

"Barrel racing?" repeated Annette. "I could ask you to expound on that, but I suppose it's self-explanatory. I can only assume she trains horses to race *around* barrels, because I cannot see how they could race *against* them. Still, I've been wrong before."

Gabrielle giggled. "Anything's possible."

"And what do you think of this latest offer to buy the ranch?"

Her sister shook her head sorrowfully. "I don't like it. But it's none of my business. She needs to discuss it with her sons. Running a ranch is a huge job." Gabrielle removed the elastic from her braid and began to separate the strands of glossy black hair. "Anyway, Sophie promised she'd talk to Andrew and Jayke. Unless she asks me for help, I can't interfere any further."

"Yes, that's all you can do." Annette rolled off the bed and hugged her sister. "You're a really good daughter-in-law, do you know that? I'm proud of you."

"Wow, what brought that on?" Gabrielle hugged her back.

"Gratitude," Annette answered serenely. "I'm glad you brought me here. It hasn't gone according to plan, but it's still been good. Maybe even life-changing," she said with a grin as she walked to the door. With her hand on the latch, she turned. "I may go home and order up some glitter shoes in every colour of the rainbow."

Gabrielle laughed and threw a pillow at her.

"Good night dear sister," Annette called, flitting into the hall.

As she entered her own room she leaned against the door and hugged herself. The rosy light of the setting sun painted the furniture in a golden hue, turning the space into a magical chamber of gilded light and shadow. A vase of fresh flowers sat on the night table. She walked to them and lifted it to her nose, drinking in the sweet scent of the huge pink peonies.

"Thank you Sandra," she whispered.

She wandered to the window and gazed out at the mountains, transforming into the silhouettes of evening.

Being here was like living in a fairy-tale. She spread out her arms and twirled, suddenly wishing she was wearing the beautiful violet dress and satin shoes. They suited this moment of beauty and wonder.

She now understood what Gabby had tried so hard to tell her. This was no place for frilly dresses and high heeled shoes. And she was beginning to realize there was more to life than fashionable clothing and art galleries. But maybe one quiet evening, all by herself, she would put her pretty things on and glory in the feeling of being a princess in a tower.

She yawned. The day's events were catching up with her. She crossed to her bed and rummaged beneath the pillow for her nightgown. It only took a few minutes to brush her teeth and wash up. She would shower in the morning. Quickly she disrobed and tugged the gown over her head. Climbing onto the bed, she crawled under the soft white comforter and fell fast asleep.

It was some time later that Annette awoke with a pounding headache. She fumbled for her phone on the table and nearly knocked over the flowers. Tapping her phone to life, she looked at the time. It was only eleven o'clock at night. She flipped the covers back and slipped out of bed, clutching her forehead. These headaches were relentless. She needed to find her bottle of painkillers. Starting to rummage through her things, she remembered how she'd given them to Gabrielle on the plane two days ago.

Groaning irritably, she clicked on the bedside lamp, and tiptoed to the door. She opened it a crack to listen. Hearing nothing, she ventured into the hallway and scampered to

Gabrielle's door. She tapped lightly, but there was no answer. Her sister must be asleep, but she knew the pills would still be in her purse. Annette let herself in soundlessly and used the light on her phone to locate the purse where it had been flung on a chair. *Got them!*

Fisting them tightly, she moved back to the door and listened again before opening it wide. She could hear voices. Closing the door except for a thin crack, she waited for whoever it was to pass. Except they didn't. Wide awake now, she peeked through the crack to see two shadowy figures standing at the top of the stairs.

"Maybe you'd like to take our discussion to the bedroom," a female voice purred. "Why don't you join me for another drink, and we can talk more about the future?"

Oh no! It was Rosa. Annette's body froze when she heard Jeff's voice reply, low and inaudible. *Zut!* She'd known it must be him. There was no one else it could be. But it was a shock. She couldn't hear what he said, but she could definitely see the two figures slowly melt into one.

Aghast, Annette looked away, unable to bear the thought that they were a couple. She hid behind the door, closing her ears to what came next and only ventured out long after their footsteps had receded.

Slipping inside her own door, Annette lifted a hand to her head. The pain had gotten worse. She went to the bathroom, took two tablets, and ran cool water over a facecloth to lay on her throbbing brow. As she made her way back to the bed, she heard a knock. Gabrielle?

Holding the cloth to her head, she shuffled to the door. She opened it a crack, ready to explain, but it wasn't Gabby.

"I see you're awake, and it looks like you're in pain. Sorry to see that," Rosa sneered, not sounding sorry at all. In the dim light, the woman's face took on a sinister glow, her cheekbones and deep-set eyes giving her a hollow, unearthly pallor. She pushed the door wide enough to enter, and slipped inside.

"This is not a good time for me to—" Annette started to explain. Rosa cut her off.

"I think it's a perfect time, and don't worry. I have no desire to stay for a girly chat." Rosa crossed her arms across her chest and regarded Annette with narrowed eyes. "I heard you in the hall just now. You might as well know, for your own good, that Jeff and I are a couple. He just doesn't want everyone to know yet." Rosa took an intimidating step closer. Annette stumbled back, but the bed was in the way and she came to an abrupt halt. Hatred rolled off Rosa in palpable waves as she leaned in so close that Annette could feel her hot breath.

"I want you to stay away from my man," she growled like some primal beast defending a den. "Jeff's too sweet for his own good. He should never have offered to keep you and your useless sister with him. In fact, I think it might be best if you both went back where you came from. Sophie has me to help her now. Besides, Jeff and I have plans," the woman spat.

The wet cloth dropped to the floor as Annette's hands went slack and her breath caught in her throat. She leaned away from this wildly jealous woman as far as she could without toppling onto the bed and clutched at the front of her nightgown, feeling vulnerable.

Rosa stepped away, a grim smile of satisfaction on her face. "Consider this a friendly warning," she said in a soft, menacing voice. "Hope you feel better by morning. Well enough to fly home, that is,' she hissed. With a glare Rosa swept to the door and closed it quietly behind her.

Annette collapsed onto the bed feeling like the rag that

lay at her feet. That was crazy. Had she really been bullied by Rosa? What a scary woman. Already the past ten minutes felt unreal. For a start, why would anyone be jealous of her? Annette took her head in both hands and winced with pain. She couldn't think about this bizarre situation now. The medication was making her feel woozy and she needed to lie down.

Annette forced herself to stand. The first thing she did was to lock her door. Next she picked up the cloth and returned to the bathroom to refresh it under the tap. Wearily, she made her way back into bed and tried to force the disturbing images of the last thirty minutes out of her mind. Only it didn't work too well.

Although Rosa's threatening behavior was alarming, strangely it was the thought of her and Jeff together that bothered Annette the most. She didn't stop until the next day to wonder why she cared.

She only knew she did.

A lot.

Chapter Nine

Annette slept much later than she'd planned. When she finally rolled over in bed and reached for her phone to check the time, it was almost nine o'clock in the morning. She moaned and flopped back on the pillow. At least her headache was gone, but the strange events of the night before came rushing back. It had taken her a long time to fall asleep. The pain of the headache had been intensified by what had happened. It was hard to believe it wasn't just a nightmare.

However, there was nothing to do but get up and face the day. What did it matter to her if Jeff and Rosa were meeting for a secret rendezvous? They were adults, weren't they? Able to do as they pleased. Rosa certainly didn't look like Jeff's type. Or maybe she didn't know what his type was since she barely knew Jeff at all, really. The two of them were welcome to sneak around as much as they desired. The fact that Rosa seemed to find her a threat didn't even bear thinking about. It simply wasn't true.

She flipped the blankets back and stretched. What would today bring? Some new calamity, no doubt. She'd never been on such a roller coaster of a holiday before. Sliding out of bed, she went about the room drawing back curtains that she'd remembered to close the night before.

The sky was a dull slate. She paused. Leaning against the arched door to her balcony, she took it all in. Heavy clouds obscured the mountaintops, and a hazy mist muted the landscape below them, turning it a somber grey. Her gaze moved to where Jeff's horses grazed in the pasture far off to the right. She smiled. Pearl was easy to spot. Her distinct dappled patterning stood out against the lush green field.

Opening the door, Annette tiptoed across the balcony floor and leaned on the railing. She breathed deep. The air was cool and moist, with the fresh smell of rain riding in on the breeze. A low rumble of thunder echoed in the distance, perhaps warning of an impending storm.

Annette shivered as the nightgown rippled across her bare knees. She hurried back into the sanctuary of her room and the hot shower that awaited her. A faint aroma of coffee reached her nostrils and her stomach rumbled. Bundling her long curls into a shower cap, she dashed into the bathroom and turned on the water. She would have to hurry.

As she had hoped, the needles of hot water against her skin were invigorating. She rubbed herself down briskly and shrugged on the bathrobe.

Now, what to wear? She consulted her suitcase, silently thanking Gabrielle for her influence. If the case had remained as it was when her sister arrived that last morning in Paris, she would be wearing the same jeans and one top every day. Everything else would have been highly inappropriate. As it was, she chose a white, V-neck t-shirt, a long-sleeve, mandarin-coloured button-up, and her third and last pair of jeans. They were slim-fitting and boasted a series of artfully placed rips along the legs. Considering she was already a bit chilly, this might not be for the best, but the others she had brought needed laundering.

Speedily, she tucked the t-shirt into her waistband, threaded her belt through the loops, and pulled on socks. She only paused for a moment in front of the mirror to add a little gold shimmer to her eyes and some mascara. Her usual beauty regimen had been non-existent since arriving in Canada.

She took one last look at her lovely room and hurriedly tossed the covers back over the bed in a poor attempt to make it before dashing out the door.

The clatter of dishes and sound of laughter met her ears as she descended, but as she rounded the corner she saw that only two people were there—Sandra and Gabrielle. It was a pleasant reprieve. The last people she wanted to see right now were Jeff and Rosa.

"Well, you finally crawled out from your lair," called her sister, rising to kiss both her cheeks and grin teasingly. She was dressed for the day in a bright pink and black checkered shirt, buttoned to her chin and flopping loose over her jeans. Her hair was clipped in a messy bun and her face was free from makeup. It didn't matter, though. Gabrielle was gorgeous with or without it. Her eyelashes were thick and her mouth, a full natural red.

Annette smiled in response and sniffed the air appreciatively. "Good morning to you both. What is that wonderful smell?"

"Fresh blueberry bran muffins." Sandra marched to the table with a plate of them in one hand, and a cup of coffee in the other. She lifted it questioningly, "This okay?"

"Yes, please." Annette dropped into a chair across from her sister. She snatched up a napkin before grabbing a hot muffin and juggling the still-steaming treat between her hands. "Where is everyone?" she mumbled through a mouthful.

"They left two 'ours ago," said Gabrielle, reaching for a muffin. She swivelled on her chair to address the housekeeper. "Why don't you join us, Sandra?"

"I don't mind if I do." Sandra threw down the dish towel she'd been using to dry a frying pan, and poured herself a coffee.

As she came around the corner, Annette couldn't help but notice Sandra's colour of the day. The lady sported a cherry red top. That, in itself, wasn't bad. It was a beautiful shade, but the enormous, fuzzy white rabbit holding a sequined strawberry emblazoned across her chest really made the sweater pop up and hit her between the eyes. Well, that and the forest green pants she wore, coupled with the dazzling red shoes of yesterday.

"I like to call this my, thank-goodness-winter's-over, outfit," she grinned at Annette. Slowly, the lady did a turn. "You know, red and green, and Christmas. Anyway, that's what I think of when I wear it." She looked down and brushed a hand over the sequinned strawberry. "I know it's a bit outlandish, but my family's gotten used to me and my love of colour…" She raised a foot and wiggled it. "And sparkle." The lady sat down next to Gabrielle with a huff of air.

Even a week ago, Annette would have recoiled at such

an eccentric get-up. Yet, Sandra, and perhaps the influence of pure mountain air had wrought a change in her attitude.

"You are *une très belle femme*," she said to Sandra. "Uh, I think you look beautiful in it."

"Why thank you." Sandra was pleased.

Annette turned her focus to the muffin, the berries bursting hotly in her mouth. "They're called *myrtilles* in French," she said thoughtfully. When Sandra looked at her quizzically, Annette raised the muffin pointedly. "The blueberries," she explained. "Whatever the name, these are the best muffins I've ever 'ad."

Sandra laughed in delight. She rested her elbows on the table and leaned toward them conspiratorially. "So…give me your honest opinion. What do you think of Rosa?"

The question took Annette totally off guard, and she could see the surprise on Gabrielle's face too.

"I—I…well…I," Gabrielle stuttered. "That is…uh, I mean…I…"

"Exactly," snorted Sandra, leaning back and folding her arms across the rabbit. "What about you?" she pinned Annette with a piercing stare.

Annette saw no reason to mince words. "I don't like 'er," she said, but then amended her statement. "Still, to be fair I don't know Rosa, and Sophie seems to think a lot of 'er." The events of last night were too bizarre for breakfast conversation and she decided to keep them to herself.

Sandra snorted again. "Sophie doesn't see it, but that…" she lifted her hands to do air quotes, "office assistant slash horse trainer woman, is after Jeffrey, that's what. I wouldn't trust her as far as I could throw her." She slammed her cup on the table with a bang.

Gabrielle was still opening and closing her mouth in a

very fish-like manner. Annette finished her muffin and took a drink before asking, "What makes you say that?"

"Because she's been mooning around behind him ever since she arrived at the Triple T. It's sickening," Sandra's mouth thinned with anger.

"You think she's after 'im for unscrupulous reasons?" Gabrielle finally found her voice. "Maybe she's truly fallen in love with 'im."

"Bah!" Sandra retorted. "Then why did I see her kissing another man just last week?"

"What! Where?" Annette and Gabrielle both chimed in.

Sandra slammed a hand on the table. "Flat on the lips," she growled, looking back and forth between them. "And it wasn't some little peck either. It was a big wet one," she nodded meaningfully.

Despite the gravity of the situation, Annette had to hold back a smile. "I meant, where did you see them?"

"Oh," Sandra grinned sheepishly. "In the city. Hubby and I went out for our anniversary to a splashy restaurant. Seated at the center table, was Rosa with some tall blond guy, and another older man, both men wearing expensive suits. We were led to a corner table out of sight, but before we were seated they all got up to leave…and Rosa smooched with the younger guy right there in the middle of the place! For all the world to see."

"*Mon Dieu*," Annette muttered to herself. In her mind she was back at Gabrielle's door, watching through a crack as Rosa invited Jeff to her room. And then they had kissed. At least she thought they had.

"I'm sure Jeff and Rosa can deal with their own affairs," Gabrielle said soothingly, then corrected herself. "Perhaps that wasn't the best word to use." Staring out the window, she took another sip of her coffee. "Do you suppose it will rain today, Sandra?" she asked, deftly changing the subject.

The lady shrugged noncommittedly. "It's not supposed to rain. Sometimes storms that hang over the Rockies blow right over us. Anyway, I'd better get back to my lunch preparations instead of gossiping," she added with an apologetic smile. She collected their empty cups and moved away, but turned back with a frown. "No," she said, shaking her head. "It's not gossip. I care about that man. He doesn't deserve to be snared by some nasty piece of work like Rosa." She stomped away.

After going back upstairs to fetch their coats, Annette and Gabrielle emerged from the house, pulling their jackets tighter around them as they stepped onto the log deck to look appraisingly at the dark whirling clouds. A flash of lightning split the western sky.

"I don't think it's wise to take horses out for a ride when a storm is brewing," Gabrielle noted. "They'll get spooked, and I don't want you to have a bad experience. Maybe we should wait here until Jeff returns and see if he can lend us a vehicle to go visit the Triple T this morning."

"That sounds like an idea." Annette said absently, still ruminating over Sandra's remarks. They settled into the porch swing, the creaking chains adding a soothing rhythm to their conversation. She decided she liked watching the interplay of twisting clouds and jagged bolts of light. The colours were magnificent.

"Have you heard anything from the galleries you applied to?" Gabrielle asked. "A couple of them seemed very interested in you."

"I haven't, but decisions are never made quickly." She twisted a strand of corkscrew hair around her finger, wishing she would have thought to tie it back. The wind was getting stronger. A moment later, her hair swirled around her face like a halo.

"I have to get an elastic," she said, trapping as much of her hair as she could in her hands. "And my sketchbook."

But she didn't have time to do either.

Without warning, Jeff's big black truck careened up the driveway, slid to a sideways stop in a shower of gravel and the motor died. Jeff lunged from the driver's seat and ran like he was being chased by rampaging water buffalos to a garage where he wrenched up the rolling door and dashed inside.

Both women ran down the steps and to the shed knowing something was drastically wrong. In a moment, Jeff was backing his old truck out of the shed and throwing poles into the back with no regard for how they landed.

"What is it?" Gabrielle screamed over the howling wind as they stopped beside him.

"Sophie called. She needs help. Cattle broke through a fence on her property. They're on the highway. Someone called the police and they're there now." He spoke in short jerky sentences, between deep grunts of effort as he tossed two and three poles at a time into the truck.

"Come on," Gabrielle hollered, seizing Annette's wrist in a steely grip. "We're going to help." Dragging open the passenger side door she pushed Annette inside and then followed, slamming the door shut just as Jeff shoved the vehicle into gear and roared away.

No one spoke. Jeff had summed the situation up in a few concise phrases and they didn't need more details to know it was bad. The truck slewed from side to side in the heavy gravel as they hit the main road. Jeff corrected their trajectory, and slammed his foot on the accelerator. The truck leapt forward, the two women hanging on tightly to one another. Tumbleweeds flew across the road ahead and got stuck in the wire fences beside them. Dust billowed behind the truck as they screamed down the road and turned onto the highway like the getaway car in a late-night movie.

And then they saw it.

At the base of the hill they'd just crested was a scene of utter mayhem. Cows and calves were all over the road and in the ditches. The flashing lights of two police vehicles were stopped on either side and officers were vainly trying to direct traffic through the maze of frightened animals. Some cattle were still in the field, but not many. Probably a hundred, highly agitated animals had flooded the area, running back and forth across the road. The bawling of frightened animals could be heard even over the relentless din of the wind and storm.

Jeff braked, and then drove straight down into the ditch on the opposite side of the break in the fence. Gradually he pulled as close to the action as he dared, threw the truck in neutral and looked at them earnestly.

"This is dangerous. Cattle aren't going to trample you unless they're scared, but right now they're terrified. I think you should stay in the truck."

"No," Annette said. "You need 'elp and we're coming with you. Right?" She turned to her sister who nodded with an ashen face.

"Actually," he said, "it would be best if one of you stayed here to drive the truck slowly behind us as we move them back. Besides, I'll need it. I've got fencing materials to repair the gap when we get the cattle back inside." He looked pointedly at Gabrielle.

"Yes. Okay," she croaked.

"Right. Let's go." Jeff leaped out and reached into the back of the truck. He threw Annette what looked like a blue plastic cane, although it had some weight to it. Then they both took off at a jog. "Use it, and extend your arms to create a barricade when rounding them up," he shouted, ramming his black hat down low on his head. "And when we get close to them, slow down to a walk. No sudden moves. We must force the cattle back over the road and inside their fence. Do you understand?"

"Yes," she yelled, but the howling wind whisked her words away into the building storm. Her hair was everywhere. There were times when she couldn't even see from it streaming over her face and covering her eyes. She twisted it into a rope, tucked it down the collar of her coat and pulled the zipper tight under her chin.

In a few moments they came upon the first of the cattle. She heard Jeff speak soothingly to the animals.

"Come on girl, that's the way. Let's go. Nope, not that way," he said, dodging to one side and holding his arms wide to prevent an escape. "Keep on going back. Everything's gonna be okay."

Annette was impressed. She followed his example and held her arms open, coming alongside him so they created a living fence that moved the animals back to safety. The first few stragglers were walking in the right direction and Annette had hope that it would all go so smoothly.

More animals joined in, and she realized that cattle were followers. If they could just keep the majority heading in the right direction, the others would come along. However, a few were excited from their newfound freedom.

They bucked, trying to run past Jeff and her, but she stepped quickly to one side. With wide-eyed looks of fear, the animals skidded to a halt and turned back.

"We don't want them to run," Jeff called to her over the wind. "We must keep them as calm as possible."

Soon they came to the crossing point where traffic had slowed on the highway. Animals lingered close to the road, and some were running across it with no regard for the passing cars and trucks. People blew their horns in frustration which only served to scare the cattle, making the situation worse. The police were directing streams of two-way traffic through using only one lane of open road.

Doggedly, she and Jeff kept the herd moving. Thankfully a four-strand fence stood on their left, belonging to the next field. It helped to provide a barrier. They were moving a substantial herd now, probably twenty-five or thirty head. Soon they would need to bring the others to join the rest of the animals on this side, and cross the road. Annette waited for Jeff to give her instructions.

Suddenly, Sophie appeared. She, Rosa, and a man Annette didn't recognize were slowly pushing the cattle toward them through the ditch. In a moment, the animals converged and with a face etched in worry, Sophie motioned that they should attempt to go over the road.

Jeff and Annette held their side while the unknown man worked his way behind the herd and began to prod them up the bank. The animals didn't want to go. They milled around in circles, no one wanting to be the first to break rank. Finally, one brave beast lunged onto the road, then another, and then five. Soon they were all climbing the bank. Jeff and the man followed with Sophie and Annette bringing up the sides. Rosa ran ahead to stop traffic and allow them space to get through.

It was the moment of truth. The first animals to cross, stopped and looked around at the strange happenings on the highway. They refused to go any further. Everyone, man and beast, were all on the highway now. Annette could see the erratic movements of the animals and their wild rolling eyes, unsure of what to do.

She had a sudden premonition of doom. They were going to bolt past on her side. She could feel it and a few moved toward her. Behind her, a long line of cars and trucks waited impatiently, angry people stood outside their vehicles shouting. These cows could not be allowed to run crazily through that. The consequences could be dire. She steeled herself, squared off, and planted her feet. Lifting her hands, Annette spoke to them as she had heard Jeff earlier. Where was he when she needed him? But somehow she sensed that it was all up to her now. Any sudden movement from any of the others could send the cattle in a frightened mob, right into the midst of trouble.

"Come on now," she said conversationally, "you don't want to do that. Your field is so nice and green and it's waiting for you down there. It's not good out here. Just keep on going." Her calm reassurance appeared to be working. "No sudden moves, Annette. No sudden moves," she repeated. Then, one or two of the lead cows plodded off down the other side. The others stood staring at Annette.

Suddenly, one butted another, sending it careening in Annette's direction. It jogged toward her, and five or six others followed, little calves trotting uncomprehendingly alongside their mothers. A smaller one lowered its head and snorted, lifting a cloven foot to paw uselessly at the pavement. Fear bubbled up in her chest, but she held her ground. Waving the blue cane, she took a step toward them, and they scattered. Back into the throng they went and then the whole herd moved as of one accord down into the other ditch and through the flattened fence.

She'd held them back. *Amazing.*

Behind her she heard the roar of a vehicle and turned to see Gabrielle drive the truck up the steep embankment and cross the road. Then down the other side she went, parking the truck across the opening in hopes of blocking any further attempts at escape.

Suddenly Jeff was beside her. Sweeping her into his arms, he twirled her around until she was dizzy. Laughter mingled with tears as shock took over her body. She sagged against him, and he held her so close she could feel the pounding of his heart. Or was it hers?

He set her down, his arms still tightly holding her. She watched his face descending to hers and tasted the salt of tears on her lips as he crushed them against his own. Her breath caught in her throat, and she kissed him back with all the fervour in her heart. Her fingers curled in his hair, and she clung to him, never wanting to let go.

And then the rain started. It came down in sheets, hard pellets of cold driving into them with fury and he let her go with a laugh. Grabbing her hand, he pulled her down the embankment to where the others were already working to build the fence again.

It was only then she realized that she and Jeff had singlehandedly held up the movement of traffic. Even the RCMP had waited until they concluded their embrace, waving the cars to proceed. A wave of embarrassment caught up with her along with the shock of what had just happened. She sank into the grass where Gabrielle found her moments later.

"You were fantastic," Gabrielle cried. "I can't believe you did that. Are you really my sister? I mean, look," she said, pointing, "you're sitting in a puddle and have grass stains and mud all over your jeans." She grinned with delight.

"Were there any accidents?" Annette asked even though she was afraid of the answer. But she had to know. She wound dripping strands of hair around her fingers and shoved them back inside her soggy collar.

"Not really. I think a cow was injured, but it still made it back into the field." Gabrielle's face fell. "There could be trouble over this. Sophie could be fined, or worse. It will be considered negligence causing a major disruption of traffic, and requiring police intervention. Although I'm no authority." She sighed. "Come on, let's go check if we can do anything to help."

It was good to hear that nobody had been hurt, and that no damage had been done to property. Though it was very sobering indeed to hear that Sophie could be in further trouble. Annette pulled herself up and walked with Gabrielle on wobbly legs to where Jeff was unloading poles and getting out tools to begin repairs.

He looked worried. Understandable, since he was concerned for his friend and perhaps since he just hugged his house guest on a public highway, and impetuously kissed her in front of Rosa, his girlfriend. Annette wondered if the woman had seen Jeff kiss her. She imagined if that was the case, she'd hear about it later. Something to look forward to. Rosa wasn't the type to let something like that go.

Annette looked for Sophie. If anyone needed a hug it would be her. She and the hired man were busy pulling the ends of the broken wire together and shooing the cattle away from the fence.

But Jeff was beckoning the sisters closer. He held a huge

hammer in one hand, and a pole he'd just gotten out of the truck was in the other.

"Seeing how you know so much already, and you're her daughter-in-law," he said, looking at Gabrielle. "I wonder if we should all be there when I tell her that this was no accident."

"What do you mean?" Annette asked. Gabrielle had already covered her face with her hands.

"I mean, the cattle didn't break down the fence," he explained wearily. "The wires were cut on purpose."

Chapter Ten

Before they went any further, Sophie was called over and Jeff showed her what he had found. Sophie digested the information, shaking her head and dealing with the shock. Jeff announced since traffic had resumed normally on the highway, he would ask a member of the RCMP to document his findings.

Two uniformed men accompanied Jeff back down into the ditch to inspect the fence. Questions were asked and pictures were taken of the clean cuts made by wire cutters and where the poles had been neatly sawn off and tossed to one side.

"It's evident," said one of the constables through the water streaming down his face, "that this accident was a result of foul play. However, we will need your formal statement, and charges may still result. Come into the station this afternoon if you can." He looked apologetic. "I'm sure sorry all this has happened to you, Mrs. Tremblay. I've been out to your ranch twice over the last week. Please know we're doing all we can to find whoever is at the bottom of it."

The two men took their time to examine the scene. However, anything that might have been a clue had been obliterated by the trampling of hundreds of cloven feet and the buckets of water that were falling by the minute. With a wave, the RCMP left.

A somber crew worked to complete the repairs. Annette and Gabrielle helped in small ways, but mostly stayed clear of those who knew what they were doing. Everyone was soaking wet, and still the rain poured on. Once everything was secure, they headed for their respective vehicles. Even the hired man, Marcus, whose name they had learned during the emergency, was invited to Jeff's home for dry clothes and something to eat.

The three of them piled back into Jeff's truck. Annette didn't even consider her place along the bench seat this time. She slid into the middle with alacrity. However, she quickly became aware of Jeff's long legs close beside her, and a faint trace of spicy aftershave that hadn't quite washed off in the rain. This would never do, she thought, purposely moving closer to Gabrielle. She would have to put the kiss they'd shared, out of her mind. He and Rosa were a couple and honestly, she wasn't even attracted to the man. It had been a random act of exhilaration after sharing an electrifying victory…or something like that.

"What a morning!" Gabrielle groaned, leaning against the door as they motored along the highway toward Jeff's ranch. "Poor Sophie."

Jeff grimaced. "I agree, but she's lucky."

"Lucky?" Gabrielle echoed.

"Definitely. If there had been an accident…" he smoothed his dripping hair back from his forehead. "Especially if people had been injured, Sophie would have been sued. She would have lost everything she had, because I don't think she has liability insurance." He gripped the steering wheel with both hands, his knuckles white.

"*Bien sûr*. I mean, of course. I 'ad not thought of that." Gabrielle subsided into silence.

The storm worsened. Dark, ominous clouds swirled above them, unleashing a violent downpour upon the ancient windshield of the truck. Jeff leaned forward, flipping the wipers on high and squinting through the relentless rain that pounded against the glass. A gust of wind caught the vehicle, blowing it to the side, but Jeff held the wheel steady and they plowed on.

Even though it was no more than one o'clock in the afternoon, the world was dark and oppressive. Annette huddled on the seat, her body soaked and shivering uncontrollably. She felt every bump and jolt of the truck as it plunged through puddles and over rough patches of road.

Jeff broke the silence. "I'd turn on the heat, but the window would fog up and it's kind of critical that I see. Sorry. Why don't you two move over and huddle together? In fact, look…" Taking one hand from the wheel he snaked an arm around Annette and pulled her close to his side. "Now, Gabrielle slides up to you and, 'we snuggle together,' as my mother used to say." He flashed them a quick grin before putting both hands back on the wheel.

Annette's entire body ignited with heat, every nerve ending ablaze. He was right, it was working. Although not for the reason he had intended. The sensation of his hard thigh pressed against hers, his muscled shoulder flexing as he drove, and the overwhelming closeness was sending her senses into overdrive.

It was with gratitude that she saw the familiar gate

overtop the entrance, *Douglas Ranch*. It wouldn't be long until they were back at the house, and she could escape to her room. The morning had left her shaken in more ways than one.

"You did very well, Annette," Jeff brought her back to the present with his words. "I was—impressed."

"Oh?" Annette blurted in a small voice.

"I agree," Gabrielle chimed in. "I was amazed at what you did out there, *ma sœur*."

"You stopped the animals from breaking away on the road. It was very brave and instinctual for someone who has never worked with cattle before. You have my thanks," he said.

Annette didn't know how to respond. Her mind was a bit muddled at the moment. "*Merci bien*," she said at length.

"I'm pretty sure that at least half of that was, thanks," Jeff laughed. "And so, you're welcome." He stopped the truck outside the house and killed the engine. As they tried to scramble out, Annette pushed Gabrielle in her haste. He arrested them by speaking again. "I think we all need some lunch," he said. "I'll ask Sandra to add something to the pot, or make a few more sandwiches to feed us all. So, we'll meet in the kitchen in forty-five minutes. Okay?"

"Okay," Annette and Gabrielle called in unison. They hurried up the steps, not even bothering to shield their faces from the rain. At least it had somewhat abated. They slipped inside the house the back way, knowing it was closer to the washer and dryer. They were met by Sandra.

"Jeff just wrote and asked me to be waiting with bathrobes for you all. Here's yours," she said, flinging the fluffy white one to Annette. "And yours," she tossed a chocolate brown one to Gabrielle. "There's a bathroom right here where you can take off your wet things and hand them to me on your way out. I'd take time to soak in a hot tub if I were you." She winked. "Oh," she said, as though forgetting something, "bring down any clothes you need washing, too. I might as well throw them all in at once." Sandra grinned and pointed to a closed door along the hall. "Laundry room is in there."

Annette and Gabrielle both dashed for the bathroom at the same time, almost getting stuck in the doorway. Giggling, Annette stepped back and motioned for her sister to go first. "Just hurry," she admonished.

It didn't take long for either of them to peel off their wet clothes and don the snuggly warm robes.

"Thank you, Sandra," they echoed and then scampered up the broad staircase to their own rooms, collected their laundry and brought it back down.

It was pure luxury to lower herself into the sweet-smelling bath salts that she sprinkled heavily in the steaming water. The heat melted away the shivering and the chill.

She sank down, almost up to her nose, closed her eyes, and just lay there, reliving the morning. It had been a personal moment of triumph. She imagined what her professors, or friends back in Paris would have thought if they could have seen her move a herd of unruly cattle across a Canadian highway. Her! It was highly out of character for her to do anything apart from focus on her art studies, painting, shopping, and eating out with friends, all while wearing the latest fashions.

Yes, saving the cows had all gone very well if she did say so herself—up to the moment when Jeff had kissed her. The sudden remembrance of it had her rearing up in the tub, feeling as if the pressure of the water on her chest was impeding her breath.

"Calm yourself, Annette," she whispered soothingly,

with the same tone as she had used with the cows. It brought a smile to her face, and she sank back down.

However, the image of Jeff's face looming over her, growing closer every moment, rushed into her mind. She could see his eyes, so deeply brown that they were almost black; the chiselled jawline, covered in several day's growth of dark beard; and the hard lines of his mouth just before it claimed her own.

Well, that was enough. She pulled the plug and stood up in the tub, her body streaming with water. Turning on the shower she pulled the curtain and reached for the shampoo. Happy hour was over. Some memories were too dangerous to contemplate, she decided, and started scrubbing vigorously at her scalp.

Later, she tiptoed from the steamy room in her bathrobe with a towel around her head and looked out her bedroom windows. The storm had passed, leaving a few broken branches strewn over the yard in its wake. Rain continued to pitter-patter to earth. Though from looking at the huge puddles brimming with water on the driveway, she could see a lot of water had fallen. Thankfully, the heavy clouds had dissipated leaving a sullen greyness behind. Leaning on the doorjamb, she searched for the horses. Pearl was missing.

Heedless of the cold and rain that still fell, Annette pushed open the balcony door and stole across the slippery deck to lean on the rail. She searched the horizon for what she considered now to be her horse, having felt a connection with the animal. That sounded silly, even to her own ears, but it was true. Concern bubbled up inside her and she resolved to look for the mare.

Quickly she dressed. Were her clothes appropriate for what she was going to do? No. Not even a little, but it was all she had at the moment. A long-sleeve, pale blue, silk blouse with ruffles at both the wrists and more running down the low, V-neck bodice went on first. And then she pulled on a pair of fitted white capris. She put her damp hair up in a bun and surveyed herself in the mirror. Ridiculous, she admitted. How would she possibly trudge out across a muddy, wet field in this?

Nonetheless, concern for Pearl outweighed the fear of ruining her clothes. When packing she had rolled a quilted pink jacket and shoved it into her case at Gabrielle's urging. She dug it out now. It was the most rugged thing she owned, and she looked at it ruefully. It wasn't even slightly rugged, as she had thought while back in Paris.

"I wonder if Canadians own such a thing as an umbrella," she muttered, and then giggled. The image of Jeff marching to the barn in his boots, cowboy hat, and jeans, holding a frilly parasol over his head leaped into her mind. That would be the day.

Zipping up the jacket, she rummaged for some socks and snuck back downstairs. She'd have to see what kind of shape her boots were in after the mud and rain of the morning. Finding them in the back entry, she lifted one between her two fingers. No. They were filthy, sodden and misshapen. Certainly not to be worn again today—if ever.

Her eyes fell on several pairs of rubber boots. Without thinking to ask if she could use them, she slipped her feet into the smallest pair, which were still far too big, and clomped to the closet. Peering into the dim recess of the cupboard, she wrinkled her nose. It smelled of cows and dirt. Hastily, she backed out, but an enormous red and black checked jacket, probably belonging to Jeff, caught her eye. It was large enough to cover most of her, and would protect her clothes. Without another thought, she put it on.

An umbrella was nowhere to be seen, but she spotted a

basket of hats. That would do in a pinch. She pulled out a dark green ball cap, the cleanest she could find, and read the logo, *John Deere*. Momentarily, she wondered who that was, and whether he'd be upset she was wearing his hat, but forgot about it as she rammed it down over her voluminous hair and stomped to the door.

The boots swam around her feet as she plodded down the outside steps and began to wade cumbersomely and ever so slowly across the lawn toward the horse pasture. She noticed the delicate flowers lining the path, that she and Gabrielle had admired earlier this morning, had been pounded flat into the sodden earth. Would they come back to life?

But that was beyond her control. She needed to ensure that Pearl was okay. The thought of lightning striking the lovely animal had her worried. As she lifted the latch and was about to push the gate open, she thought of the barn. It had to have been Pearl that she saw Jeff put inside that first day when they'd arrived. Maybe she'd check there first, just in case. She dropped the latch back in place and slogged in the other direction.

The huge sliding doors were closed. Throwing her weight into it, Annette was able to push one aside enough to allow her entry. Then she struggled to close it behind her. At least the barn smelled nice. She took a deep breath of the fragrant hay and the distinctive smell of horses. The lights were even on, offering a warm ambiance. Rain pattered high above her on the tin roof. It was a comforting sound. Not like the lashing torrents of water from before.

She slopped toward Pearl's stall, swinging each foot out wide in a semi-circle before placing it on the ground like an automaton. The thought of what she must look like made her giggle.

"Who's there?" asked a gruff voice.

She stopped dead in her tracks. Oh no, it was Jeff and inwardly she groaned. He was absolutely the last person she wanted to see right now. Well—maybe Rosa was the last, but Jeff was right up there at the top of those she least wanted to be around.

"It's me," she quavered. "I was worried about Pearl. I couldn't see 'er in the pasture you see, and I thought…"

Emerging from the stall, his forehead creased into a frown, and he growled. "You thought what?" He looked different without his hat. Less intimidating.

She drew herself up to her full height as his eyes travelled down her costume and one eyebrow lifted quizzically. "I thought she might be 'urt. I was worried about lightning, if you must know, and I came out to check on 'er." She met his gaze head on, refusing to allow his arrogance to get the better of her.

"You…came to check on her," he said in a disbelieving tone. "In that?" His mouth lifted in amusement. "I barely even recognized you." He chuckled.

"Is there something wrong with me being here?" she asked haughtily. Brushing past him she galumphed to the door of Pearl's stall to assure herself the horse was okay. Inside, Pearl lifted her head from a small bucket and whickered at her.

"Oh, she likes me!" Now it was Annette's turn to sound disbelieving. "She was 'appy to see me." Swivelling toward Jeff on one enormous boot, she felt happiness gurgle up inside her chest. "Is that true? Or am I imagining it?"

"Yeah, she likes you," he agreed. He came to stand next to her and his voice softened. "It's real nice that you came out here to make sure Pearl was okay. I'm just surprised, is all."

"It shouldn't surprise you to know that I care," she remonstrated. "Can I brush 'er?"

"Sure," he shrugged. "That's what I was doing when you came in." He handed her a brush and gestured that she should move inside. "I don't like seeing the old girl out in a storm. She's too important to me. I'll get a seat and join you..." He turned to leave and then paused. "If you don't mind?"

He was actually asking her rather than making another mocking remark which surprised her. What a switch? "Of course. Do whatever you want." She heard his footsteps die away as she began to briskly brush Pearl's beautiful coat and run her free hand down the horse's soft neck. She leaned close to Pearl's ear. "You're beautiful, you know that?" The ear flicked back and forth as though answering.

Presently Jeff returned and she glanced at him as he placed a bale of straw inside the box stall and took a seat. At first there was silence, apart from the swish of her brush, and Pearl snuffling for leftover grain in the bucket before grinding it between her teeth. Then Jeff spoke.

"Do you like it here? In Canada?"

"Yes," she shrugged. "I didn't know what to expect. Gabrielle tried to prepare me. Mostly with what not to wear," she threw him a rueful smile. "But I really 'ad no idea 'ow beautiful it would be until I arrived." She paused and stared out the window to the greyness beyond. "It 'as captured my 'eart." She patted Pearl. "And this girl 'as part of it too."

"Wow, you sound quite poetic. You're an artist, right? Not a writer?"

"That's right. I just finished four years of university in Paris. At Beaux-Arts de Paris."

"Sounds impressive," Jeff pulled a long strand of yellow

straw from the bale and stuck it between his teeth. "What do you do with that?"

"What do I do?" she stopped to look at him questioningly.

"I mean, what sort of job can you get with that training?"

"I 'ave applied to several art galleries in Paris. And I paint. It's not a lucrative occupation, but it makes me 'appy." Annette moved around the other side, ducking under Pearl's neck.

"You've never worked with horses before? Cause you're really comfortable with them."

"I'm comfortable with Pearl," she said, puffing with exertion. "I don't suppose it would be that way with other 'orses."

"Perhaps not," he agreed. "Hopefully tomorrow I can give you another lesson. I believe Jessica would be happy that Pearl is being loved and ridden again."

"I'd like that." She hesitated a moment and then asked a question she knew might challenge the tentative friendship they were forging. "What 'appened to Jessica, and your father?"

It was long minutes before he replied. She thought he might not answer at all, and was kicking herself for her intrusive query, but at length he cleared his throat and began.

"She was fifteen, as I told you, and very much into showing horses. Dad helped her with that. He was the best horseman this area had known for many years. He could get a horse to do just about anything, but he was gentle with them, you know. When Dad worked with a horse they *wanted* to please him..." Jeff's voice trailed away. Annette stole a quick peek over Pearl's back to see him chewing on the straw and staring into space, his legs crossed in front of him as he leaned back on the wood wall of the stall.

"Jessica was a happy accident, you might say. Born to older parents whose only other child, me, was seven years old when she was born. They'd thought they were done having children. But then she appeared, and we all doted on her. Consequently, I was twenty-two and full of myself when it happened," he said, bitterly. "I should have taken her to the event that day, or tried harder to stop them at least...but no, I had other, more important things to do..." He paused, sinking into a world of regret. "It was a day much like this. Raining so hard you couldn't see the front of the truck. Still, she wheedled Dad into taking her. He loved to make her happy."

Jeff sighed deeply and bent over double, resting his face in his hands. His damp hair fell forward, curling around his face to give him the appearance of innocence and vulnerability...much like the young man he must have been on the day the accident took place.

"The weather was terrible, visibility poor, and they were pulling the horse trailer home that night, after the show. Pearl wasn't with them that day, because she'd come up lame that morning. Jess had an older, more experienced horse with her. Anyway, she and Dad came over the crest of a hill and there was an intersection on the highway. A semi-truck and trailer didn't see them until it was too late. He pulled out right in front of them." Jeff brushed at his eyes and stopped.

Annette felt terrible. Why had she asked such a painful question? "I am so very sorry, Jeff," she said, coming out from behind Pearl and taking a seat beside him. "I should not 'ave asked you to speak of such a painful time. Please forgive me." She took his hand in hers and squeezed, feeling the torment he must have felt that dreadful night flood through him into her. How he and his mother must have suffered to learn that half of their family was gone forever.

"It's okay," he managed, after a time. "The counselor said it's cathartic to talk about what happened. And particularly to remember the good times." He took her small hand in both of his large ones and intertwined her fingers with his. It was reflexive, she knew, and meant nothing other than maybe a distraction from the memories.

"So, with that in mind," he continued, "I'll tell you something that brings me happy thoughts of my sister, and of Dad." He glanced at her quickly and then looked away.

"She would have been about six years old that winter, and me, thirteen. It was just before Christmas and at the breakfast table that morning Dad announced that we were going on a winter ride. Right after chores were done, he said. We kids were thrilled. It was always too cold to ride much at that time of year, so this was a surprise. While he and I did the chores, Jess caught and saddled her little pony, Princess. Pearl was too spirited for her to handle back then."

Annette let the brush drop onto the ground beside her and leaned back onto the wooden walls of the stall with Jeff as he settled into a more comfortable position. She looked at her hand, still trapped within his two, but made no attempt to pull it away. He drifted back in time to that perfect day.

"The snow was deep," he began again, "blanketing the land in dazzling white up to the horses' knees. But it was powdery and not too difficult for the horses to get through. Dad was on his old horse, Champ, Mom on her horse, Tina, and I rode my pinto, Chief. We headed across the pasture and wove our way into the forest near here. Frost glittered like diamonds on every surface, from the dark, towering pines to the bare branches of the poplars and even on blades of grass that rose above the snow."

"The air was cold and crisp, but the sun shone and warmed our backs. As we rode, Dad pointed out tracks of the animals he saw: deer, moose, rabbit, fox, coyotes, and, most exciting, the huge paws of a cougar. He told stories of his youth, and how his father had taken him on a similar ride in this same spot. 'It's now a tradition,' he'd said happily. 'You kids have to carry it on.'" Jeff stopped and brushed roughly at his eyes.

"Anyway, pretty soon Jessica complained that her feet were getting cold. Dad had anticipated this, however, and was prepared. He had me dig under the snow for long prairie grass while he searched for wood. Soon we had a blazing fire. He fashioned seats for everyone out of logs and propped Jess' little boots on a forked stick to warm them near the flames." A smile curved Jeff's lips.

"To top it all off, Mom had packed a picnic lunch for us. She pulled sandwiches and a thermos of hot chocolate from her saddlebags along with tiny plastic cups. We basked in the warm glow of the fire, we talked about everything and anything, and we enjoyed the lunch. My heart was full of love for my sister and parents..." Jeff expelled a long, drawn-out breath. "I think that was the best meal I've ever had."

With a grunt, Pearl lowered herself to the sawdust, breaking the flow of Jeff's reminiscence. He shrugged and gave Annette's hand one last squeeze before placing it back on her knee.

"That's a beautiful memory," Annette whispered, feeling she was still with Jeff in the midst of the forest.

"Yes," he agreed. "But that's about enough talking for me today. What about you?"

"Me?"

"Of course. You owe me a childhood story of equal or greater length," he grinned down at her. "It's only fair."

Annette was still affected by the intimate details of Jeff's family. It was rather shocking to think that he'd just unburdened his soul to her, and she felt moved. She cast about in her memories to come up with a story for him. She had no traumatic tales to tell. Her parents were both alive and her childhood had been without incident. Growing up in southern France, with the occasional trip to Spain or Italy, had been quite normal events in her world.

Wait. That was it. Her life in France might be quite interesting to Jeff. If visiting the Rocky Mountain foothills of Canada was such a unique experience for her, it stood to reason that her life might be thought-provoking for him.

"I grew up in in the southwest of France, in a city called Toulouse," she began slowly. "My parents are people who work each day in professions they love. They raised Gabrielle and me to believe that this was important; to enjoy each day doing what brings you joy and contentment. They also wanted us to understand other cultures and lifestyles. When we were young we travelled to various countries in Europe. We were exposed to good music, the theatre, fine art, and museums. During the summer breaks we visited my Aunt Elyse who owned a vineyard north of Marseille. That is in Provence."

"Sounds very grand," Jeff observed with a chuckle and a regal flourish of his hand.

She considered this a moment. "I suppose it does, yes, but it was just normal life for us. Anyway, it was on one of these visits that I was first exposed to the work of Vincent Van Gogh. My aunt took us to Arles, which is a city not far from the Mediterranean Sea. There we walked along a path dedicated to the famous painter. Van Gogh went to Provence, like many painters before and after 'im have done, seeking the vibrant colours, intense light, and sunshine of the south. We saw many places around the city where 'e set up 'is easel and painted the changing landscapes, the daily life of peasants or the men who worked on the Rhone River. Everything this man saw, inspired 'im and appeared on 'is canvas." She looked up at him guiltily. "Sorry. I get carried away."

"Not at all. It's very interesting. And so, was this what motivated you to become an artist yourself?"

She nodded. "I 'ad always loved to draw, and they bought me children's paints when I was very young. But after that trip I knew it was what I was meant to do. My parents enrolled me in lessons, and after I graduated from *lycée*, the word in English for this escapes me…"

"High school?" Jeff supplied.

"Yes. When I was finished with 'igh school, I went immediately to Paris to begin my studies."

"Four years ago, right?" Jeff asked. "So, you're what? About twenty-two, twenty-three?"

"I will be twenty-three this fall," she answered, frowning. "Does it matter? 'Ow old are you?"

He laughed. "*Touché*. It doesn't matter at all, and in the interest of full disclosure, I'm thirty years old."

She leaned away and squinted at him. "So, what you are telling me is that you could 'ave broken many old and brittle bones that day I fell on you." She tapped a thoughtful finger to her chin. "I must be more careful with someone of your advanced age."

"Hey!" he cried, giving her a little push. "That's a low punch."

Just then the outer door to the barn slid open and someone stepped inside.

"Jeff," Rosa called. "Are you in here?"

Jeff got to his feet and went to the door of Pearl's pen. "Yep, just visiting with Pearl," he said. "Anything wrong?"

Rosa appeared in the doorway and scowled at Annette. "What's she doing here?" the woman said unpleasantly. Pearl lunged to her feet and shook herself sending bits of dirt flying.

"Annette was concerned about Pearl and was talking with me," Jeff sounded angry. "Is that a problem?"

"Of course not," Rosa gave a tinkling laugh, flipping the switch to turn back into her syrupy sweet alter ego. "I just didn't recognize her in that peculiar outfit." She waved at Annette without even looking her way. Laying a hand on Jeff's arm, she said, "I just came to tell you that lunch is ready and we're waiting for you before we start. Also, Sophie wanted to talk about checking the rest of her fence line that borders the highway in case any other wire was damaged."

"I see." Jeff strode back into the stall and gave Pearl one last pat before stooping to pick up the brush. "We should go have lunch," he said to Annette. "Feel free to come out here anytime to visit Pearl. I'll leave her brushes outside the door."

Wheeling around, he held the gate open, waiting for her to exit the pen.

She shook her head. "Actually, I think I'll take a few more minutes with Pearl, if that's alright?"

"Of course. See you back at the house." He and Rosa walked away, talking in hushed tones. She was glad she hadn't gone with them. It was an uncomfortable situation that she had no desire to be caught up in. Whatever sort of relationship they shared was none of her business.

Sagging against the wall, she stared at Pearl who was nosing around the fallen pail.

"You'd like a bit more of that, wouldn't you my girl?" Annette said in a low voice. "Maybe later, once I learn what it was he gave you, and where he got it from, I could bring you some." She stood up and moved to Pearl, running a hand down her soft neck. The horse curled her head around to nuzzle her. "You're so sweet." She stroked the incredibly soft muzzle and smiled.

"Talking to yourself?" came a strident voice from the alleyway. Both Annette and Pearl jumped. A shadowy figure stepped up to the bars of the gate.

"Rosa?" Annette said in astonishment. Inwardly, she groaned. *Not again.*

"I just came back to have a chat since you didn't seem to understand my English the first time," the woman purred, her voice dripping with venom "I wanted to make it quite clear that Jeff is mine. We have plans to be married and you…" the woman took a deep breath and continued, as she arrogantly flipped a dismissive hand at Annette, "with your little French accent, and childlike innocence, are so ignorant. You wouldn't last here five minutes. If you think by kissing him, or looking for secret ways to catch him alone, that you'll win him over, you're wrong. He's in love with me."

"I'm not…"

Rosa interrupted. "I don't want to hear what you have to say," she snarled. "Just stay away from Jeff you trollop."

She turned on her heel, stomped out of the barn, and slid the door closed behind her with a bang.

Chapter Eleven

After her heartbeat slowed, Annette took several calming breaths. *Trollop? Unbelievable.* She wasn't even sure what the word meant, but obviously it wasn't good. That had been intense. She'd known if Rosa had seen the impromptu kiss on the road this morning there would be repercussions, but this had been another full-frontal attack. How did no one but Sandra see this woman for what she was?

Sure, she'd seen plenty of jealous girlfriends before, because of Gabrielle. Young men had always paid attention to her. They fell over themselves staring at her beautiful sister wherever she went and openly admired her beauty. Normally that wasn't a problem unless the men were already in a relationship. If they were caught ogling a gorgeous woman by their girlfriends or wives, there was trouble. Annette had witnessed plenty of fights between couples left in her sister's wake, while Gabrielle breezed right on by oblivious. No one blamed her for being beautiful. She had the looks and personality that men adored.

Annette, however, was different. No one had ever been jealous of having her around their men. Yes, she'd had a few half-hearted boyfriends, but always suspected they hung around just to get closer to Gabrielle. Being plain had been hard to accept when Annette was young and wanted to be pretty like her sister. Over the years though, she'd come to terms with being ordinary. Her self-worth became tied to her art and how she dressed. It was hard to believe Rosa found her threatening at all.

It had stopped raining. She opened the barn door just enough to squeeze through and made sure she shut it behind her. Dragging the hat off her head, she scrunched her hair to accentuate the curls. At least she had one nice feature.

She picked her way carefully around the puddles, then suddenly realized what she was wearing on her feet. Since it relieved the tension she felt, she sloshed right through the worst of them with careless disregard for her white capris. Realizing she couldn't avoid going back inside, she let herself in the back door, kicked off the enormous boots, and put the hat and coat where she'd found them. Pausing, she listened to the steady hum of voices coming from the dining room. At this moment, she didn't want to see anyone, particularly Jeff and Rosa.

It was tempting to avoid lunch altogether and just sneak upstairs to her room. Still, she couldn't lurk there all day, besides she had nothing to feel ashamed about. She hadn't asked him to kiss her or to even talk to her for that matter. It was Rosa who should feel shame over her actions, but as the woman's voice rose in a wild cackle of laughter above all the rest, she knew Rosa had no such concerns. She was in high spirits after marking her claim.

Tilting her chin and taking a deep breath, Annette entered the room. Everyone was busy eating at the long table, even Sandra. A lively discussion of the morning's events was taking place, in fact, as Annette approached the table, Sandra cheered. Even the bunny on her shirt looked impressed.

"Good for you, Annette!" she exclaimed heartily. "I've heard no end of praise for what you did this morning."

Sophie rose to her feet. She must have gone home to change, because she was wearing a pair of black trousers and a crisp white blouse with a rose-coloured sweater overtop. Her hair had been neatly combed and she even wore a little pale pink lipstick. She enveloped Annette in a hug.

"Thank you, my dear," Sophie said. "I was too busy this morning to offer my thanks, but I so appreciate you and Gabrielle jumping in to 'elp as you did. That could not have been easy. Jeff tells me you stopped a group of animals from turning the whole herd in the wrong direction."

"You're very welcome," Annette said breathlessly. "I didn't expect thanks. It's the least I could do after all the kindness you and Jeff are showing me."

Sophie kept an arm around her as they walked to the table. "Come," she said, "I saved a place for you, right beside me." Bemused, Annette allowed herself to be pushed into a chair. A bowl of steaming tomato soup was set in front of her.

"*Merci*," she said. "I mean, thank you." She stared at the beaming faces around her, all except for one, of course. Thankfully, Rosa sat on the same side and at the far end, out of her line of sight.

"No translation necessary," Jeff chuckled from across the table. "We all know the meaning of that word. Oh, and Annette, this is Marcus." He waved a hand toward the blond man sitting beside him. "He just started working for Sophie. No time for proper introductions this morning."

Marcus had the biggest, bushiest moustache that Annette had ever seen. It curved down from his upper lip to disappear under his chin. His hair was still wet from their escapades in the rain and stuck out at right angles from his head.

The man looked up from his soup with bright blue eyes and gave her a nod of acknowledgement. "Nice to meet you," he said in a deep voice. Picking up a plate of sandwiches, he handed them to her. "I advise you to try the chicken salad on the bottom. They're delicious. However, the toasted cheese is good too." He grinned and she smiled her thanks as she accepted the heaping platter.

Now that she had smelled the food, she found that she was ravenous. Good thing she hadn't ducked upstairs. She took one of the recommended chicken sandwiches and took a bite as conversation flowed around her. Surreptitiously, she watched Jeff. He'd changed into a chocolate brown t-shirt that accentuated his broad shoulders and muscled arms. The man was, in a word, hot. Jeff's hair was still damp, and it curled past his ears. He could easily be cast as a pirate in a swashbuckling movie. Rosa didn't deserve him. He was too nice, funny, and kind for her. She forced herself to look away and tune back in to the conversation. What did it matter if the man was good-looking?

Talk centered on the fence, the injured cow, who had slipped and hurt a leg as the animals all rushed across the slippery road, and what might happen with the charges. The whole incident had caused a major disruption on a public highway and blame could be laid squarely in Sophie's hands, as far as the authorities were concerned.

Breaking away from the main discussion, Rosa stood

from her chair, went around the table and laid her hands on Jeff's shoulders. "You were marvelous out there this morning," she cooed. "The way you gave orders and took charge of those beasts was simply masterful."

Gabrielle kicked Annette under the table. Good, she thought, quelling an urge to roll her eyes at the sickening flattery, Gabby sees it too. Thankfully, she wasn't the only one who had noticed Rosa's overt tactics to win Jeff's affection. Marcus also looked disgruntled.

In turn, Jeff looked distinctly uncomfortable with the flowery praise. "Thanks Rosa. However, I think it was a joint effort," he said with a cough. "In fact, we just did what we knew we had to do, it was these girls…" he brandished a cheese sandwich at Annette and Gabrielle, and continued, "that were the real heroes. They'd never been in a situation like that before, yet they stepped up and made a difference."

Rosa flashed a venomous look at both of them. Sliding her hands down his arms in a too familiar gesture, she gave him an extra little pat before walking into the kitchen for a glass of water. "Whatever you say," she said lightly. "I just know what I saw, and I believe something terrible would have happened without you there."

"I'm grateful for you all and that no one was 'urt," Sophie said, dropping her spoon into the empty bowl in front of her and pushing it away. "That would 'ave been a catastrophe. I don't think I could 'ave lived with myself."

Although no one said it, Annette was certain they all knew the perpetrator of the crime had hoped that if the animals ran amok, it would cause that very situation. Clearly, whoever was behind the crime had no scruples. An accident involving vehicle damage, or worse yet, injuries to people, would have spelled the end of Sophie's ranch. That was most certainly their goal.

The conversation turned to ideas as to who could have pulled this latest attack in the succession of strikes on the Triple T Ranch. Sadly, that was all it was, thought Annette as she listened to them talk—speculation. No one had any evidence or idea who was doing it.

"Do you 'ave liability insurance?" Gabrielle asked quietly, while the others continued talking among themselves.

Sophie shook her head. "Malcom always carried it, but I 'ad to let it go after 'e died. It was expensive, you see, and there were so many bills to pay." She pushed crumbs from her sandwich into a pile on her placemat and toyed with them, her eyes downcast. "Many important matters were neglected in the months following Malcom's death. I am grateful that Rosa is 'elping me deal with them now. She is very good at keeping records and making sure the bills are paid. And 'er skill at training horses is well-known in the barrel-racing circuit, particularly in Alberta. The animals she is working with will be worth a lot of money next year and should recoup a little of what 'as been lost."

It was plain to see that Sophie put a great deal of faith in the younger woman. Annette hoped it wasn't misplaced. From her perspective, Rosa's main interest was in capturing the handsome next-door neighbour. However, she wasn't at the Triple T to see what Rosa did every day. She must be a great help for Sophie to trust her so implicitly.

Sophie leaned over her empty plate and spoke to them in hushed tones. "We need to spend time together, just the three of us. I am so sorry all of this 'appened just as you arrived. Perhaps you would like to accompany me into town today? A stop at the police station will not be fun. Still, it shouldn't take long and then I must do some shopping. We could even stop at a lovely little *boulangerie* I know."

Gabrielle looked at Annette for approval and then nodded. "Yes, that sounds wonderful. I'm glad I changed into something presentable." She looked lovely, as usual, in a fuchsia round-necked sweater dotted with bobbles of black fluff and black, slim-fit jeans. It was a gorgeous outfit with her black hair.

"You could wear a bathmat, two garbage bags, and curlers…and still turn heads," Annette said with a laugh. "It's me that has to work at it."

"*Bonne*." Sophie pushed away from the table, pulled on a long black jacket she'd slung over the chair and belted it around her waist. "I'll take Rosa and Mark back to the ranch and return for you in about thirty minutes. It will be fun."

Soon, Annette and Gabrielle were the only ones left in the kitchen with Sandra.

"You know I don't like it when you put yourself down," Gabrielle said, coming up to Annette and resting a hand on her arm. "You don't see your beauty, but the rest of us do." She lowered her voice to a whisper. "I believe Jeff sees it also."

With a sniff of derision, Annette patted her sister's hand and turned away. She knew the truth and didn't want to invite any more lectures from Rosa.

As the door closed behind Jeff, and the grumble of the engines carrying Sophie, Rosa, and Mark faded away, Sandra took off the yellow rubber gloves she was using to wash the stovetop and tossed them on the counter. Marching to the window she looked outside as though assuring herself everyone was gone.

"*Humph!*" she exclaimed, crossing her arms across her chest. "Do you girls want to hear something strange—no, bizarre is more like it. Just wait till I tell my husband." She peered out the window once more and then used the cuff of her red sweater to wipe at a nonexistent smudge on the spotlessly clean glass.

Annette, who had been gathering dishes, and Gabrielle, who was pouring leftover soup into a bowl, both stopped to look at the housekeeper expectantly.

"Well, he's not going to believe it, that's what," Sandra continued, waving her hands in the air. "I just wish he was here to see it with his own eyes. He'd be able to tell me I wasn't seeing things. Of course, I was the only one who saw them, so I guess maybe he wouldn't. He'd sure be shocked though and—"

"Saw who? What are you talking about?" cried Gabrielle, interrupting. Tomato soup dripped onto the counter as she took a step toward Sandra and missed the bowl altogether.

Sandra looked up as though just realizing the sisters were still there. "Oh," she said apologetically. "I'm just a bit puzzled is all." She marched toward them, lowering her voice as though still worried she'd be overheard. "I'm sure I won't be telling you anything you don't already know when I say that Rosa has her heart set on being mistress of this here ranch. Correct?"

Both women nodded in agreement.

"And we've all seen her practically throw herself at Jeff every time he's in the vicinity?"

"Yes," they answered in unison. Gabrielle set the pot on the counter and Annette let the cutlery fall back to the table with a clatter as they both converged on Sandra, sensing this was momentous.

"You know how I told you I saw Rosa having dinner

with two men in the city." Again, they nodded. "Well, that Marcus fellow we just saw sittin' here nice as pie and actin' like he doesn't know her from a hole in the ground, is very familiar to me. I'm almost positive he's the young man I saw kissing Rosa at the restaurant in the city. Smooching for all the world to see, I tell ya."

Chapter Twelve

Annette sat in the back seat of Sophie's spotlessly clean, yellow pickup truck, as they bumped along the gravel road on their way to the closest town. She stared out the window at the passing hills and pondered what Sandra had said. Perhaps the housekeeper was mistaken. By her own admission it had been a quick furtive glance in a restaurant, two weeks ago. It wouldn't make sense for Rosa to be outright chasing Jeff, if her boyfriend was there beside her. Still, Rosa had been seen kissing *someone*, if not Marcus, who?

"Sophie, how did you find Marcus?" she asked. "And didn't you hire two new people to work on the ranch? Where's the other one?"

"I advertised on a job search platform. Actually, Rosa did it for me since she's better at computer things." Sophie slowed to negotiate a sharp curve. The road was muddy and quite slippery after all the rain. "And I hired Tristan as well, but he couldn't start work until tomorrow. His wife is sick or something."

Gabrielle continued the questioning. "But you interviewed them, right? Or did Rosa do that too?"

"Of course I interviewed them," Sophie cast them a sideways glance. "What's with all the questions?"

Annette looked at her sister. Should they tell Sophie what they knew? Gabrielle gave her a quick nod.

"It's just that…you see…Sandra might have…" Annette stumbled. It all sounded too farfetched when she tried to put it into words.

Gabrielle intervened. "Annette is trying to say that we all know Rosa likes Jeff, but Sandra saw Rosa with two men in the city a couple of weeks ago, and she kissed one of them…I mean Rosa kissed the man, not Sandra, and today Sandra says that the man Rosa kissed looked just like Marcus." It all came out in a jumbled rush.

Sophie laughed. "Well, of course, he did. I'm sure it was him."

"What?" the two sisters said in unison. They looked at one another in shock.

"You know about this?" Annette gaped. "Doesn't it concern you?"

"Why should it?" Sophie said equably. "Marcus is her cousin."

Both women flopped back in their seats. Annette whistled between her teeth. Well that explained a lot. Sandra must have been mistaken about the sort of kiss that was shared between the two. Annette felt unaccountably relieved and at the same time her heart fell. Rosa had a perfect right to warn her away from Jeff. They were a legitimate couple. She couldn't help but wonder why Jeff would also kiss her, though. It must have been the excitement of the moment that brought it on.

"So, Rosa convinced you to hire her cousin? Who is the

other guy, her brother?" Gabrielle wasn't about to let the subject rest.

Sophie smiled at her. "I appreciate the concern I hear in your voice, but it's not like that, I assure you. She asked me to consider Marcus, and I did. He had very good credentials, and drove out to the ranch to meet with me in person. Rosa was working with a young filly we have great hopes for, so she was nowhere around. I made the decision alone." She flipped on her signal light and came to a full stop before entering the busy highway. "Tristan answered the advert and came later the same morning. He's no relation to anyone."

"Well, that's something I guess." Gabrielle didn't sound convinced. She drummed her fingers on the armrest.

"And I entirely approve of a union between Rosa and Jeff," Sophie said firmly. "She's a wonderful person and has been there for me through all the hardships of these last few months. I don't know what I'd do without her."

"What about Jayke?" Gabrielle asked. "I'm sure he would be here if he knew how difficult it's been."

"A long letter has been written and I'll mail it to him today, if that's what you're wondering," Sophie said. Her voice was starting to sound annoyed. "I've already explained why I don't want him to be dragged back here."

Annette exchanged a look with her sister in the front seat, knowing what she was thinking. *A letter. Fantastic.* That meant it would take a few more days for Jayke to be notified of the troubles his mother was coping with. And that was if she'd told him the full extent of it. Sophie was stalling, of course. Hoping that things would rectify themselves, so Jayke could be reassured that everything was okay. Gabrielle had asked her mother-in-law to simply call her son—not write him a letter.

Brightly, Sophie changed the subject. "How about I leave you two at the shopping centre where I get groceries, and you can look around the various stores until I'm finished leaving my statement with the RCMP?"

Annette rummaged through her purse, looking for her designer sunglasses and popped them on. As the day wound down, the sun had come out in full force. "That would be great. Thank you," she said. "Is there a pharmacy?"

"Yes, I'll drop you off there. Now, please tell me about your graduation from the prestigious school of art. Did you love it?"

"I did." Annette warmed to the subject change, telling Sophie about the classes in art history, which were her favourites, and how much she had enjoyed studying the post-impressionists including Van Gogh, Paul Cézanne, and Henri de Toulouse-Lautrec.

"I sent my resume to several art galleries in Paris before I left. It is my dream to work among the paintings I love. I have yet to receive a response though," she finished.

"You will," Sophie assured her. "And I've seen some of your original work. You are a very accomplished painter in your own right."

"Andrew and I are very proud of her," added Gabrielle.

"Of course," Sophie hastened to say.

Moments later, they entered the outskirts of town. Soon the girls were arranging a time to meet Sophie outside the grocery store and waving as she motored off through the busy parking lot. They spent an enjoyable two hours poking around clothing stores, curio shops, choosing some lilac-scented soaps to take home, and wandering through a huge cosmetics store sampling perfume.

Soon it was time to meet Sophie. They found her easily. She stood with a loaded shopping cart waiting for them.

"I can hardly wait to tell you my news," she said gleefully. "First, let's put the groceries into the truck and I'll take you to my favourite coffee place." Pushing the cart, they rumbled outside to the truck and stuffed all the food into the opposite side to where Annette sat. As they unloaded, Sophie explained. "I cornered Sandra at lunch and made her tell me all the things she needed. It's not fair that Jeff treats us like guests in his home and feeds us too. So, I bought food to help out."

It illustrated exactly what Annette had been thinking: what a lovely lady Sophie was. They piled into the truck and drove to the tiny café.

It was quaint and almost French in appearance. With a tiny weather-beaten facade of creamy-white bricks, the coffee shop was tucked between two buildings that overshadowed it on either side. If not for the sign over the door, '*Lulu's Café*' in bold green letters, it would have been easy to miss.

Underneath the sign were long windows, almost completely covered with trailing vines that appeared to curl through the door and continue growing on the inside. Although both the exterior and interior showed the patina of age, one could see in an instant that it had been lovingly preserved. Down the walls on either side were tables for four covered in white linen tablecloths, while antique chairs with ornate backs were pulled up underneath. It was a busy spot. Happy customers filled almost every table. Young couples with children were perched in high-chairs, white-haired seniors chatted over steaming drinks, and a group of boisterous teens laughed in a back corner.

The floor was a burnished mahogany, dark and worn from years of passing feet. Plants hung from baskets and trailed around the inside of the windows and on both walls were shelves filled with interesting things—sparkling glasses, old books, and small antiques of every sort.

It was a welcoming, homey shop. Despite the ambience, it was the wonderful smells emanating from the kitchen that must be drawing the crowd. The rich aroma of coffee beans, fresh baked bread and pastries made an alluring combination.

An elderly man came out from behind a swinging door, rubbing his hands on his apron.

"Sit, sit," he invited with a broad grin, gesturing about the room. Sophie and Gabrielle moved immediately to the only empty table. It was a lovely setting near the windows where natural light flooded through the greenery.

Annette was drawn to the front, where a massive glass case housed the most delectable pastries she'd seen outside of Paris. On display were lemon tarts piled with gooey meringue, cream pies topped with plum red raspberries, slices of apple cake flecked with cinnamon, four layers of chocolate cake with fudgy icing, flakey croissants, crisp, curling palmiers, cookies of every description, long eclairs slick with chocolate and sprinkled with powdered sugar, and strawberry tarts piled high with glistening fruit. Behind the counter were baskets and shelves of fresh bread. She drank in the air. It was wonderful. She made her way to the table they'd chosen, aware that Sophie was ordering coffee for all three of them.

"I hope that's alright?" Sophie said anxiously, as the man shuffled away. "The coffee here is wonderful, and I saw that you drank it before."

"This is perfect," Annette said, clasping her hands, her eyes dancing. "What a wonderful little place."

"When snowdrifts are up to your waist, and the temperature outside is so cold that the simple act of breathing hurts your lungs, this place is a delicious oasis of warmth and happiness," Sophie explained. "The people that own it are both in their eighties. They have a son that makes the breads and likely he will take over one day. But for now, the couple makes everything themselves. They would not dream of using frozen, prepared foods."

"What a remarkable pair!" Gabrielle looked around with appreciation. "Andrew and I came here often when we were visiting the ranch. I knew you would like it, Annette."

"Like it?" Annette joked. "I want one of everything I saw up there."

Everyone laughed, Sophie the loudest. She beamed at them. "I must tell you what I learned today." She fanned her face against the glaze of tears that sprang to her eyes.

"As you know, there was some question as to whether or not I would be fined for negligence when the cattle escaped this morning," she said. "When I arrived at the police station, I was met by the same nice constable that was at the scene. He took me into his office and told me in light of all that had been happening, they would not press any charges or fine me. They feel I've been through enough and it's clear someone is trying to sabotage me and the ranch. Isn't that kind?" Reaching for a paper napkin, she dabbed her eyes.

"That's fantastic!" Annette cried.

Gabrielle, who was sitting beside the older woman, took her in her arms. "I'm so glad," she said. "This calls for a celebration. Annette, what's the most decadent and fattening thing you saw?"

"You need to look for yourselves. I can't make such a very important decision. All I know is there's a strawberry tart over there with my name on it."

As the two women hurried over to the counter to select

their own treats, Annette subsided into a reverie of her own. Sophie had received some good news, but the underlying fears remained. The perpetrators of these crimes had not been caught. They were still at large, and most likely devising their next attack. Everyone was aware of it, but no one said it out loud.

The day ended pleasantly with Sophie dropping them and the groceries with Sandra. She had hurried back to the Triple T Ranch to check the cattle and take another drive past her fence lines. She was a much more relaxed woman after their trip to town and it was nice to see.

After helping Sandra put the groceries away, Gabrielle announced her intention to take a nap and call her husband, but not necessarily in that order. Annette chuckled. She understood this. It had been four years since the pair had married and they were nearly inseparable, although Gabrielle's job took her away from the wine shop every day. It was good to see her sister so happy.

Annette grabbed her sketchbook, stuffed a couple of pencils and an eraser into a pocket, and went back downstairs to find those same enormous rubber boots. She giggled again as she stepped into them and galumphed out the back door.

Although she wanted very much to sit on the bale of straw in Pearl's stall to draw, it held a sour note for her since Rosa had cornered her there. So, she turned and walked along the gravel path to the garden. A cloud scudded across the sun, obliterating its warmth for a moment. She shivered, even in her quilted jacket. A wooden bench sat near a tall wire support that had been created to allow climbing flowers to weave their way up and over the pole fence that surrounded the yard.

She sat and flipped through her book. A slight breeze curled down from the mountain. It whispered among the velvety pink and purple flowers, wafting their sweet perfume over her. She remembered from her childhood they were called sweet peas. Tall, lush fronds of corn rustled in this same breeze, and she gazed upon the fresh clean landscape, feeling her heart soar. It truly was a stunning part of the world. She hadn't expected to like it so much in Canada. And all without even one party to dress for and attend. She smiled at her naivety of a mere three days ago.

The old red barn stood stoic and silent with the mountains surging skyward in the distance. How many storms had it endured? Her gaze slid sideways to see that Jeff had turned Pearl out to join the horses who dotted the lush field close by and she smiled. Now she would draw.

It was some time later when she heard the tires of a vehicle crunch in the driveway. It must be Sophie returning. She dreaded the sight of Rosa, but knew she couldn't escape. If only she could make the woman understand she had nothing to worry about as far as Jeff was concerned.

Closing her book, she tucked it under her arm and strolled to the front of the house. But a sleek grey car was parked there. She considered retreating and had even turned away, but a booming voice arrested her.

"Hey, you there! Where's Sophie Tremblay?" A large beefy man stumped around the front of the car, and, in wide-eyed amazement, Annette found herself wondering how he had managed to fit behind the wheel.

He wore a pair of enormous jeans cinched around his ample girth with a belt, and blue striped suspenders stretched over each shoulder as an additional means of support. It was topped off with a pale green shirt with buttons very near to bursting, and a white straw cowboy hat tipped rakishly to one side. His face was florid and puffy, revealing to the casual observer that self-indulgence was no stranger to this man. Pale watery eyes nearly bugged out of his head with rage. He was angry, but the question was why?

"I 'ave no idea where she is. She does not live 'ere," answered Annette with her best get-out-of-my-face attitude. Honestly, self-importance and arrogance were rolling off this man.

Her terse reply did not stop him, and he advanced on her rapidly, considering his bulk.

"Well, you just tell her I came round to see her, you hear me? She ain't at the Triple T and I know very well she's been hidin' out here on account of the water problems at the ranch. Maybe if she knew what she was doin' she wouldn't be driving that place into the ground. Women shouldn't be runnin' a ranch. That's a man's job." He came to a stop in front of her, placed meaty hands on his hips, and stared down at her. "That assistant of hers told me to look for her here. I don't aim to search the countryside for her. You just give her my message and I'll…"

Annette felt her blood boil. She drew herself up to her full 5'3" and with barely concealed fury she stopped him with a raised hand. "I would not repeat a word of that garbage, even if you paid me to do it. I don't know who you are, and I can assure you I don't want to know. I think you should leave."

If possible, the man's face grew even redder, and he took a step closer. "Now you look here Frenchie…"

"I think you'd better do as the lady asked," said a voice from behind the man. It was Jeff, striding toward them.

"That's no way to talk to anyone, let alone my guest and friend. I'll tell Sophie you called in to see her. Now it's time for you to go."

Spluttering and swearing, the man allowed Jeff to take his arm and turn him back toward his car. Only he shook Jeff free and rounded on him. "You lookin' for trouble, Douglas? I won't be pushed around by you or anyone else," he shouted. "I'm not someone to mess with and you know that."

"Indeed, you're not," agreed Jeff calmly. "And it's Mr. Douglas to you. Now, before you say anything more you'll regret, I'm asking you to get off my property."

Without another word, the man stomped back to his car, wrenched open the door, and fired off a few parting words. "I'll be back to talk to Sophie tomorrow. You make sure she's somewhere I can find her."

As the car peeled away in a shower of gravel Jeff turned to Annette. "Are you alright?" he asked solicitously.

"I'm fine, apart from feeling very angry. Who was that boor?"

"That, my dear Annette, was Jim Danbury. One of the men who wants to buy the Triple T Ranch."

Chapter Thirteen

"And you don't think 'e is capable of breaking the law?" Annette asked, lifting her brows incredulously. "That man was 'orrible. I can easily imagine 'im doing whatever it takes to drive her away?"

"I don't know," Jeff sighed. "Of course it's possible. Anything is possible." He took off his hat and scratched his head. "It's true, Jim and his son have caused problems in the district for years. Nothing they did was as destructive and underhanded as these incidents, though. Poisoning Sophie's well and driving her cattle onto a busy highway could have cost lives. It's hard to believe even Jim would do that." He rubbed the stubble on his chin. "Plus, you just can't go around pointing fingers without solid evidence."

"Humph! Then we must find the evidence." She crossed her arms over her chest and looked mutinous, her mind racing. Could they somehow follow the man every time he left his property? His son would need to be tailed too, of course, although she'd need to see a picture of what he looked like. Too bad they didn't have the sort of private investigator equipment spies used in movies. She was busy devising strategies to capture this awful criminal of a man, and came back to the present as she heard Jeff's next words.

"I've never seen you like this. You're quite the firecracker when you get riled." He bent down and looked into her face, his eyes dancing with fun, then his countenance grew serious. "You are a rare beauty, Annette." He caught her eyes and held them a moment before a strange little smile twisted his lips. "I suppose you hear that all the time." His focus moved to the mane of hair that blew across her eyes. "Your hair is almost glowing. The sunlight's turning it into living flames." He took a long strand between his fingers, moving it away from her face. "It's beautiful."

Annette froze. Her breathing became shallow as he stepped close and lifted her hair in the setting sunlight. Her eyes fluttered shut. Had anyone ever said such things to her? She couldn't remember if they had. Her heart longed to hear more.

Then, a wave of self-consciousness washed over her, and she thought of the warning she had so recently received.

She coughed and stepped back, her hair running through his fingers like liquid fire as she pulled away. "I—I think it's time..." her face flushed. "I, uh, should go in now," she stuttered.

"Of course," he said, becoming brisk. "And I must attend to several more chores before dinner." He wheeled around and strode down the path.

"Jeff," she called, breaking into a run to catch up. He turned abruptly and she ran into him. His body was solid and immovable. No wonder Jim had backed down.

Catching her breath, Annette stepped hurriedly away, fighting a wild urge to run into his arms and hug him for what he'd done for her just now. No one had ever protected her like that before. True, it had never been necessary either, but that wasn't the point. There was something caring about Jeff. She felt safe when she was around him. Shaking off the bizarre impulse, she made do with simple words instead.

"Thank you for coming at just the right time to rid me of that man."

Jeff grinned. "Any time." Reaching out a calloused hand, he brushed her cheek, then turned and was gone.

Annette stood there long after he'd disappeared. She lifted a hand to the spot where he'd touched her. The thought came that perhaps she wouldn't wash that spot for a while. Then she gave herself a shake. What was she, fifteen? She was a grown woman with plans and a future. And Jeff was already entangled in some sort of relationship with the hostile Rosa. Besides, a commute between France and Canada was out of the question. No relationship could withstand that level of separation. She would put all such ridiculous notions out of her head and focus on the immediate problem of how to help Sophie.

She needed to discuss it with Gabrielle. Maybe there was some way to do their own surveillance on Sophie's land. She knew where the Danbury Farm was located. It was worth a try anyway and a much better plan to be proactive rather than waiting around for another catastrophe. The next one might truly end everything for the Triple T Ranch.

She marched into the house and made her way upstairs. Pausing outside Gabrielle's room, she heard talking. Her sister must be on the phone with Andrew. Figured. Those two shared everything with one another.

Annette stole past and entered her own room, wondering if Gabrielle had told Andrew what was happening with the ranch. She collapsed into the cozy chair by the arched window and gazed at the view, refusing to allow herself to go over what had happened near the garden. The parts that involved Jim Danbury, she stuffed away for later contemplation. Instead, she went back to what Jeff had said to her.

Why had he? She knew she was no beauty at all, let alone a rare one. Standing, she walked to the bathroom mirror and made a face at herself. Yes, she looked the same as always. No fairy godmother had visited her while she slept in this princess boudoir, suddenly making her beautiful. She was the very same, freckle faced, hazel-eyed girl she'd always been.

So, why would he tell her that? It didn't make sense. She flopped onto her bed, meaning to check on Gabrielle in ten minutes, and fell fast asleep.

Annette woke to an incessant tapping on her door. Lazily she rolled over, realizing she'd pulled the comforter over herself, and it had tangled around her legs. She toppled to the floor with a thud.

"Ow," she yelped. The door opened.

"Are you okay?" Gabrielle whispered, hurrying to help. She dragged the blanket away and threw it across the bed. "How long have you been sleeping?"

Annette yawned. "Not sure. I was waiting to talk to you, but you were on the phone with Andrew."

Gabrielle jumped onto the bed and sat cross-legged, leaning her chin in her hands. "Oh, it wasn't Andrew. I forgot what time it was there. He would have been in bed long ago."

"Then who?"

"It was Mom, and she called me. Couldn't sleep apparently and she wondered if we were enjoying our holiday."

Annette propped up the pillow and sat with her back against them. "You didn't tell her all this, did you?"

"Don't be silly. She'd be worried sick."

Annette chewed on a fingernail wondering how to convince her sister that they should take action. Just saying it flat out was likely best. "Gabby," she began in her most persuasive tone. "While you were on the phone I met Danbury, the guy who wants to buy Sophie out. He is a terrible person and I think he could be behind all the things that have been happening. I'd like to do a little investigating of our own." She added quickly, "For Sophie's sake."

"Investigating? What could we possibly investigate? And what do you mean you met him? I need details."

Annette explained what had happened when Danbury showed up, leaving out the interaction between herself and Jeff. "So, that's why I think he needs to be watched," she concluded.

"I see," Gabrielle fell back, her hands under her head. "You could be right. He certainly sounds awful. But how could we watch him?"

Annette explained, "As far as I understand it, the attacks have been escalating. It seems to me that something major happens every two days. When we arrived it was the water well, two days before that her hired help walked off the job, and today it was the fence. Each one of those events happened two days apart."

"That's an interesting observation," Gabrielle mused. "How can we do anything to prevent it, though? Jeff has a surveillance company at Sophie's every night and they must be doing their job."

"I'm sure they are. However, they won't be specifically

watching the Danbury ranch and the latest incident didn't take place at the Triple T. Probably because the culprit knows it's guarded and chose to attack elsewhere. We can do more than watch Sophie's yard. We can watch the suspects, otherwise known as the Danburys, and perhaps catch them in the act."

"Attacks? The culprit? Suspects?" Gabrielle's eyes widened. "Maybe you've been watching too many late-night movies. I think we should leave this up to the RCMP."

"Jeff said they already questioned the Danburys, remember? And they didn't learn anything. I have intuition about the father though. Tomorrow night we should watch him."

"And if I go along with this crazy scheme, how do you propose we get there? We can't walk all that way and spy on the man from his own yard. And we can hardly ask Jeff to take a vehicle out in the dead of night. Do you propose we lift the keys from his pocket, push it down the driveway when he's sleeping, and start the engine once we're out of earshot?" Gabrielle giggled. "This is starting to sound like a second-rate detective show."

Annette rubbed her temples, screwing her eyes shut as she racked her brain for ideas. "No. You're right, that would be crazy. I'll think of something, though, just you wait and see. Now, let's go down to dinner. I smell something wonderful."

Sandra had created a spicy pasta dish, green salad, fresh buns, and an apple crumble with vanilla ice cream for dessert. The meal was delicious. However, the people around the table were sombre, especially after Jeff told Sophie that Jim Danbury had come to see her earlier.

"That man!" she fumed. "Why can't 'e listen to me? He

rang me today and I told 'im I was not selling. When 'e became rude and abusive, I 'ung up."

"I wondered why 'e arrived angry," Annette said. "Now I know." She relayed the conversation that had ensued between her and Danbury, and how Jeff had appeared at just the right moment to escort the man back to his car. "If Danbury's son is anything like 'im I think they are both capable of underhanded tricks."

"I have a bad feeling about him, too," Rosa said. "Personally, I wouldn't put it past Jim or his son, Dillon, to be behind the terrible things that have been happening." Annette looked at her in surprise. Rosa had agreed with her, really? Had she mellowed since this afternoon's threat? Sitting beside Jeff at the table, Rosa laid a hand on his and smiled up at him. "Good thing you were there to save the day."

"Uh, thanks," he said. "Annette was dealing with him just fine, though. She really didn't need me."

Rosa's face soured and Jeff pulled his hand away. He patted hers companionably. They sat quite close. Granted, that might be because she was leaning into him, but still.

Annette eyed them with interest. They didn't act like a couple. Perhaps she misread what had happened outside her sister's door. Or maybe they didn't want anyone to know about their relationship.

"I am so sorry you had to cope with 'im," Sophie said remorsefully, interrupting Annette's train of thought. "At this point, Jim Danbury is the last person on earth I would sell my ranch to...Oh, by the way Jeff, the water safety report from Alberta Health should be back tomorrow or the next day. If everything checks out, we can go back to the Triple T and leave you in peace."

"Excellent news about your water, Sophie. Just know

that you're all quite welcome to stay here as long as you want. I've enjoyed the company." Jeff pushed his chair back and patted his flat stomach under the thin material of his t-shirt. "Thanks for another wonderful meal Sandra," he called to his housekeeper. "We'll clean up. You head on home to that long-suffering husband of yours."

Sandra dried her soapy hands down her apron before pulling it off to reveal the rabbit on her sweater in all his splendor. Ducking her head she checked the bunny to make sure nothing had been splashed on his pristine faux fur. Once satisfied, she smiled at her employer and wished them all a good night.

When she was gone, they carried their dishes to the kitchen and worked together to tidy up. Everyone except for Rosa. She'd disappeared, muttering something about a headache and went to lie down in the living room. When they all came in later, she was watching television.

Patting the sofa beside her, she spoke exclusively to Jeff. "Come sit. You've had a hard day. Would you like me to massage your neck?"

"Actually, I am pretty beat," he yawned. "Think I'm going to take a quick check outside to make sure everything's alright with the stock and then head to bed. Maybe take a quick run back to the Triple T as well."

Rosa's disappointment was obvious, but she recovered rapidly. "Want some company?" she asked. "I'd like to check on something myself."

"Sure," he said. She jumped up to get her coat and Sophie made to stand as well. "No," Jeff held up a hand. "You stay here and visit with your company. You've barely had a chance to see them with what's been happening. If something's wrong I'll call."

Sophie subsided back in her chair, her face expressing

gratitude. "Thank you, my dear. I'm actually quite tired. I'd love to spend more time with the girls and then I think I'll also have an early night. I'll leave my phone on, though."

With a wave he marched across the room for a coat that was hanging by the door and held it for an exultant Rosa, who called, "Good night, don't wait up," before disappearing outside.

Annette was glad to see Rosa leave. However, it bothered her for some inexplicable reason to see the woman go with Jeff. Still, without them there, the three women chatted for the next hour about family in France, the ranch, and barrel racing. Annette learned quite a bit about the sport just by listening and was enthralled with her sister's knowledge on the subject. She noticed, however, that Gabrielle kept the topic away from discussing the recent troubles on the ranch and her feelings on whether Sophie had called Andrew yet.

Sophie couldn't possibly have written him a letter too. It wouldn't make sense considering his wife was here and seeing what was happening with her own eyes.

After a while, Annette felt herself drifting off to sleep and realized she still wasn't quite over jetlag. Checking the time, she realized it was only past nine on Wednesday, the third day. Their holiday had been so packed with activity that it was hard to keep track of the days.

"I think I might go up to my room," she announced, when there was a lull in the conversation about how quickly Rosa was training a horse called Trixie. It was clear that Sophie was impressed with Rosa and her abilities. Maybe the woman had some fabulous personality traits that Annette hadn't been made aware of yet. It was doubtful though.

Suddenly, she jerked to wakefulness with an idea. She

could hardly wait to share it with her sister. "*Bonne nuit,*" she said, getting out of her chair with a groan. Jeff had been right. Her muscles really were sore today. She flexed her shoulders and then moved to her sister and Sophie, giving them a kiss on each cheek. "I'm too tired to stay up any longer. See you in the morning."

When Sophie and Gabrielle came up to bed half an hour later, Annette was waiting. She slipped into her sister's room behind her.

"I have an idea," she said in a loud stage whisper, causing Gabby to jump. They slipped back into French now that it was just them.

"What about?" Gabrielle turned on the lamp by her bed and drew the curtains.

"I think we should take horses to investigate Jim Danbury's ranch tomorrow night." Annette crossed her arms feeling a bit smug.

"Horses!" screeched Gabrielle.

"Shhh!"

"Horses?" she hissed again. "You've had one riding lesson in your entire life, and almost crushed your instructor trying to get on. How in the world do you presume to ride several kilometres in the middle of the night?"

"I have all tomorrow to practise," Annette said airily. "Besides, Pearl likes me, and I like her. I'm confident I can do it." She leaned toward her sister and whispered dramatically, "Will you join me?"

"To do what?" Gabrielle asked in exasperation. "Patrol past this man's house for several hours? In the middle of the night? If he *is* the one doing these things, how do we know when he might do his dirty work?"

Annette shrugged. "We don't. That's the only problem. But if I was going to pull a stunt like that, I'd do it between the hours of two and five. People might stay up late, and on a ranch they might get up early, but not many people will be awake between those hours. I'd say that's playing it safe. Remember though, we'll have to go to bed super early tomorrow, so we can be up half the night. So, will you do it with me?" she asked eagerly.

Gabrielle came to stand in front of Annette, a furrow appearing between her lovely eyes. "Alright," she agreed with a heavy sigh. "It's crazy and I don't like it one bit. I know I'm going to regret this, but I'll go with you…if only to pick up the pieces when you topple to the ground and break your neck."

"Thanks," Annette said dryly. "Your confidence in me is overwhelming." Wishing her sister a good night, she went back to her own room, ruminating on the task she'd set before herself. Gabrielle was right. It was a crazy idea. It was highly improbable that they would uncover the plot, or catch the men who plotted to drive Sophie from her home.

Still, she was so sure the Danbury men were at the bottom of Sophie's troubles that she was willing to risk it if things went sideways. Come to think of it—sideways was exactly how she'd fall if she couldn't stay on Pearl as they traipsed through a field, in the dead of night. After only having two lessons riding a horse, it sounded ludicrous, even to her. Despite that, she was determined to catch them in the act and bring them to justice.

How that would be done was another matter.

Chapter Fourteen

Annette snuggled beneath the puffy white comforter on her bed, relishing in its softness and warmth. She covered her eyes with an arm against the blinding light that streamed into her room, momentarily disoriented. It was never this bright in her Parisian apartment. What was happening?

She sat bolt upright, remembering where she was, the plans for today, and moreover, the proposed scheme for tonight. Flipping the covers back, she leaped from the bed and moved quickly to the windows.

Morning sunlight streamed through a gap where she'd neglected to pull the drapes fully shut. As was always the way, that shaft of light had fallen right across her pillow. But it was actually a good thing, she realized as she pulled the heavy fabric aside and saw how high the sun had climbed into the clear blue sky. It was late—again.

Gone were the heavy clouds of yesterday's thunderstorm. She moved to the door of her balcony and flung it wide, inhaling the crisp morning air. It was so clean and fresh, compared to the city. Stepping outside, she walked to the railing and rested her arms on it, uncaring of how her diaphanous pink nightgown swirled around her legs in the gentle breeze. No one was around to see her here.

Her only companions were the majestic Rockies, their peaks glistening with snow under the bright sun. The rolling hills were a vibrant green, the tall grass freshly washed after the rain. Straight ahead was the massive red barn, sheds, and corrals—empty now. Though she was sure they would be full of animals when the cold winter winds blew. Off to her right were the horses, grazing and swishing their tails. Even dear Pearl, her coat looking the purest white. It was a breathtaking scene that would remain etched in Annette's memory forever.

A banging sound emanated from one of the sheds and Annette scampered back inside. She didn't wish to be caught in her gown. Closing the door, she readied herself for what lay ahead. Sandra had kindly laundered all of her clothes the day before, which meant she had a supply of jeans again. She scrabbled through her bag for a different top to wear. Surely there was one fashionable shirt that wasn't all about functionality. Considering she was a girl that prided herself on her wardrobe, she'd set her fashion sense aside when packing. Still, it hadn't been all that bad to forget about her appearance these last four days, she reflected.

Choosing a rather rumpled, moss-green, long sleeve, crop top from the jumble of clothes, she threw it on the bed and pulled on some jeans. Once dressed, she dragged a wide-toothed comb through her curls and left them flowing free. She could always tie up her hair for the ride later. Right now, it was important to get downstairs. Makeup didn't matter, after all she had no one to impress.

Bursting into the kitchen, she looked around with surprise at finding herself alone.

"Jeff told Sandra to take the day off," Gabrielle called from behind the swinging doors leading into the living room. "He said she's been working too late and needs to spend some time relaxing with her husband. Anyway, I found a cupboard full of cold cereal. I ate a sugary, yet tasty bowl of something called Captain Crunch. Help yourself."

She walked in and took a seat opposite to Annette at the table and leaned her chin on her hands, looking quite beautiful in a cherry red, peasant style blouse tucked into her slim jeans. Annette admired her sister's simple, yet elegant outfit as she shoveled a spoonful of the crunchy cereal into her mouth.

"Are you still determined to follow through with your plan to spy on the neighbours?" Gabrielle asked.

"Yes. *You* weren't accosted by that horrible man yesterday. All he wants is to get his greedy hands on Sophie's farm. I'm sure he's guilty of the attacks. I'll practise riding on Pearl today and tonight...we become French spies."

Gabrielle grinned and shrugged expressively. "Then I must tell you that Jeff is busy all morning and can't give you another lesson until later in the afternoon, if then. So, your idea of galloping across the midnight range may not go as well as you had hoped. And Sophie has asked us to come to the Triple T for a visit this morning. She'd like to show you around and have us watch Rosa train the horses for barrel racing. Jeff left us a vehicle to use."

"Wonderful. I'd love nothing better than to stand around watching Rosa perform her magic. Must we applaud and throw flowers as well?"

Gabrielle arched her eyebrows. "You and Rosa seem to have a growing dislike for one another. Why?"

Annette countered with a question of her own. "Do you think she and Jeff are romantically involved?"

"I haven't considered it. I suppose they could be. It's obvious she really likes Jeff, but I can't tell if he feels the same about her."

"Well, she warned me away from him."

"Oh," Gabrielle drew out the sound with added meaning. "That's strange, I agree. What happened?"

"We were sitting in Pearl's stall talking and she came in." Purposely, Annette left out the night where she'd seen them in what looked like an embrace and the confrontation afterward. It was just too messy and unpleasant to bring up, and Gabby would want all the details. It upset her to think of it.

"That hardly seems grounds for issuing a warning. Anyway, you don't care, because you don't like him, right?" Gabrielle watched her sister's reaction closely.

"Right," Annette stated without conviction. Before more questions were asked, she rose and carried her bowl to the sink.

After doing the few dishes, the two women went outside to find that Jeff had left the keys in his old truck for them. They climbed in, rolled down the windows, hit the gravel road, and revelled in the pine-scented breeze that rushed through the cab.

"I have two things to thank you for," Annette said suddenly. "Bringing me here and making me repack."

Gabrielle laughed. "You're welcome. Sometimes your older sister knows best."

"But not in matters of espionage," Annette said with a chuckle.

Gabrielle just shook her head and grunted. Minutes later they pulled up to the house at the Triple T Ranch.

Sophie, in deep discussion with Marcus and another man they assumed was Tristan, waved them over.

By the time they parked and reached her, the men had moved on to a huge steel shed near the barn.

"I keep everything locked now," Sophie explained, nodding at the men as they paused to open a padlock that secured big double doors. Then, as they slid open, Annette saw a tractor and other machinery. "I'm doing everything possible to try preventing whatever might happen next. But enough of my worries," Sophie said with forced brightness. "I'm so glad you're here."

To the left of the house, Sophie had a similar hip-roof barn to Jeff's red one. It wasn't as big as his and the paint was chipped and faded, but wide doors were open to an interesting looking loft. Across from it and down a path sat another huge structure almost twice its length. It was where Sophie was taking them.

"Rosa's working outside today," she explained as they followed her in through a side door, "but when it's winter, very windy, or raining, she brings the horses in here for training." It was gloomy and dark until Sophie flipped a large metal switch, and the building was flooded with light.

It was an arena of gigantic proportions. The floor was covered in sand with a pole fence and a couple of wooden gates blocking off either end of the building. Furthest away from them were three barrels. Two were placed opposite to one another on either side of the arena close to the open gate, and one barrel was in the center and closer to where they stood. The barrels formed a triangle shape.

Gabrielle turned to her sister, eyes gleaming with pride. "This is where Andrew and Jayke used to practise team roping and steer wrestling," she said. "They won prizes all over Alberta in rodeos when they were young."

Annette tried to look suitably impressed. She had zero idea what those activities were, although they sounded impressive. She did know that Andrew had caught a criminal on the streets of Paris using some of the tactics he'd learned while roping and wrestling cattle. Yet, while that was cool, she didn't understand what he had done. She promised herself she'd ask for a proper explanation once she and her sister were alone.

"Yes," Sophie agreed, "I am very proud of my boys." Her eyes took on a faraway look. "Not just for that, you understand," she hastened to add. "I will always be proud of my sons for who they are. I miss them." Turning swiftly, Sophie flipped off the lights and led the way back out into the sunshine.

"This way," she said. Next, they entered the barn. It smelled of cows and Annette wrinkled her nose before she could stop herself. Following Sophie, they trooped along a narrow alleyway, passing several box stalls on their way toward a large pen in the back of the gloomy building. Only a row of small windows down each side allowed a small amount of light to filter through. It took a few minutes for her eyes to adjust to the shadowy interior, then she leaned her arms on the wooden rails like Sophie had done, and looked through to what was inside.

Three bedraggled cows stood in a bed of straw, their heads hanging low. Even Annette could see that they were very sick. "Dr. Roberts says we might lose them yet," Sophie said quietly. "We're doing all we can for them, but the next couple of days will determine whether they make it or not."

"I'm so sorry," Gabrielle laid a hand on Sophie's shoulder. "I wish there was something we could do to help."

Sophie continued as though she hadn't heard, "It's strange that the rancher, Weaver, from up north still wants to buy them." She turned to Gabrielle and lifted her hands in mute appeal. "Why?" she asked finally. "I don't understand it."

They turned from the dismal sight and walked back toward the doors. "He called to repeat his offer to take the ranch off my hands this morning. That's two men in the space of a month that have offered to buy me out." She stopped with her hand on the doorjamb and her head bent. She peered up at the sisters with a bleak look in her eyes. "I think Weaver is interested in the location. When he was here, you know, to look at the animals I had for sale, he seemed to fall in love with the place. He offered me far more than it was worth then, and still more now." She shook her head in bewilderment. The lines on her face appeared to grow deeper by the day. No matter how she tried to hide it, Sophie and the Triple T Ranch were in trouble.

She shrugged. "I might have to accept it," she said, staring at the ground as though she'd forgotten she wasn't alone. "If anything more happens..." Her voice trailed away.

Gabrielle put an arm around Sophie's shoulders. "We aren't going to think that way, not now at least. Whoever is at the bottom of this will be brought to justice, I just know it. And then everything will go back to normal."

Annette noticed that Gabby didn't mention Sophie's two sons. The letter would not have reached Jayke yet, and presumably Andrew still didn't know. She studied the firm set to her sister's jaw and wondered if she would simply take matters into her own hands. Both men should be informed.

Sophie took a deep breath and straightened. "Anyway, I didn't ask you here to whine about my troubles," she said, passing a hand across her eyes. "I wanted you to see Rosa in action." She glanced at her watch and hurried around the corner of the barn and down a narrow lane between corrals. "I believe she'll be working with Trixie right now."

They passed a series of pens built with metal poles and sheds for housing animals, and skirted a few puddles of scummy black water, remnants of yesterday's storm. Annette began to hear the thumping sound of a horse's hoof beats and despite her feelings for Rosa, felt a thrill of anticipation.

Finally, they came to another sandy arena surrounded by a high wooden fence painted a striking white. Inside were the expected barrels and at the far end were trees shivering in a slight breeze. At both ends of the huge oval pen were metal gates, but the one closest to them was open and Rosa was poised on a tall, glossy brown horse with black mane and tail.

As usual, she wore denim from head to toe, but today she had a broad felt cowboy hat pulled low over her eyes against the late morning sun. Sophie put out an arm to halt them in their tracks and raised a finger to her lips as Rosa whistled and kicked the horse into action. She crouched low over the horse's withers, urging it to greater and greater speeds with her hands and voice. Trixie flattened her ears against her skull and snaked her head out in front as she galloped toward the first barrel. They rounded it at breakneck speed, the horse's legs nearly sliding out from under her. Rosa's one foot almost touched the ground on the inside as they took the barrel so close that it swayed for a moment.

As they sped to the second barrel, Rosa slapped her reins on the horse's rump. Sophie, in a low voice, explained, "Trixie is a Quarter Horse and she just turned three. When she was two, before I hired Rosa, I sent her to a local trainer to learn the basics. Now, that Rosa is here, she's been working with Trixie and three more horses every other day, schooling them on the barrels. It's quite thrilling isn't it?" She turned to look at them, her face glowing.

Both women were mesmerized and only nodded in response. It really was electrifying to watch. Annette lifted her phone and took several pictures. This was a scene she'd like to draw and perhaps paint later, when she was home in Paris.

"After another month, Rosa wants to start taking them to competitions to fine tune their skills. Then, when their training is complete, I hope to sell each one for around $10,000." Sophie folded her arms across her chest as Rosa rounded the third barrel and came racing back, driving Trixie to go faster and faster.

"You see," Sophie went on, clearly loving this sport, "the quickest time wins. Rosa keeps a stopwatch with her, and she feels Trixie has the most potential of all the horses she's training."

The horse thundered toward them, her mouth open, grunting with effort as she hurtled herself and her rider to the alleyway that marked the finish line.

Then, in a cloud of dust, Rosa pulled the horse to a sliding stop and consulted the watch in her hand.

"She did it in fourteen point nine seconds," Rosa called. "That's better than last week. She's improving every time I take her out." Leaning forward she patted Trixie's neck and murmured words of encouragement. It was the first time Annette thought perhaps the woman wasn't as bad as she previously believed. At least she had one redeeming quality.

"Wonderful!" Sophie yelled. Turning to Annette and Gabrielle, she motioned for them to go back the way they'd come. "I don't want to interrupt her," she explained. "Rosa is very strict about her training regime, and I wouldn't want us to throw it off."

Ending up back at the truck, Sophie said sorrowfully, "I'm sorry that I can't ask you to come inside for a drink. I only bring a few bottles of water and a thermos of coffee with me when I come here." She sighed. "The water test wasn't completed today, so we'll have to spend one more night with Jeff. But then I feel sure we can all come back here tomorrow. It will feel so good to be at home again. Although I appreciate Jeff's kindness, I'm looking forward to having you here, where just us girls can have a proper visit and I can show you around the property. There are some lovely rides up into the mountains. Oh…" Sophie paused and regarded Annette with concern, "I forgot, you can't ride, can you?"

"I'm learning and doing very well," Annette said with more confidence than she felt. "And I'd love to go with you and Gabby. Just…maybe not on a barrel horse," she laughed.

Sophie chuckled, her expression lightening. "I have many horses here that you could ride. They would be quite suitable. Perhaps Lassie?" She looked questioningly at Gabrielle.

"I agree. Speaking of riding, I believe Annette has a lesson soon," Gabrielle offered, glancing at her phone. "And Andrew just tried calling me, so I'd like to ring him back if that's okay?"

Sophie nodded emphatically. "Yes, my dear. We'll have plenty of time for visiting when you're both here. I'll see you back at Jeff's for dinner, yes?"

"Yes," both women parroted.

As they waved and drove out of the yard, Annette considered what Sophie had said. All four women would be living here tomorrow. That meant there was no choice. Tonight, they would have to make their move, because the Danburys place was close to Jeff's not the Triple T Ranch. They could never make the trek from here in the dark.

Unbidden, it crossed her mind that when they moved over to live with Sophie, she would not see their handsome host each day either. But why should that matter to her? It was ridiculous and she pushed it from her mind.

What was important to consider was what the night might bring. She felt a shiver of fear and excitement trickle up her spine. Would she fall off Pearl and break her neck, as her sister predicted? Or would they catch the Danbury men in the act of sabotage? Only time would tell.

She must focus on tonight and prepare herself for what might happen next.

Chapter Fifteen

When they arrived back at the Douglas Ranch, Jeff was striding across the yard, heading toward the barn. Annette's eyes lingered on him. It was a warm day, and he'd rolled the sleeves of his black button-up shirt over his elbows to reveal strong, muscular forearms. It fit loosely, but there was no doubt his body was in perfect shape beneath the material. The shirt was tucked into the waistband of snugly fitted jeans and a belt. She pushed the hair away from her face and forced a nonchalant expression to her face, suddenly wishing she would have at least worn a little makeup.

"I've just had a bowl of beef-barley soup and a sandwich," he called as they hopped out of the vehicle. "Go inside and help yourself to lunch while I saddle up. I have a couple of hours to spend on another lesson. Okay?"

Annette was aghast. "No!" she shrieked.

Jeff stopped, a puzzled frown creasing his forehead. He tipped the battered black cowboy hat he always wore, back on his head. "No? You don't want to try riding again?"

She forced herself to be calm, took a breath and

answered. "I mean, I need to be with you because I want to learn everything about catching Pearl in the pasture, riding, and saddling her today."

"Oh," he said a grin flashing as he wiped a hand across his chin, dark with stubble. "I have other things I should do right now. Come find me when you're ready. Actually, hang on a minute," he fished a small phone out of his breast pocket and clicked it to life. "Can you use your phone in Canada?"

"Yes," Gabrielle replied on Annette's behalf. "I 'elped 'er with that since…uh, well, since she might be 'earing from someone while she's 'ere. We 'ave a limited number of texts to use, but…" she explained and shrugged, "we also 'ave no one else except you or Sophie to use them with while we are 'ere."

Jeff and Annette exchanged numbers. He slid his small flip-phone phone back into his pocket and buttoned it closed. "Great," he said, patting it as though assuring himself her number was safely guarded. "I use a phone that's easily replaced when I'm working. In case it gets destroyed," he explained a bit self-consciously. "Now it will be easy for you to shoot me a text when you're ready and we'll go out to the pasture for Pearl together."

He turned away. "Jeff?" she called tentatively. He swivelled around and waited; eyebrows raised. "I want to thank you for taking the time to teach me. It really means a lot."

A grin of pleasure eased the worry lines on his forehead. "You're welcome," he said, "It's always a treat when I can help a beautiful artist from a foreign country learn to ride a horse." Playfully he scratched his chin and squinted at the sky. "Actually, that's never happened before, but I'm enjoying it now." With a deep chuckle, he walked away, calling over his shoulder, "Text me."

Annette rounded on her sister as soon as he was out of earshot. "Why would he say that?" she demanded.

"Say what? That you're a foreigner?"

"No, of course not," she snapped. "Why would he call me beautiful?" Just repeating the words brought a prickle of tears to her eyes, and she spun quickly away to hide them, blinking hard. No one had ever said that to her before. Was he mocking her?

"Why?" repeated Gabrielle, her voice rising to a squeak. "Because it's true," she said with conviction. She grabbed Annette and swung her around. Taking her by her upper arms, she leaned in and looked deep into her sister's eyes. "I always tell you this, but you never listen. You. Are. Beautiful. I'm not going to list all your attributes, mainly because I'm hungry and that soup sounded good," she giggled. "But you're very, very pretty."

"You have to say that," Annette protested, her shoulders sagging. "You're my sister. It's the law."

Gabrielle laughed. "See! Case in point. You never listen to what I have to say." She dropped her hands and they both started walking to the house. "Maybe you'll listen to Jeff," she said slyly.

But that wasn't worth replying to, so Annette ignored it. They mounted the steps to the front door and let themselves inside. Jeff's house was becoming like home to her now. She kicked off her boots and walked through the huge living room, admiring the sunlight streaming through the massive windows on both sides, and how it took on a homey, comfortable feeling at every hour of the day. It must be so cozy to sit beside the roaring fire during the winter, when cold winds whistled down from the mountains and snow blanketed the land.

Together they passed through the space and into the

kitchen. They heated the soup that was waiting in the fridge and found ham and cheese for quick sandwiches.

Seating herself in her usual spot at the table, Annette sank her teeth into the homemade bread and closed her eyes. "Sandra's a marvelous cook," she exclaimed with gusto. "Too bad I'm in a hurry and can't dawdle over lunch."

"You're anxious to see Jeff again?" Gabrielle inquired innocently.

Annette grimaced. "You know that's not true." She slurped a spoonful of the piping hot soup and burned her tongue. Scraping back her chair, she hurried for a glass of water. "Want one?" she called.

Gabrielle nodded and Annette filled two large glasses to the brim before carefully shuffling back to the table so as not to spill. "This afternoon I want to learn everything I can about riding and getting ready to ride," she said, feeling this explanation was unnecessary. She clunked the glass down in front of her sister. "You know why."

"Yes," her sister sighed long and loud. "I know why. I still don't agree with this wild idea of yours, but I can't let you go alone either…or I fear you would do just that."

Annette nodded her head in the affirmative, too busy eating to answer. They both made short work of the meal, keeping talk to a minimum. Annette learned that Gabrielle intended to ask Jeff if she could take Panda out for a ride again.

"I might as well get accustomed to him if we have to go for an extended midnight ride," she confirmed in a monotone voice.

As they cleared away their dishes and prepared to leave, Annette corrected her sister, "Not midnight. Remember, I'll come to get you at about one, so we have time to catch the horses and saddle up before heading over at two. Get it?"

"Got it."

"Good," quipped Annette as they hurried back outside.

She fumbled with her phone to send Jeff a text. Hers was cumbersome compared to his small one and after it sent she wondered where it would be safe. Her only options were a back pocket or under her shirt held in a bra strap. Neither were good. Tonight, she'd have to bring a cross-body purse since she might need to take photographic evidence of the Danburys' nighttime criminal activities.

Both women strolled toward the barn, knowing it might take a few minutes for Jeff to appear from wherever he was working. With Gabrielle's help Annette slid open the big double doors and they stepped inside the barn.

"We might need a little encouragement for them to come to us," Gabrielle suggested. "Something like a few oats in a small pail or in our pockets. And of course, we'll have to take their halters and lead ropes too."

"Okay," Annette remarked uncertainly. "That's the strappy thing that goes around their heads, right?"

Gabrielle tilted her head and rolled her eyes heavenward. "We're in trouble," she groaned. "Go look on the wall beside Pearl's stall for the halter. She was likely wearing it the last time you saw her."

"Right. Oh, it's pink," Annette remembered happily, and found it hanging on the wall. Attached to it was a long rope. *Success.* She heard footsteps approaching and swivelled around to see Jeff's shadowy form fill the door with his broad shoulders and large hat. Well, not really, but it looked that way to her. She licked her lips and lifted the halter proudly.

"Found it," she said.

Gabrielle appeared at her side with Panda's in tow and they followed Jeff back outside into the sunshine. He was holding a small pail that he swished back and forth. Grain rattled against the sides.

"Pearl is usually good about being caught," he said, "but Panda, not so much. So, we'll take them a little incentive."

"Where did you get it?" Annette blurted. Gabrielle rolled her eyes and Jeff narrowed his gaze quizzically.

"Out of that bin of oats over there." He pointed. "Why? You need to catch them for a moonlight ride that I don't know about?"

Annette's startled gasp caused her to choke and splutter. Gabrielle slapped her on the back with a bit more vigour than was actually required. "*Est-ce que ça va ma sœur?*" she asked with exaggerated concern.

Coughing, Annette smiled through watering eyes and tried to smile. "I'm fine," she croaked. "Must 'ave been a crumb from lunch that went down the wrong way."

Jeff didn't question it any further. Instead, he led them to a small metal gate built into the fence. They passed through and stopped.

"Don't we 'ave to walk out there?" Annette asked.

"Naw," he said. "Cover your ears." Lifting two fingers, he placed them in his mouth and blew. A piercing whistle shattered the air and every horse, far away in the field, lifted its head. First one began to trot toward him, and then they all broke into a gallop and thundered toward them from across the pasture. It was quite a sight. Annette shrank behind Jeff for fear of being trampled.

He laughed. "It's a fact that horses fight over oats," he explained. "And without meaning to they could hurt you. Why don't you and Gabrielle stand just outside the fence until I catch them?"

The women did so, Annette arching her eyebrows at her sister. How was this going to work in the middle of the night? It posed yet another issue she hadn't considered. Twenty horses hurtling toward them in the middle of the night wasn't ideal. She'd have to think about this.

Meanwhile, Jeff caught three horses and beckoned to them. Hesitantly, the sisters stepped through the gate, and each took a lead rope.

"Are we all going for a ride?" Annette asked. Pearl looked bigger today and she was beginning to feel the first flutters of fear.

"I don't think Gabrielle will want to hang around with us," he said with a grin. "She can go for a ride on her own. You and I will start off in the pen. If you feel comfortable, we'll go for a little ride in the closest pasture to the yard. Okay?"

His eyes searched her face. She knew she must look tense and made an effort to smooth her features into a brave smile. At least she hoped it resembled confidence and not a grimace of pain.

"Sure. That sounds good." They led the horses inside the barn.

It took half an hour to brush, saddle, and bridle Pearl. Jeff stood back and directed while Annette did everything herself. There were a few mishaps like when she clanked the bit against the horse's teeth and she flinched, or when Annette didn't lift the saddle high enough and plowed it into the side of Pearl's stomach. Though overall, it went well. She stepped back and surveyed her efforts with pride.

"I did it," she exclaimed, as though there had been grave doubts about it.

"You did," Jeff said, patting her on the back. "Now, lead

her out into the same round pen we were in before. I'll get you started and then I'll saddle my own horse."

She led Pearl out the big barn doors, around the corner, and through the open gate of the round pen.

Annette felt a good deal of apprehension when she placed her foot in the stirrup and prepared to mount. She had no desire to take another tumble. Memories of lying on top of a handsome gasping man in the dirt caused her to blush all over again. Still, she took hold of her courage, seized the saddle horn, hopped three times on her left foot, and threw herself up and over the saddle.

It worked! She felt like a pro. *No, it wouldn't do to get too cocky. Settle down.*

"Perfect," Jeff said with another pat, this time to her leg. She was happy, but realized these innocent little pats were messing with her senses. Each time he did it, a trickling sensation of awareness went through her body. It was as though he'd left his imprint on her since, even later, she could still feel his hand.

Shaking her head to rid herself of these wayward thoughts, she concentrated on the job at hand. She would learn to ride today if it killed her. And it very well might.

He watched as she gathered her reins and moved Pearl forward by the slight pressure of her heels to the horse's sides. They walked sedately at first. Annette struggled to remember all that Jeff had taught her: don't slouch, relax your back but sit straight, hold reins gently, heels down and balance your weight in the stirrups, toes in, be aware of your horse.

By the time Jeff left the barn with his own saddled steed behind him, she was feeling almost ecstatic. Everything had gone according to plan so far. She'd even tried trotting and put her weight in her stirrups, rising up and down in rhythm like Jeff had directed her. She spoke to Pearl as they went round the pen. The horse's ears flicked back and forth as though she were listening to every word. The steady, rocking rhythm of Pearl's gait, the warmth of the sun beating on her back, and the connection she felt to the beautiful animal was surprisingly enjoyable.

"*Tu es une jolie fille,*" she said, leaning down to rub a hand along Pearl's smooth neck. It was an exhilarating feeling to be atop such a gorgeous animal. How lucky she felt.

Jeff leaned his arms on the top rail and watched her. When she got close to him he called, "How is it going? Feel like taking her out for a little spin in the field?"

"*Oui, merci,*" she responded, concentrating so hard on riding procedures that she forgot to speak in English.

"Great" he said with a grin. "You're looking good up there. I must be an excellent teacher." He polished his fingernails on his chest with a laugh. "I'll go get Champ."

Annette made a few more circles in the round pen while waiting for him. She giggled, feeling a freedom and joy she'd never felt before. She was riding a beautiful horse in the gorgeous Canadian Rockies with the most handsome man she'd ever known. Could it get any better?

When he returned with his big chestnut gelding, something triggered her memory. "You named your 'orse after the one your father rode didn't you?" she asked curiously. "It could not be the same horse.

He smiled, but his eyes looked sad. "Yes." He stroked the animal's neck with obvious affection. "When he was born, he reminded me so much of Dad's old horse that I couldn't help myself."

She looked at Jeff, emotion flooding her heart. He was a complex man. Who would have thought he was so sentimental? He opened the gate and stepped back as she and Pearl joined him.

Jeff closed the gate behind her. This would be her first true riding test. She took a deep breath and willed herself to be calm. Jeff mounted his large chestnut gelding, and led the way along a narrow corridor beside the barn. He dismounted to open one last gate as they passed a series of pens, several sheds, and a small outbuilding.

He swung himself effortlessly into the saddle, not even bothering with the stirrups. She was impressed.

"Okay," he said, his voice changing to instructor mode. "I want you to keep a close rein on her. Not tight," He added hurriedly, as she pulled back in alarm. "I just mean you need to be aware of your horse and unexpected situations that may arise, so you can correct her."

"Situations?"

"A sudden movement, an unfamiliar noise, that sort of thing. Horses will shy away when startled and you could be unseated." He looked at her with narrowed eyes, evaluating her comfort level. "We aren't going to progress past a walk. Not today. And we'll stay in this pasture. Try to enjoy yourself—relax and get to know Pearl before we try anything further."

They walked a few paces and Annette asked, "What do you mean by 'correct 'er?' I 'ave so many things to think about already, I don't think I can 'andle anything else."

He laughed. "Maybe I'm trying to tell you too much at once. Just relax. I'm here with you and nothing bad will happen."

"No, that's not 'ow this works," she said tensely. "I need to know what to do, because you won't always be with me."

His expression sobered. "True. Okay, you remember how to let Pearl know you want to stop, right?"

She nodded.

"That's all I mean by correcting. If a horse gets spooked or frightened, their first instinct is to run. You have to be ready, and prevent that from happening by stopping them using what I told you about how you sit, your legs, the words you use, and pressure on the bit in the horse's mouth."

This was valuable information indeed and Annette soaked it up. Now she could try to relax.

The bit jangled as Pearl tossed her head and snorted, protesting at the swarms of pesky flies that buzzed around her in lazy circles. In the distance, the jagged peaks of the Rockies stood tall and proud like silent sentinels guarding the humans and wildlife below.

Everything but the brilliant blue sky was a vibrant shade of green; from the tall grass swishing with each steady step of the horse's hooves to the trembling leaves of the nearby aspens that shimmered in the warm breeze.

Annette couldn't help but revel in the beauty of her surroundings, feeling small yet somehow connected to this picturesque scene. Pearl's horsey smell only added to the perfection of the afternoon. The sun warmed her shoulders, and she lifted her face to it, smiling. *What a wonderful day!*

If she lived here, she'd wear a cowboy. The image of herself dressed head to toe in denim with an enormous hat pulled down to her ears, made her smile. Could she ever look like that? The girl to whom fashion was like a religion. Perhaps—if the conditions were right. Inadvertently, she looked across at Jeff. He caught her eye and held it, swinging his horse in closer.

"Did you have a nice visit at the Triple T?" he asked as his leg brushed hers and she flinched, but he didn't notice.

Champ walked faster than Pearl and they stepped into the lead immediately.

"Yes," she called, raising her voice. "Sophie gave us a little tour and then we watched Rosa take a horse through the barrels. It was interesting."

"I'm glad. Rosa wins a lot of competitions on the rodeo circuit each year. She's gone most weekends. If you're here long enough maybe you could go see one."

"That would be fun."

They fell into an awkward silence. His horse walked so fast that every five minutes Jeff would stop and wait for Annette and Pearl to catch up.

The second time this happened, Jeff was using the cuff of his jacket to polish the saddle as she pulled up beside him. Casually he asked, "So, are you waiting for a call from your boyfriend?"

Annette was so taken aback that her mouth fell open. She shook her head. "Waiting for—what did you just ask me?" She stopped Pearl and swivelled in the saddle to look at the man.

"Your boyfriend," he repeated slowly, turning his attention to his horse, who also halted. A tiny piece of dead grass was tangled in Champ's mane and painstakingly Jeff worked to get it free. "Gabrielle said you were waiting on a call and that's why she made sure your cell phone worked. I was just wondering if that was why." He tossed the grass to the ground as though it had been a manoeuvre vital to his horse's well-being.

"No. I don't have a boyfriend," she said at length. Why was he asking her such a thing? She was flustered now and began to babble. "I think I told you I applied for work at several art galleries before I left Paris and if one of them should try to reach me, I want to be available."

"Ah, of course. That makes sense." They set off in a companionable silence.

The horses rounded the far end of the pasture and Jeff, in the lead again, stopped to wait before turning Champ toward home. Everything had gone well, and Annette was as relaxed as Pearl. Looking toward the distant mountains, she saw a herd of Jeff's white cattle lying contentedly on a hillside. It was a peaceful scene, the white animals a stark contrast against the green. Champ swished his tail at flies. Annette thought that the picture Jeff made on his horse, hat low over his eyes against the sun and gazing out across his land, deserved to be captured on canvas. She etched the image in her mind, thinking that later she would paint it. Perhaps that was something she could do to repay all of his kindness. The thought made her both happy and sad.

As she approached he swivelled and grinned at her, before moving off toward home. The brush was thicker on this side of the field with a stand of trees ahead and Jeff indicated that they should keep away from the bushes and stay more to the center.

"Keep a good grip on Pearl, since she'll be anxious to get home," he called over his shoulder.

Without warning, a flock of frenzied prairie chickens erupted from the tall grass, their wings flapping wildly as they scattered directly in front of her.

Pearl snorted and went up on her hind legs. She lunged to the left, narrowly avoiding the chaotic birds, and charged into the underbrush in a blind panic. Annette lurched sideways, screaming. She dropped the reins in a wild attempt to grasp the saddle horn. Frantically she hauled herself upright and clung to the saddle for dear life as Pearl hurtled herself under the low-hanging limbs of the poplars. The animal was terrified.

Branches smacked Annette in the face and chest as Pearl plunged through the undergrowth. Twigs scratched her, branches and twigs snapped, and then one supple branch drove into her long curls, lodging itself, tight.

Annette screamed. She let go of the horn and grabbed for her hair, the momentum of the horse's plunging stride laying her flat back against Pearl's rump. With a loud crack, the branch broke. But thankfully the horse had come to a stop.

Annette groaned in pain and her heart pounded with fear. She could hear Jeff's calm voice speaking to the animal, reassuring both her and the horse. Pearl shifted her hindquarters side to side and Annette moved with her, almost slipping off, the movements wrenching at her snarled hair. Slowly she pulled herself upright to see that Jeff was off Champ and holding Pearl's bridle. The horse's breath was laboured, her body heaved and quivered, but she didn't move.

A moment later, Jeff was at her side, his fingers working gently to free her. Twigs snapped, and branches broke as he struggled to release her hair. Clearly he was trying to cause her as little further pain as possible.

"Hang on, my sweet," he soothed. "You'll be free in a moment. Don't move. Be patient. It's almost there."

How kind he was to the horse, Annette thought. Tears stung her eyes, from the pain and a sudden, irrational longing to hear those same words spoken to her.

Jeff eased the last branch free and put a strong hand beneath her back to help her sit up. She felt her head. Her scalp hurt as though hair had been ripped out by the roots. She moaned again.

"Th-thank you, J-Jeff," she sniffled. "Could you please

'elp me down from 'ere? I—I need to stand on the earth for a moment."

Without a word, Jeff placed his hands on her waist and lifted her away from the saddle. Setting Annette on the ground beside him, he pulled her close and held her shaking body against him. One hand softly stroked her back. She laid her face against his torso and leaned on him. Her arms crept around his waist, and she let out a shuddering sob.

"I—I was s-so scared."

"I know you were," Jeff's deep voice reverberated in her ear. "You're safe now." And tenderly, his hands glided up to cradle her face. He tipped her head away and searched her eyes, his own dark and unfathomable. His thumb followed the delicate curve of her cheek, then slowly dropped to boldly trace the fullness of her lips. He bent to touch his mouth to hers.

His lips were soft and sweet as they moved against her own. She sighed with pleasure. In a moment though, a fire ignited and the kiss was deepened. They moved closer, clinging to one another, until Pearl stepped sideways, crushing Jeff's toes.

"Ouch!" he yelped, breaking away and giving the horse a shove. His breathing ragged. Annette lifted a hand to her heart, willing it to stop its frantic racing. She stepped away and turned from Jeff to run a hand down Pearl's neck.

Later, she wondered if it had been merely the shock and adrenaline of the accident that had fueled this intense connection. Though in that moment she hadn't cared. It was a perfect storm of passion bringing an antidote like honey to the chaos that surrounded her.

Taking a deep, restorative breath, she reached for the reins that Jeff had looped around a branch. "Thank you for saving me…again," she croaked. Clearing her throat she continued, "I'm sorry I wasn't prepared like you said I should be." She shot him a watery grin. "It was one of those famous 'situations' you spoke of earlier."

Jeff's arm snaked out and caught her wrist as she unwound the reins. "Are you okay? How's your head?" Without waiting for an answer he said, "You don't have to ride again if you're hurt. We could lead the horses back to the buildings, no problem. I'm so sorry that happened." He ran a hand through his dark hair. Somewhere along the way he'd lost his hat.

"No." Annette couldn't look at him. She had this wild urge to run back into his arms. Turning her gaze to Pearl, she focused on the purpose of this lesson. She had to accustom herself to riding, so that she could go out tonight. It was not supposed to end in disaster, or an illicit *tête-à-tête* among the bushes. Jeff had no business kissing her. He was dating someone else, and she was leaving for Paris in a few days where her fabulous life and career awaited her. At this moment it didn't feel so great, but she knew it would be.

"No," she repeated. "It's important that I get back on the horse and face my fears after a fall. Didn't you tell me that was a popular saying in this country? And besides, I didn't fall, I was swept off the horse." She'd meant that last remark to be humorous, but all it did was serve to remind her of Jeff's powerful hands around her waist.

She led Pearl out of the trees and stopped, listening as Jeff pushed his way clear of the underbrush to come stand nearby.

"If you're positive," he said, "I'll make sure you're safely on and then I'll follow from behind the rest of the way back to the barn."

Annette waved away his offer to help her mount. Having Jeff touch her again was the last thing she needed right now. After a couple of tries, she made it onto Pearl. She took her time to adjust her feet in the stirrups and steeled her confidence. Thankfully, Pearl was well-trained and stood still for these operations as opposed to Champ who danced around them—throwing his head up and down, and prancing sideways, eager to get started for home.

"You would think we'd been gone for weeks, the way this guy acts," Jeff laughed, but his voice sounded strained and not at all like his usual self.

They rode in silence back to the barn. Jeff opened the gates, and she filed through, leading the way back to Pearl's stall. When she arrived, she slid off and patted Pearl.

"You're a good girl," she murmured into the horse's ear. "It's not your fault those silly birds flew out in front of you."

"Are you and Gabrielle interested in riding tomorrow morning?" Jeff asked, stopping in the alleyway behind them. "If so, why don't you both leave Pearl and Panda in the barn overnight? It'll make things easier."

"*Quelle bonne idée.*" Annette couldn't believe her ears. With a shake of her head, she amended. "I should say, what a good idea. Thank you, Jeff. For everything. You've been more than kind."

"I'm happy to do it," he shrugged. "But are you really alright? You have a nasty scrape on your cheek and I'm sorry to say your hair looks like a nest." He reached out as though to soothe the scratch, but thought better of it and hastily withdrew his hand. "I'll see to Pearl. You go inside and take care of yourself."

Annette shook her head emphatically. "No. This is all part of learning. I'll do it."

With a shrug, Jeff looked at her in admiration. "Okay. Just take her tack off and brush her like I showed you. I'll be back." He led his horse down the alley then called over his shoulder, "Don't forget to tell Gabrielle to keep Panda in, too."

"I won't forget. *Merci.*"

Jeff disappeared and Annette sagged against the wall of the box stall. What began as the perfect afternoon had turned into…what? She didn't even know what that had been. Lifting tentative fingers to her face, she felt dried blood and knew she must look like a wild woman. Of their own volition, her fingers slid to her lips, still sensitive from Jeff's mouth and the roughness of his beard. What happened out there? Yet, there were no answers that she could understand. Pushing herself away from the wall, she sighed heavily.

She would take care of Pearl and then herself, so that she'd be ready for whatever the rest of the night threw at her. The hard part was yet to come.

Chapter Sixteen

Annette's pillow buzzed. She opened her eyes just a crack and peered around the room. It was dark. She punched the mound beneath her head, trying to make the vibration stop. Her eyes closed as she prepared to ignore the annoying phenomenon. Then, the merest hint of a tune began to play, and she reared up in bed. It was her alarm. She flipped it off and the small bedside lamp on.

Soundlessly, she dressed.

Last evening, around seven, she'd pleaded a headache and retired to her bedroom. She'd laid her clothes on a chair and forced herself to sleep early. Gabrielle had done pretty much the same thing. Now, she hurried to the bathroom to braid her hair as Gabrielle always did. She couldn't afford to get it caught in a branch again. Her scalp still ached. They needed to move quietly into a surveillance position without any major catastrophe. Plus, it had been extremely painful to leave a handful of hair behind on that tree. The whole incident caused her to doubt her ability to ride a horse that distance, but it hadn't weakened her resolve.

Splashing cool water on her face, she patted it dry, surveying herself in the mirror. She'd been a fearsome sight after returning from the ride yesterday. It was fortunate no one but Jeff had seen her. Somehow, she'd managed to sneak into her room and tidy up first, but there was no way to disguise the long scratch across her cheek. Gabrielle was shocked when she saw it.

Hurrying back to the bed, she picked up her phone and sent a text to her sister. *Are you up? It's 1:20 am and I'm ready to go.*

Gabrielle replied immediately. *I'm ready and waiting. This is idiotic.*

Now that the time to leave was upon them, Annette almost agreed. The plan did seem crazy, but stuff like this always worked in the movies. Why not for them? She was convinced that Danbury was guilty. They would collect evidence of some wrongdoing tonight; she was sure of it.

Stealthily, she crept outside her door and closed it softly behind her just as Gabrielle appeared from hers. Together they tiptoed down the stairs and made their way to the back door using the lights from their phones. They pulled on jackets and boots, unbolted the latch, and slipped outside.

Neither of them said a word until they were safely inside the barn.

Gabrielle slid the door shut and leaned against it with a grunt of displeasure. "It's one thing to talk about doing this in the cold light of day, and quite another to execute it in the middle of the dark night. I'm cold, I'm sleepy, and I want to go back to bed," she complained bitterly.

"It will all be worth it when we catch them," Annette said with a confidence she didn't quite feel.

It took a while to saddle the horses, since Gabrielle had to double check that Annette had done everything correctly. Though before long they were mounted, heading past the house and down the winding driveway enveloped by the inky darkness of the night.

Above, the sky was cloudless, and the breeze had stilled. Countless stars glittered in the vast emptiness of space and a full, luminescent moon hung high overhead with its pale light bathing the earth in an ethereal glow. Annette gazed up. She'd never seen the sky like this. It was amazing.

"It's called a Strawberry Moon," Gabrielle called softly, her voice barely audible over the rhythmic clopping of the horses' hooves. "Sophie was telling me about it today. It's named for the North American tradition of harvesting strawberries in June. Pretty isn't it?"

An owl hooted in the distance, its haunting call echoing in the night and Annette jumped. However, it was nothing compared to the eerie howling of coyotes that suddenly splintered the air. Their mournful cries sent chills down her spine.

"The moon is gorgeous," Annette murmured. "But the howling is freaking me out."

"I've been on a couple of midnight rides with Andrew," Gabrielle said. "It's nothing to worry about." She exhaled noisily. "Still, I wish he was with us now."

"Have you told him?"

"If you're talking about the Triple T and his mother, no. I will though, if Sophie doesn't. He and Jayke need to know what's going on."

"I wonder how long it will take her letter to reach Jayke," Annette pondered. She heard, rather than saw Gabrielle shrug. It was a question no one could answer.

The saddle creaked with the swaying movements of the

horse, and she reached down to stroke a hand along Pearl's neck. She really loved this horse. It would be sad to leave her behind when it was time to go home. She'd barely even noticed horses before this trip, but now found herself wondering if there were any places she could go riding near Paris. It would be a poor facsimile for this place, though, since it was magical.

They reached the main road and turned to the left. Annette looked at her phone; almost two o'clock in the morning Perhaps they shouldn't be riding down the middle of the road like this. What if the Danbury men went roaring past on their way to pull the next stunt? She didn't want to be seen. In fact, what if they spun past her and Gabrielle, disappearing into the night. How could they follow on horseback when she couldn't get past a slow amble without falling off? Maybe this was even less of a good idea than she'd previously thought.

"I'm sorry," she said. "I shouldn't have dragged you out here like this. It is kind of crazy."

"No," said her sister, "it's not kind of crazy. It's absolutely, positively ludicrous." She giggled. "It is an adventure, though, and a fantastic night for a ride. I'm actually enjoying myself, so don't feel bad."

Annette smiled to herself. Trust Gabby to find the positives. Feeling better, she looked ahead and caught the gleam of the wooden Danbury sign.

"There it is," she hissed. Standing up in her stirrups she could see the yard light not far from the road. She reined Pearl to the right.

"Wait!" There was an urgency in Gabrielle's voice. "I thought we just decided this was a bad idea. It's been a lovely ride, but I think we should turn back. I don't want to go in there."

"We're so close," Annette wheedled. "Please, let's check things out. Just because this wasn't the best plan, doesn't mean they aren't guilty. Maybe we'll see them leave or learn something incriminating that will bring them to justice. Besides," she gestured to a field on the far side of the driveway, "there's no fence over here. We could ride up to the house undetected."

With an exaggerated groan, Gabrielle turned in behind Annette. They rode down the ditch and up the other side into the pasture, heading toward the dreaded Danbury ranch.

Apart from two lone lights that stood atop poles, one near the house and the other perched on a low building off to the right, the house stood completely dark. It didn't appear as though anyone was awake and planning a rendezvous with danger.

Annette urged Pearl to come alongside Gabrielle and Panda. "See that knoll to the left? If we can lead the horses into the trees up there and maybe wait an hour to see what happens, I think we'll have results. We came this far, so let's spend just a little time watching."

"*Ugh!*" Gabrielle replied in exasperation. "I'll give it thirty minutes and then I'm going back."

They turned to the side and made their way up a small embankment toward a bluff of trees. It was actually a perfect vantage point to watch the farm undetected and Annette was pleased. Before they reached the bushes, however, she stopped and slid to the ground.

It was much easier to lead Pearl on a winding path through dense brush than it was to ride her. Soon they stopped in a spot overlooking the house. She tied the horse to a tree and sank to the ground, head in hands to watch. After a moment, Gabrielle joined her.

"I'm timing this," her sister whispered testily, dropping down beside her.

Fifteen minutes passed. The ground was littered with rocks, twigs and other debris causing them to shuffle to find a more comfortable position. The horses moved restlessly. Annette began to feel cold and damp. She was just about to suggest they leave, when a set of headlights swung onto the driveway from the road and proceeded up to the house at breakneck speed.

It slammed to a halt with a shower of gravel. After cutting the engine, someone got out and slammed the door. Suddenly, a light went on inside the house. The front door was thrown open and an enormous figure loomed in the doorway. Two men exchanged angry, unintelligible words, but they were too far away to make out.

"I'm going down to see if I can hear what they're saying," Annette whispered.

"Have you lost your mind?" Gabrielle grabbed her arm and shook it. "You'll get caught."

"Listen, if you can lead both horses out of these trees and wait for me below, we can make a fast getaway if necessary."

"I can't believe I let you talk me into this. A fast getaway...*argh!*" Gabrielle groaned. "Be careful." Turning, she untied the horses and disappeared into the night.

Annette moved cautiously down the rise, staying under cover in the bushes. Fortunately, the men were shouting too loud to hear her approach. She recognized the arrogant voice of Jim Danbury and could only assume the other man was his son, Dillon.

She slipped once and sat down hard on a thistle which jabbed her bottom and legs mercilessly, but she didn't make a sound. Her objective was to reach the arguing men and listen for incriminating evidence. As quietly as she could, she pushed herself up and continued to creep closer. Finally, after what felt like an eternity, she reached the last few shrubs available to hide under and found she could hear the men quite easily. Mainly because as they talked their voices rose higher and higher.

"You've been there all evening?" Jim shouted, pacing back and forth on the porch. "Why did you insist on leaving without telling me what you're doing?"

"Because I'm not a kid anymore, Dad. And I have a mind of my own, that's why. And if it took me the whole night, what business is it of yours?"

"If I'm paying for it, then it damn well is my business."

Annette felt like screaming. *What business did you pay for?*

"Look," Dillon said in a calmer tone, "I got the job done didn't I? Isn't that what matters? Who cares how long it took, or what time I'm home."

"Okay. Do you think it'll work?" barked Jim. "I've put a lot of effort into this."

Dillon crunched through the gravel to take the steps of the porch two at a time. He was heavyset, but not so massive as his father and appeared agitated with his father's imperious words. "*We've* put a lot of effort into it," he corrected. "This is my future too and I…"

At that very moment, Annette's phone rang. She froze in horror. Louder and louder it grew as the dulcet tones of Gene Autry singing, "Home, Home on the Range" burst into strident voice. She'd added the ringtone as a joke before leaving Paris. Only now it filled the still night air with orchestra music and Gene's crooning wish to return to where the buffalo roamed.

Both men came to a screeching halt and whirled to face Annette where she crouched in the shrubbery.

Dillon leaped from the porch to the ground hollering, "What the hell is that?"

"Someone's in the bushes," Jim bellowed. "Don't just stand there, Dillon. Go get them!"

The younger man charged straight for Annette.

Her body came to life. The deer and the antelope were just warming up on Gene's lips when she switched her phone off, scrambled to her feet, and ran for her life back up the hill. Sheer adrenaline gave her feet wings. Dillon crashed through the trees after her, cursing and swearing. She ran, heedless of branches that tore at her clothes, poked her face, and ripped her hair for the second time in the past twenty-four hours. Her breathing came in huge, wrenching gasps, and her legs felt like jelly, but fear drove her to a much greater speed than the cumbersome Dillon who followed just behind ordering her to stop.

Of course, he had no idea who he was following, or that she was a girl, evident by his word choices. Luckily for her, it took a lot of his energy to yell such curses and make so many demands while running. He was slow and it gave her an edge.

She crested the hill and flung herself down the other side, only able to hazard a guess at where Gabrielle might be since the moon had gone behind a cloud. She paused for a moment, grasping a tree for support, her chest heaving, breath dragged out of her body with every gasp. She listened. Ahead of her down the hill she heard a low whistle. It was Gabby. Thank goodness, she knew where they were.

But Dillon wasn't far behind. Annette summoned every bit of her remaining energy and raced down the hill. The cloud moved past, and Pearl's gleaming coat came into view. She flung herself at the horse, loving her more in this moment than ever before. Gabrielle had knotted the reins over Pearl's neck and Annette took them, knowing she would have to guide her horse and ride as she had never done before if they were to escape. She rammed her foot in the stirrup, made a wild grab for the saddle horn and hauled herself up. Then she gave Pearl a jab with her heels, and they were off.

Fortunately, Gabrielle had gotten them out of the bluff and into a clear space where the horses could gallop. And gallop they did. Jeff's steady voice spoke in her ear and his smiling face floated in her memory, telling her to grip with her knees and to find the rhythm of the animal. It helped only a little. Mostly she just clung on for all she was worth as both horses thundered across the meadow and back toward the road.

Annette knew it was only a matter of time before Dillon got back down the hill and came after them in his car. What to do?

Gabrielle solved it for them. As they raced off the Danbury property, down the ditch and up the other side, she crossed the road at a dead gallop, pulling her horse up short at Jeff's gate on the opposite side.

"Take my reins," she shouted, threw them to Annette, and hurled herself at the gate. In a moment it was down, and Annette was urging both horses through. In no time, Gabrielle fastened the gate again, leaped onto Panda, and they were off once more, headed for a small stand of trees not far away.

Annette knew what was coming and braced herself.

"Get as low as you can over Pearl's neck and hang on," Gabrielle called, as she herself did the same thing with Panda. And then they smashed into the first saplings and the horses stumbled through the low scrub brush. The density of the bluff pulled them up short and the animals waded through, pushing into the interior of the thick growing poplars just as headlights flashed toward them. The engine screamed as the vehicle slid from side to side along the gravelled road. Even from here Annette could hear the tires spinning as the car rushed down the road in search of the intruders.

As it hit the main road, the driver braked sharply sending the car sideways, and swung it wide into the road, so that the sweep of headlights lit up a large area. Clearly knowing the trespassers couldn't have just vanished into thin air, Dillon stopped the car and got out to inspect first the ditch, and then the road in the powerful beams of light. The heavier man clambered out of the passenger side. They were looking for tracks, Annette thought with a sinking heart. *Oh no!* She and Gabrielle would be found. Back and forth the ponderous figures of both men paced, heads down, eyes searching the gravel for telltale signs.

They followed the fresh trail of hoof prints across the road and up to Jeff's property line. Dillon shook the gate viciously. Annette held her breath. Any minute now they would open it and drive in to capture them. She and Gabrielle would be dragged off to the police and thrown in jail for trespassing. But nothing happened. Eventually, with more hollering, the men climbed back into the car, turned it around, and slowly drove back down their drive.

Neither woman said anything for a long time. They remained in the bushes, the horses puffing, their sides heaving as everyone strove to calm down.

"I can't believe that just happened." Gabrielle finally chanced a whisper. "Did you at least hear anything worthwhile?"

Annette nodded, then, realizing her sister couldn't see a nod, she answered in a croaky voice. "I believe I did, yes.

Nothing conclusive though. I have no idea what Dillon was doing tonight, but I'm sure he was at Sophie's. There were no clues as to what part of the ranch he attacked. Then my phone rang, and I was chased by the son. Oh Gabby, I was so scared." She took a shaky breath. "But they're guilty alright. I heard them talking about it."

"I believe you. Too bad you didn't hear anything definite. We need evidence before we can talk to the authorities. But we can't lurk in the shadows all night. We'd better go."

On the ride back to the ranch, Annette considered what she'd heard. Dillon's words, "I got the job done didn't I?" echoed in her brain. What had he done? To what and where? She didn't know any more than what they did when the night had started. If only her stupid phone hadn't rung.

Fishing it out of her pocket, she flicked it to life and stared at the fluorescent blue screen as the missed call popped into view. Her arm went limp, and she almost dropped it into the dirt.

She'd been called by the Musée d'Orsay, her favourite art gallery in Paris where more than twenty-four of Vincent Van Gogh's paintings were displayed. It could only mean one thing.

Chapter Seventeen

Annette was trapped. The Danburys had cornered her at the center of Pearl's stall and were marching around her, their faces twisted in sneers, and her ears filled with unearthly laughter. In their hands they held enormous, black cell phones on which they endlessly tapped out the telephone number for Air Canada, the airline that had brought her and Gabrielle here.

"Go home where you belong, Frenchie. Go home where you belong," they chanted over and over. She twisted and turned, trying in vain to evade them; to block out the incessant tapping, to run and hide, but it was to no avail.

The tapping grew louder and louder. Finally, summoning all her nerve, she yelled, "No!"

Then she snapped awake and sat up in bed.

"Annette?" Gabrielle's insistent voice drifted through the closed door. "Can I come in?" She hammered on it as though she were using her fist. "The door is locked, and I need to talk to you," she hissed.

Annette flew out of bed and rushed to let her sister in.

"Old man Danbury is here," Gabrielle said through clenched teeth. "I saw him pull up to the big shop where Jeff keeps his farming equipment."

"What!"

"Yes. I escaped up here." Gabrielle hurried to the windows, flicked back the curtains, and peered apprehensively outside. Sunlight blazed into the room. Turning away, she sank down on the bed.

"Do you suppose he suspects it was us and came to question Jeff?" Annette felt familiar fingers of fear creep up her spine. How could she possibly explain her actions to Jeff?

"Maybe," Gabrielle shrugged. "But honestly, why would Jeff's French guests go for a secret midnight ride and spy on the neighbours from the bushes?"

"Why indeed?" Annette said dryly.

"I think it's more likely he was informing Jeff that there are dodgy people in the area, trespassing on both properties."

Annette sighed for the lost opportunity that was last night. "I suppose you're right," she admitted.

"Anyway, do you realize it's ten o'clock in the morning? Everyone's been asking where you are."

Annette looked at her suspiciously. "Who is everyone?"

Gabrielle shrugged and picked invisible lint off the comforter. "Me mostly," she grinned, peeping up at her sister through thick eyelashes. "I think Sandra did mention it once, though. The others were gone shortly after seven."

"Why didn't you sleep in? The sun was already coming up by the time we got to our rooms."

"I slept for a while. Did the art gallery call you back?"

"No," Annette had checked for a message before going to sleep last night, but there had been nothing. It was one of the places she'd left her resume. Though she just couldn't imagine they'd actually want her to work for them. They must have called for some other reason.

"I have news," Gabrielle said, her eyes sparkling. "I wanted to see Sophie before she left, so I set an alarm. And guess what?" Without waiting for a response, Gabrielle answered her own question. "We're moving to the Triple T this afternoon. Isn't that great?"

"Yes. Uh, great," Annette plastered a smile on her face for her sister's sake, but had mixed feelings about leaving. She'd miss this bedroom, this ranch, Pearl, and…Sandra's cooking. She wouldn't allow herself to consider anything else she might miss about this place.

Gabrielle hopped off the bed and gave Annette a quick hug before holding her at arm's length and looking seriously at her. "You tried your best last night," she said. "And on behalf of Sophie and Andrew, I thank you. But I really believe, once we get to the ranch, it will all be okay."

Annette merely smiled and kissed her sister three times before shooing her out the door, so she could get dressed. She didn't share Gabrielle's optimism, and didn't think that the misfortunes of the Triple T would cease. However, nothing could be done at the moment.

She looked at the pile of discarded clothes by her bed. There was a hole in the sleeve of her coat and if she wasn't mistaken a twig was poking up from the knee of yesterday's jeans. She quickly dressed in the wide-leg jeans that Sandra had washed, and dug through her suitcase until she found her most casual top—a pale pink, cropped hoodie.

She made the bed and packed her things, then leaned over the sink to study her reflection before brushing her teeth. Her beautiful hair had really been mangled yesterday. She turned sideways to inspect it at all angles. Oh well, nothing could be done now. She combed the snarls out and tied it back with a matching pink satin scrunchy.

Carefully she performed her morning rituals, being gentle with the angry red scratch across her cheek. She added a little shimmery silver eyeshadow and some mascara, then gathered her case and her coat, and went downstairs without looking back. She'd miss the Douglas Ranch.

After promising to come back soon to visit Sandra, the women went outside with their luggage to look for Jeff. Jim Danbury was gone, which Annette was grateful for. They found Jeff sprawled underneath a tractor with various tools strewn around him. He crawled out and grabbed his hat from off the ground where he'd thrown it, hitting it on his hip to clean off the dust and debris. Annette stared shamelessly at his wavy black hair, and the way it fell around his face as he leaned forward. She had a sudden urge to push it back in place for him. She admired the way his dark maroon t-shirt clung to his muscled chest and how his smile made her heart sing.

He shoved his black hat down on his head. "Ready to go, are you?" he asked, picking up a rag from off the tractor tire and wiping his hands. He tossed it to one side and fixed them both with a searching look. "I have some good news and some bad news. Which do you want first?"

"The good," Gabrielle said.

"Okay," he smiled. "I talked to Sophie about it and Annette, I'd like to lend you Pearl while you're there. We can take her over in the trailer right now and you can keep her in Sophie's barn to use every day. Would you like that?"

Annette clapped her hands with joy. "*Vraiment? C'est merveilleux!*" she said, forgetting English in her enthusiasm. "*Merci beaucoup.*"

"I'll take that response as a resounding yes," he said and laughed. "Now for the bad news."

Both Annette and Gabrielle sobered. Had something more happened at the Triple T?

Jeff took his hat back off and scratched his head. "Jim Danbury was just here with a remarkable tale," he said, looking at them closely. "He said at least two people were spying on him in the middle of the night from the hillside beside his house. He said he wouldn't have even known they were there except that one of them received a phone call at approximately three o'clock in the morning. And when this phone rang, it played an old cowboy song from the late 1940s, which, I'm sure you'll both agree, is quite unusual. Anyway, after that the spies took off running. Both Danburys gave chase, but the intruders were on horseback and got away."

Jeff turned his attention to his fingernails, as though their cleanliness was a matter of great importance. "Funny thing is,' he continued nonchalantly, "these intruders, as he called them, opened the gate to my property and disappeared inside. He thought I should be aware of it, so I could keep a watch on my own yard. People like that can't be up to any good—can they?"

Both women ardently shook their heads.

"Maybe they were innocent people out for a moonlit ride who lost their way," suggested Gabrielle, a little too quickly. Her face flushed.

"I wondered that myself, although there isn't another ranch for several kilometres." Jeff smiled benevolently at them, and Annette felt like an errant child being reprimanded by an all-knowing teacher. "So, no. That doesn't make a lot of sense, now does it?" He chuckled as though finding this a great joke. "The other peculiar thing I noticed, long before Danbury's visit, was that Pearl was in a completely different stall this morning than when we'd left her yesterday afternoon. And I know you both went to bed early, so it couldn't have been you. Quite an unusual phenomenon, wouldn't you say? I wonder how she managed it."

"The 'orse is an intelligent animal," Annette said evenly. "I will be sure to take very good care that Pearl stays in one place while she is at Sophie's ranch."

With old-world charm, Jeff tipped his hat to her. "I'd appreciate that," he said. "Now let's get her loaded and take you over there."

Long after Jeff had left them at Sophie's place, Annette stayed with Pearl. She brushed her dappled coat while sitting on a small stool in the large box stall as the horse munched on a sheaf of fragrant green hay.

Annette wasn't against being here. After all, this was where they'd been coming in the first place, and she liked Sophie. She couldn't put her finger on it, but she felt uneasy. Jeff's beautiful log house had become home over the last few days and now she felt displaced. She was happy for her sister, however. Gabrielle had gone inside immediately to spend time with her mother-in-law.

Annette yawned. Thankfully, nothing had been found amiss on the ranch so far today. Whatever Dillon had done the night before still remained a mystery.

She took a few photos of Pearl and then flipped through the other pictures she'd taken so far. When she was back home in Paris, a few of them would make great drawings, maybe even paintings. She lingered over one she had taken of Jeff on the first rainy day when she'd seen him leading Pearl into the barn. The lush green of the grass, the mountains in the distance, and the misty rain all lent a magical charm to the man in the cowboy hat who cared for his sister's old horse.

Her throat constricted. Who was this woman she'd become in just a few short days? From avidly following Paris Fashion Week and trying to emulate each new look of the season. Always dressing elegantly for dinner at the finest restaurants and perusing the pages of glossy magazines for the latest chic trends, to crouching in a dilapidated barn, wearing a filthy jacket with holes in the sleeve as she spent the best part of her day talking to a horse. What an extreme contrast.

Come to think of it, she felt happier in this environment —lighter somehow. Annette crossed her arms over her stomach and leaned against the wall, shutting her eyes, and enjoying the tranquility of the moment. It was late in the afternoon and soon she would go inside. Until then, life was peaceful.

The bang of a screen door jerked her upright. She knew it would be Gabrielle, looking for her, so she roused herself, gave Pearl a final pat, and left the barn.

As she suspected, her sister stood on the porch. "I want to show you your room, so you can get settled in," she said, waving impatiently. "And Sophie would like to spend a little time with you too."

The house was old and the steps uneven, yet it retained a charm that newer buildings would never have. It was painted a pale yellow with white trim and boasted a quaint veranda that wrapped around one corner affording the comfy, deep cushioned chairs and love seat a prime position to take in both the morning sun and the pink and gold of the sunset. Rose bushes were profuse, and their scent saturated the air with sweetness.

It was a two story, full of angles and nooks with tall windows in unusual places. Annette was curious as to which one might be hers. Dutifully, she followed her sister inside. They entered a boot or mud room first and Annette pulled off her jacket, and kicked her scuffed boots to one side. Trailing after Gabrielle, they walked into a lovely living space decorated in a mixture of Victorian and old country elegance. At least, that's how she would describe it if asked.

It wasn't a large room, but it felt homey and lived in. Filmy white curtains were tied back to either side of the double windows. Two of the walls were a deep teal, but the high ceilings and crown moldings were painted a warm creamy white. Bookcases filled one whole wall and an ornate, and rather antique looking fireplace lay waiting with a pile of wood in a wicker basket, while a corresponding mirror hung over top. Two cozy armchairs and a deep sofa in a paler version of the teal, along with light oak end tables and a huge square coffee table, were arranged before the fireplace. A huge bouquet of roses sat on a cream-coloured sideboard, while an assortment of plants squatted on the bookcases and sprang from hanging baskets. The air was sweetly scented. Pictures of country scenes and the inevitable mountains graced the walls.

They didn't linger here, but walked straight through to where a staircase was tucked on the other side of one of the teal walls. Annette plodded behind, realizing her sister must have already carried both of their bags upstairs. After they reached the landing three closed doors waited.

"Thank you," she said with feeling as Gabrielle threw open the door to her left and ushered her inside.

"For what? Looking all flustered and guilty when Jeff

questioned us about the horse?" Gabrielle said. She gestured toward Annette's bag and purse which were already waiting for her on a blue velvet chair.

"No. For bringing my bag up, but now that you mention it, yes. I do appreciate your effort to cover up my misdeeds." Annette smiled at her sister. "Can you forgive me? I know attending the cinema and art galleries are more our thing. Still, you have to admit it was rather thrilling."

"Thrilling?" Gabrielle squeaked. "I am *not* a detective. I get enough thrills riding the metro, thank you very much." She sounded outraged, yet gave her sister a quick hug on her way out. "When you're settled, Sophie and I plan to be downstairs in the kitchen. She's making supper and Rosa is out with the horses. So, if you want a little quality visiting time before the barrel racer arrives, I'd come now. Oh, and the bathroom is on the main floor, bottom of the stairs and to your left."

The door closed behind her sister with a soft click. Annette swivelled around to examine the room. It was small yet packed with charm. The ceiling was sharply slanted on two sides meaning she could only stand up in the very center. Every wall was covered with a delicate rose wallpaper with a pale blue background, which might have looked overdone in a newer home. It was lovely.

A desk with an antique chair and lamp were situated under an old-style casement window, its frame painted white with diaphanous white curtains pulled back on either side. She stepped to it and bent over the table to peer outside. She looked toward the barn, the arena, and the jutting purple mountaintops above the roofs. *Wonderful.* Wrapping her arms around her middle she moved to sit on the bed, testing it for softness. She bounced up and down a few times and declared it just as cozy as the last one. Pushed under the eaves on one side, it was piled high with pillows and a thick blue comforter.

Annette was pleased. Taking a few more minutes, she unpacked and hung her clothes in a small, empty wardrobe that stood beside the door. Lastly, she unfolded her lavender dress and caressed it lovingly before hanging it. It was badly creased, but that could be rectified. She placed the matching shoes on the floor beneath the dress and shut the door.

The remainder of the evening went by in a blur. Sophie was a faultless host, and prepared a delicious meal of steaks, stuffed baked potatoes, and a green salad. She appeared to be in high spirits, considering all that had happened. Annette wondered how the woman did it and asked her as much.

"If I worried about the future I would drive myself crazy," Sophie said soberly. "There are never any guarantees in this life." She lifted her shoulders in an expressive shrug. "I cannot prevent what may happen next. Still, I have faith in the goodness of people. So many of my neighbours have called me or dropped in to offer their help. They are watching the property for me and so are the RCMP. At this point, it's all I can do."

Annette was impressed with the kindness of the community.

The three of them talked and laughed at the kitchen table for over an hour. Eventually, however, Sophie said she had work to finish outside, and needed to feed and water the poisoned cattle. Happily, they had improved and were now outside in a corral.

"I need to tell Marcus what time to start work in the morning," Sophie said, shrugging into a light blue jacket that had seen better days. "The new fellow should be here too—finally. I must remember to text him."

Long after the meal had been cleared away they sat in the living room talking. Even Rosa had been congenial Perhaps now that Annette was no longer a guest under Jeff's roof, she could afford to be pleasant.

Talk turned to the wine shop in Paris, Annette's plans for her future, and stories of the Dordogne where Sophie had grown up. Apparently, Sophie hadn't been back to the area for over fifteen years. Her eyes glowed when she spoke of its beauty.

However, the previous night's activities were beginning to take their toll. Around ten o'clock that evening, Annette's eyes started to droop. "If you will excuse me," she said, "I must go to bed. It 'as been a long day."

"*Bien sûr.*" Sophie glanced at a large clock on the wall. "I would like an early night myself. Rosa," she said, turning to the younger woman. "Will you go out with me to check on the animals one last time?"

Rosa yawned. "Sure," she said. Pulling on her customary denim jacket from where it had been draped over her chair, she shot Annette a tight little smirk. "It was so sweet of Jeff to lend you his sister's old horse, hey? He's always taking pity on people."

"You think he pities me?" As soon as she asked it, Annette knew she shouldn't have given Rosa an opening to say more.

"Yeah, he's always helping people he doesn't really know, like you…sometimes too much and they take advantage of him. We've talked about it, but he'll never change. I love him for it, though."

Sophie smiled benevolently at the horrid woman, as though she hadn't heard the backhanded insult, and waited to follow her out the door. "We'll see you girls in the morning," she called. "Sweet dreams."

Annette wished her sister a good night at the doors of their respective rooms. Apparently, Gabrielle had the room next to hers and Rosa occupied the third room on this level. She glared at Rosa's door. It was innocent but she felt like giving it a swift kick. Before she acted on such foolishness, she escaped into her own lovely space.

She felt the scratch on her cheek and thought of how Jeff had kissed her. Rosa was probably right. Jeff was taking pity on her. He'd felt sorry she'd been hurt and comforted her, that was all.

She undressed and kicked her clothes viciously into a heap in a corner of her room. Then, after donning her nightgown, she slid beneath the sweet-smelling sheets, forcing her mind away from such pointless thoughts. But the air in the room was stuffy and warm. She needed fresh air to sleep. Padding to the window, she studied how to open it, and with a bit of difficulty, lifted the bottom window up several centimetres. After a quick search, she used a book on horsemanship she found in the desk, to keep it propped it open. A cool night breeze wafted through, billowing the curtains. She looked for a shade or blinds, anything to prevent the early morning sun from waking her up. Only there was nothing. *Oh well.* She crawled back into bed. Sleep was instantaneous.

It was much later that something woke her. She opened one eye. The ceiling was awash with a strange light. It flickered almost like a candle. Was this the Northern Lights she'd heard so much about? That would be exciting to see. Should she investigate? It was so comfy under the blankets, and she was so tired, but maybe she should just look outside to check.

Flipping the covers back, her feet hit the cold floor. She shivered and tiptoed to the window, feeling her way by grasping for the bedposts. The light outside, whatever it was, was getting stronger. She bent over the table and leaned her elbows on the table to peer outside.

Sophie's barn was on fire.

Chapter Eighteen

Bright orange flames had engulfed the far corner of the old building and were licking greedily up the side.

"Jeff!" she screamed, flicking on the lamp so she could find her clothes. Where was her phone? Where were her jeans? She seized her phone from the bedside table. Who to call? She didn't know the emergency number for Canada. Stay calm, she told herself. Stay calm!

"Oh God, please save Sophie's barn," she begged, as she brought her phone to life and found the number Jeff had given her. She called him, clicked it to speaker, and threw the phone on the bed while she bent to drag on her pants, tucking her nightgown into the top. It was ringing.

"Answer, damn it!" she yelled, then lunged to the wall over her bed and hammered on it, knowing Gabrielle was on the other side.

"Hello? What's wrong?" Jeff's booming voice flooded the room and Annette caught a sob in her throat. Shaking, she snatched it up.

"*Appelez les pompiers!*" she shouted.

"Take a deep breath and tell me, in English, what's happening," came his steady, but now thoroughly alarmed response.

"The people to fight fire," she hollered. "Get them. Sophie's barn is on fire." She clicked the phone off, dragged on her boots and flung herself out the door.

She rushed to Gabby's door and rattled the knob. Locked. She beat on the sturdy wooden door with her fists, hollering, "Wake up! There's a fire. Get Sophie and Rosa." Gratified, she heard Gabrielle's feet hit the floor inside.

"I'm here. Yes!"

Wheeling around she slammed her fists into Rosa's door. "Get up! Fire!"

Unwilling to take any more time, she threw herself down the stairs as fast as her feet could move, trying desperately to think of what she could do to stop the flames. Was there a garden hose outside? Had she seen one in the flower bed? Despite her panic, a horrifying thought slammed into her heart like a ton of bricks.

Pearl.

She unfastened the locked front door and ran into the night, straight for the big double doors beside the blaze. In the moments she'd taken to rouse everyone, the fire had spread further. It had reached the roof top now, moving fast in the breeze that swirled down from the mountains. Fingers of scorching red flames consumed the dry wood, making it snap and crackle under the pressure.

Annette ran to the door, heedless of the danger as fire raged above her across the front of the barn. The heat was searing. Yanking her night dress out from her jeans she wrapped it around her right hand and reached for the door handle to slide it free. Even through the fabric the heated handle scorched her hand. She flinched, but didn't let go. A terrified neigh gave her the strength to haul the door wide even as flames, whipped into a frenzy by the growing wind, rained sparks down on her head.

She raced to the box stall where Pearl lunged and dove, seeking a freedom that was unattainable. Her eyes rolled wildly in her head, the whites showing, and her ears laid back. She whinnied again when she saw Annette.

"It's okay," she soothed, striving to keep her voice composed. "You're safe now girl." In a flash she'd undone the gate and grasped Pearl's halter. In terror, the horse lunged through the gate, dragging Annette with her. But she saw what lay ahead and pulled back with all her might. The door she'd just come through was consumed with flames.

Wait, there must be a back entrance. Dragging the frightened horse with her, Annette turned and ran down the long alleyway toward the rear, praying there would be an opening for them to escape. If not, they would both die in the inferno behind them, and it was gaining momentum fast.

The only light she had to see by was the terrible orange glow of the fire that fed on the dry old walls around them. With considerable effort, she tried to slow the panicked animal she held and feel her way along the corridor. Dimly, she could see the outline of a door in the glow of the raging light cast from the fire outside the barn.

She ran frantic hands down the center and with a sob of gratitude, found the latch. It was barely warm, and she was able to swing it wide open. She and Pearl fled to freedom. She released the horse, knowing they could easily find her again. The most important thing was to get her to safety. Pearl galloped away.

Annette took great gulping breaths of fresh air and looked up. Glowing embers rose high in the midnight sky, filling the air with an eerie glow. Suddenly the wailing sound of a fire engine filled her ears, and she heard voices shouting. She sagged with relief. Perhaps the barn couldn't be saved, but the rest of the buildings could.

Except she was too close to the barn and needed to consider her own safety. She broke into a jog, soon coming to a corral fence that she climbed and perched for a moment on the top rail. Looking around she noticed a shrouded figure to her left. The person moved swiftly away and melted into the shadows of a small stand of trees between the barn and the arena. Someone had been lurking there this whole time, watching and waiting.

It all became clear. The fire had been set. It was the latest in the string of terrible misfortunes designed to drive Sophie from her home. A rage filled Annette's heart and she took off after the hooded figure. There was no time to get help and she didn't stop to consider it. It was up to her, as she had felt it would be, to catch the perpetrator once and for all.

She moved stealthily. Keeping to the cover of the sheds and fences, she edged her way to the bluff. Somehow she knew that whoever it was, they wouldn't be watching for her. No, their eyes would be trained on their handiwork—the raging inferno of Sophie's barn.

Closer and closer she followed and just as she was about to enter the bluff, the shape of the person emerged from the other side. They began to make their way around to the house. If Annette didn't move quickly, her chance of catching this evildoer would be lost. She broke into a run, calling upon every ounce of power in her legs, adrenaline giving her yet again another burst of energy.

By the time the hooded figure heard her coming in all the commotion of fire engines, people, and the crackling embers of the conflagration, she was upon them. Throwing herself, arms outstretched, Annette bodily tackled the person. They both tumbled heavily to the ground. Annette was up first, and she pinned the struggling person to the ground with her weight.

"Let me go you fool!" rasped a familiar voice. With a quick flick of her wrist, Annette tore the hood from the veiled face.

"Rosa?" Annette was taken momentarily off guard. The barrel racer heaved her body sideways, dislodging Annette and sending her tumbling to the ground. Then Rosa was off, running through the assembled onlookers where she came to a stop.

Annette picked herself up and limped to where her sister stood on the driveway with an arm around Sophie. A puffing Rosa was busy explaining how she'd slept through the uproar and had only made it downstairs now. She was certainly convincing. If Annette had not just followed the young woman, the story would have been quite believable.

"*Elle ment*," Annette snapped, coming to stand in front of all three women, but speaking French for just two. "*Elle a allumé le feu. Elle a tout fait.*"

"What did she say?" Rosa screeched. "You can't believe her. I was sleeping this whole time and only just woke up."

But Sophie had turned to stare at Rosa in horror. In the flickering light of the fire destroying her livelihood, she confronted the young woman. "*Est-ce vrai?*" she asked quietly. "Is it true, Rosa? Did you set the fire?" Rosa shook her head violently, but her wide frightened eyes gave her away.

Sophie continued, shock and revulsion entering her voice. "You poisoned the water and killed an animal. You could have killed me. And you cut the fence in hopes of causing a major accident that would hurt others." Her voice rose with each new revelation, and she stepped away from the woman, distancing herself. "Why?"

But as the barn succumbed to the power of the ravenous flames behind them, collapsing in an explosion of sparks and burning embers, Rosa whirled around and fled into the night.

Chapter Nineteen

The three women stood, arm in arm on the porch, as firefighters, a few neighbours, and of course Jeff, worked to extinguish any remaining embers. Then, a wet, filthy, and very tired group of men were thanked profusely by Sophie as they prepared the firetruck to leave. The sun was rising in the eastern sky by this time, its golden rays throwing the remaining plumes of smoke into sharp relief.

Only a huge, steaming pile of wet ashes marked the spot where the barn had been. When the truck at last rolled out of the yard, Sophie, followed closely by Annette and Gabrielle, walked out to meet Jeff, whose face was barely recognizable as he turned to face them. Without saying a word, he opened his arms and Sophie sobbed as he folded her within his embrace.

He held her until her crying ceased. Then he bent to look earnestly into her face.

"It'll be okay," he said with conviction. "You'll see. We'll build it back bigger and better than it was before."

She managed a feeble smile. "I don't think so." She

blotted her tears with a sleeve. "Did you know that Annette caught the person responsible for the fire?"

Jeff stepped back to flash a look at Annette, his brows furrowing. "No."

"It was Rosa. I cannot believe it. 'Ow did you figure it out?" Sophie looked expectantly at Annette.

"When I was be'ind the barn with Pearl, I saw someone sneaking away and 'iding in the bushes to watch the barn burn. The person was wearing a black sweater with an 'ood. I didn't know who it was until I tackled them." She shrugged as though this sort of activity was commonplace for her.

"You tackled Rosa?" Gabrielle asked. Her eyebrows nearly reached her hairline.

Annette nodded.

Gabrielle grabbed Annette by the shoulders and moved so close their noses nearly touched. "You, the sister I've known since 'er birth, who wouldn't play outside for fear of getting 'er shoes scuffed or grass stains, or 'er hair out of place—you physically threw yourself at someone and knocked them to the ground?"

"I suppose so. I wouldn't 'ave put it just like that, but yes."

"I believe it," Jeff said with a hint of pride in his voice. "Where is Rosa now?"

"She ran," said Sophie dispiritedly. "And I think you'll find that her cousin Marcus was in on the scheme too. If he even is her cousin." Sophie rubbed her temples and drew a deep breath. "The police should be called. I'll go do that now. Then I think we should try to get some sleep." With slow steps, Sophie walked back into the house and mounted the stairs. The screen door slammed behind her.

A sudden jolt went through Jeff's body. He whirled away

from them and took a few faltering steps toward the blackened ruins. "Pearl?" he croaked hoarsely. "She was in there. Oh no…"

"She wasn't," Annette flew to his side and placed a hand on his arm, looking up into his frightened face. "I went outside as soon as I'd called you. I got into the barn and found a way out the back to set her loose."

"You what?" he asked incredulously. He grasped her arm, hope brightening his countenance even through the grime. "You're telling me she's alive?"

"Yes. I don't know where she is though since she bolted as soon as I got 'er out the door, but…"

Jeff didn't wait to hear more. His strong arms went around her, and she was lifted into the air to be kissed soundly. Oblivious to their surroundings, Annette kissed him back. He tasted of soot, smoke, and sweat. He was filthy and wet from the spraying water, and his hands were black from fighting the dreadful flames. Though she didn't care about such trivial things. She wanted to stay in his arms forever.

When he finally set her back on her feet, they were alone. "I'm going to look for Pearl," he said, holding out a hand. "Do you want to join me?"

The pain in her right hand, from wrestling with the hot door handle, was barely noticeable in light of this wonderful development. She held out her left one to his and he held it tight. Her heart surged with a brand-new feeling she couldn't quite believe. Was she falling in love with this man? How could that happen after less than a week of knowing him? Yet stealing a glance at his profile as they walked through the dewy grass with the first streaks of gold in the sky, she knew it to be true. She loved him.

They found Pearl wandering in a back field and led her

back to be put into a corral with food and water. She looked no worse for her terrifying experience, for which Annette was grateful. They walked in silence for the most part, holding hands the whole way. She wasn't sure what any of this meant, because Jeff appeared to be lost in his own thoughts. Though for the moment she was happy.

Still, so many questions were left unanswered. Who was Rosa and the strange kissing cousin Marcus? Why had they carried out a series of attacks on Sophie's farm? And did the Danburys still have something to do with it? Until they were all caught Annette knew none of this made sense.

And no one was safe yet either.

Chapter Twenty

Sophie had been right. The next morning, Tristan was the only person who showed up for work. The RCMP questioned him, but he was adamant that he hadn't known Marcus or Rosa prior to meeting them on the ranch. Everyone had given a statement, in particular, Annette. The police officer told them that a massive search was underway for Rosa and Marcus. Fortunately, Annette could provide them with a picture of Rosa—taken from when she'd been riding Trixie. They could only describe Marcus as there were no pictures of him.

The three women sat around Sophie's kitchen table, cradling mugs of coffee.

"We can only hope the RCMP are successful, and it ends soon," Sophie said. "I'd like an explanation. More than that I'd like my cow and my barn back and all the money I've spent returned. It was all so needless." She looked toward the window where plumes of black smoke still rose from the wet, smoldering embers. "After all this, the Triple T will have to be sold in order to cover my bills.

There's no way I can afford to build a new barn, and this winter I'll need one."

"What about the arena? Couldn't you use that?" Gabrielle asked. "And aren't the horses Rosa was training worth a lot of money?

"It's true that the horses will fetch a few thousand, but I'm talking about figures upward of $120,000.00. There's no way I have enough money to build a barn comparable to the one I had. Or even take out a loan for one. And the arena is not equipped to calve out cattle. It would take so much renovation…" Her voice trailed away. Then she lifted her hands in a gesture of defeat. "I'm so sorry to burden you with all this. What a terrible holiday…"

"I'm glad we're here," said Annette. "Where else could I have gone where there was a mystery to be solved, or where I could learn to ride a horse, or wrestle people to the ground?"

Sophie reached across the table and squeezed her hand. "Thank you, my dear." She sighed and leaned back in her chair. "In any case, I'm seriously thinking about calling Jim Danbury."

At that moment, an imperious knock came at the door. Sophie almost spilled her coffee. Setting it down, she scurried to the window, peeked out, and turned an ashen face back to the girls.

"Speak of the devil," she said, lifting a hand to cover her mouth. "It's him."

Annette and Gabrielle both hurried to the door behind Sophie as she opened it to the man in question. She held the door for him to enter and his considerable bulk loomed in the opening.

He cleared his throat, readying himself to make an

announcement and hastily took off his lopsided straw hat as though just remembering his manners.

"I'm here to make you an offer you can't refuse," he said in a booming voice.

Sophie held up a protesting hand and the girls stepped forward to offer their support as she asked the man to leave.

"I appreciate yo—"

He cut her off abruptly by raising his voice over hers. "Hear me out is all I ask."

He moved inside and turned to shut the door. Before he got it closed, however, the group heard the spluttering roar of a tractor being started and several other engines firing up. A horn honked and suddenly loud voices filled the air.

"What is 'appening out there?" Sophie said, trying to edge past the burly man and get to the door.

"Never you mind," Jim barked. He brandished his hat and nearly knocked a picture off the wall. It swung back and forth crazily as they all waited for the man to continue. Narrowing his eyes, he advanced further into the room and the women all backed up together.

"My offer is this," he said, puffing out his chest. "I propose to do the neighbourly thing after all these years. My father thought a lot of your husband's folks and I aim to reconcile our two families by organizing a barn raising and doin' all I can to help you out. I'm real sorry you lost Malcom. Don't think I ever told you that or came to pay my respects. I, uh, I humbly apologize. Consider it done." Jim put a finger under his collar and pulled to relieve the pressure his vast neck created. "I've been payin' for my son Dillon to take night classes at the college in carpentry. Guess that'll come in handy now." Jim inclined his head as far as possible and pressed himself against the wall in order to usher the women past him. "Now let's go outside," he ended graciously.

With a little manoeuvring, they shuffled past him and stepped onto the porch. And they stopped.

The yard, indeed even the driveway back as far as could be seen, was filled with trucks. Lumber filled each truck bed or was loaded on flat deck trailers being pulled behind. Men and women swarmed all over. They were busy unloading wood and piling it. Some were organizing groups already carrying toolboxes to begin building. A bulldozer was hard at work clearing the ashes of the burned barn into piles, its metal tracks unaffected by the heat of the still-red coals lying below the ash. Another tractor was dumping the gathered debris into the back of a gravel hauling truck.

Sophie fell back into a chair on the porch and gaped at the scene. Helplessly she looked up at Gabrielle and Annette, tears streaming down her face. People, seeing her, called out, expressed their sympathies, or waved, but all of them continued on their mission to rebuild Sophie's barn.

Annette looked for Jeff. He was nowhere to be seen, which she thought was odd. Another vehicle pulled carefully through the maze of automobiles. It stopped, almost in the rose bushes and out hopped Sandra.

"Don't you start worrying about feeding all these people," she called, opening the back door of her van. "I've got that covered. A few of the ladies, the owners of *Lulu's Café* and I got together this morning and made enough food to get us through a famine." She began to carry a box up the steps and, as though she'd been in a daze, Annette suddenly came to life.

"I'll help," she cried. Gabrielle, laughing with joy, followed her sister and the two of them spent the rest of the afternoon in the kitchen with three other ladies from the district, preparing meals.

The camaraderie and sense of community was outstanding. Annette had never seen anything like it. By dinnertime that evening the cement floor of the barn was clean and the bare bones of four walls stood waiting for more construction the next day.

Folding tables had materialized from somewhere and the whole community sat on the grass or in collapsible chairs eating and laughing.

And in the midst of this scene of brotherly love, a big black truck pulled up. It was Jeff. She'd wondered all day where he might be. It was strange that he hadn't come to lend a hand. Seeing him, Annette's heart leapt. She stood to her feet, as did Sophie, and they walked together to greet him until suddenly the passenger door was thrown open and a tall young man jumped out. Sophie stopped. A strangled cry erupted from her throat, and she flung herself at him.

"Mom!" he cried. Rushing forward he wrapped his arms around Sophie and lifted her off her feet. "Oh Mom, I've missed you so much."

Standing on her tiptoes, Sophie kissed his face over and over. She'd pull back for a moment, holding his cheeks in her hands to look at him as though reassuring herself he was real, and then pulled him into her arms again.

The assembled crowd cheered and clapped. Sophie, her face rosy and wet with tears of joy, pulled him over to Gabrielle and Annette.

"It's Jayke," she said, her voice wobbling. "My boy 'as come home."

"I'm so 'appy you are 'ere," Annette said. Stepping close she kissed his cheeks, as did Gabrielle who looked ecstatic.

"It's great to see you, Jayke," Gabrielle said. "You could not 'ave come at a better time."

"That's thanks to Jeff," he said, turning to include the man waiting so as not to intrude on the family reunion. "I was planning on driving out when I got Mom's letter, but when Jeff called and said I needed to catch the next plane, I came right away. He was waiting when I arrived."

Jeff's eyes found hers and for a moment, Annette felt shy. Her emotions were rather raw and new. She was unsure if she should hug Jeff or wait to see what happened. He took the decision out of her hands. His eyes were dark with emotion as he swept her into his arms and kissed her for all the world to see. And the crowd once again cheered.

Flushed and smiling, Annette looked out on them all, feeling part of a community she'd never known existed.

Later that evening, she and Jeff rocked back and forth on the porch swing, sitting as close as two people possibly could. As the sun sank behind the mountains, they had talked of their childhood dreams, their interests, and even one or two past romances. She even told him of the call she'd received from *Musée d'Orsay*. He showed interest and encouraged her aspirations.

"So, you were never attracted to Rosa?" Annette asked. "I thought I saw you kiss her one night."

He looked surprised and shook his head. "I've never even touched the woman," he asserted strongly. "She, of course, touched me every chance she got. The woman wasn't shy. I knew exactly what she was hoping for." His face took on a sour expression. "Oh, she's cute enough, I guess, and she was good with horses. I can, however, say no.

I was never attracted to Rosa. I didn't give her any indication I was interested either."

Annette was pleased.

He lifted her hand to his lips and kissed it. "I have to apologize for my rude behavior when you first arrived," he said ruefully. "It was a mixture of worry for Sophie and irritation that she hadn't said anything to anyone about what was happening. I didn't think she ought to have allowed guests to visit."

"It's true." Annette shuffled uncomfortably. "I thought the same thing myself. I even suggested to Gabrielle that we return to France the next day."

"I'm grateful you didn't. Did I tell you yet how proud and in awe I am of you?" he asked, sliding an arm around her shoulders, and pulling her close.

She laid her head on his shoulder. "About five times," she said. "You can say it again if you'd like though."

"Good, because I intend to do just that. I'm so amazed that you persevered until you learned who was behind all the attacks. And that you went into a burning building for Pearl is beyond amazing." He caught her lips for a kiss, then pulled back and sobered. "Jessica would be so grateful, and so am I."

"You're both welcome," she said softly. "I love Pearl too."

"I need to know one thing," he said, suddenly turning to her with a serious expression. "Did you, or did you not, talk your sister into riding over to the Danburys that night? And did you actually spy on them from their own yard?"

Annette swallowed the wrong way and choked. Coughing and spluttering, she was seized with guilt and covered her face with her hands. But she felt Jeff shaking with laughter beside her.

"You knew all along," she cried, giving him a shove with her shoulder. They laughed together.

"It will remain our little secret," he promised solemnly. "Jim will never know. He and Dillon turned out to be decent guys after all."

Shifting around to face her, Jeff gently took her face in his hands. With infinite attention, his eyes travelled over her face as though committing every detail to memory. His thumb began a slow caress of her soft cheek.

"You," he began, with emphasis and in reference to what had just been noted of Rosa, "are not cute." Annette's eyes dropped as low as her heart at his words. She had always known it, of course. But hearing it from the lips of the man she loved was far more difficult than she could ever have imagined. Though Jeff hadn't finished speaking.

"You are the most beautiful woman I've ever seen. Your eyes are exciting. They dance with vivacity and life. They sparkle dangerously when you're angry and glow with love when you care." He touched the tip of her nose. "Your nose is sweet and pretty with its dusting of freckles and your mouth…" He paused to kiss her tenderly. "Your mouth is like a pink Christmas bow just waiting to be kissed, yet strong and determined when the need arises." Next he took a lock of her corkscrew auburn hair and let it run through his fingers. "Yes, your mane of hair is gorgeous, and I love it, but your face—I will never be able to stop telling you how beautiful you are."

Tears brimmed in her eyes. She blinked, willing them to disappear. Instead, they spilled over and trickled down her flushed cheeks.

"Honey," he said tenderly. "What is it? Are you okay? Is it the stress from the fire? Of this week?" He gathered her into his arms, and she drew a deep shuddering breath against his chest.

"No one has ever said such things to me before," she managed at last.

"I find that hard to believe," he said in surprise, leaning back to search her face. "You are stunning! I'm sorry if what you say is true, but you had better get used to hearing it because I intend to tell you every day how lovely you are. I have seen the real you," he said, holding her closer and whispering into her ear. "The woman you are on the inside is as wonderful as the woman people can see outwardly. I see your creativity and artistic nature, your care for defenseless creatures to the degree that you'd risk your own life for them, your devotion to family, your sense of justice and right from wrong, so much that you'd ride a horse in the dead of night to try to discover the truth and to help save your friend. I see this and so much more, dearest Annette. You are a remarkable, gorgeous woman. Never forget it."

Annette's hands crept around his neck and spread across his strong back. Even though there were many things she could say about him too, she was beyond speaking at the moment. She sniffed and strove to bring her emotions under control.

"And now," he pulled back to smile into her eyes, "I'd like to ask you out on a proper date. Should we go buy you a dress? I have a fabulous restaurant in mind that's in the city. What do you say? Will you go with me tomorrow night?"

She nodded. A wobbly smile breaking through her tears. "I—I don't need to buy a dress. Remember, I came prepared for parties."

He laughed and pulled her close again. "So, you did," he said. "Then tomorrow night is ours."

Chapter Twenty-One

Just as the first shaft of sunlight slanted through Annette's window, she heard trucks pulling up to stop in the yard and the barn building began again. It was unbelievable. The way people had gathered together in this time of crisis to help out a fellow human being and neighbour was a testament to the goodness of mankind. Annette was used to the impersonality of a city and its inhabitants. Where you nodded to your neighbour without ever knowing their name. People minded their own business to the degree that life became narrow and self-centered. She loved her city. Yet this was something special.

She looked outside at the beehive of activity and realized it was going to be a hot day. Finally, she could bring out a summery outfit and take a little more time with her appearance. After all, Jeff thought she was beautiful.

Dressing in a Boho style, cold-shoulder top with wide ruffled trim, in a print of apricot and rust-coloured flowers, cut-off jean shorts, and a gold necklace with a heart-shaped locket given to her by her parents, she made her way downstairs to find Sophie pacing the floor. The older woman had her hands folded as if in supplication with her head bowed. When Annette entered the room Sophie ran to her, her face flooding with happiness.

"I have the most marvelous news," she cried in French "The police just rang. They captured Rosa and Marcus on the highway between Calgary and Edmonton during the night and this morning the two of them broke down and confessed to everything."

"*Oh la la*," Annette's shoulders sagged with relief.

"The wealthy landowner and oil magnate from northern Alberta, who was buying the heifers, was behind it all. It turns out he is Rosa's father, and Marcus is her boyfriend, not a cousin. I believe she was after Jeff solely in order to gain control of his ranch too. She would have discarded him in the end. Apparently this man, Weaver, is accustomed to getting what he wants, and when he wants it. He took a fancy to my ranch and decided he would have it at any cost. He has been buying up huge tracts of land all over the province with no regard to people or property. When I wouldn't sell, his daughter and her fiancé were pressed into doing his dirty work. He also offered a huge amount of money to the men who had been working for me. Which is why they left without notice. I suppose money talks." She sighed. "Weaver thought to drive me from my home, but thanks to you, Gabrielle and my dear friends, he failed and will now pay with time in jail."

"It's the sort of bizarre story you only hear about on the news," Annette mused. "Not something that happens so close to home."

"Exactly," Sophie continued. "Rosa admitted she harboured some wild notion that she could win Jeff over and secure 'is ranch for their evil use too. It's shocking what people will do for possessions or wealth."

Impulsively, Annette hugged the older woman. "This is wonderful," she said. "He will be brought to justice and his greedy monopoly will end."

Sophie nodded gleefully. "But that's not the best part," she said mysteriously. "Jayke and I talked last night. He wants to be here with me and run the ranch. It was a case of miscommunication between us, but it's all been solved. He always wanted to take over the ranch one day, but felt that perhaps it wasn't what I wished to happen."

"Oh Sophie," Annette breathed. "This couldn't be better." She clapped her hands with delight. "He will settle down here with you and you won't have to worry or struggle alone anymore."

"Yes," the woman laughed. "My heart overflows with happiness this morning." She dropped into a chair at the table and patted the one next to her. "Come sit down and tell me what's happening with you and Jeff. Well, only if you want to, of course," she amended.

"I'm not really sure about the future," Annette confessed. "As you know, Gabrielle and I are leaving in two days' time. For now, I am just happy to have met him and…"

Sophie interrupted with a sly smile. "You love him, don't you?"

Annette lifted a shoulder. "Can someone fall in love that fast?" she asked. "It seems impossible to me. I know I've never felt this way before, but…"

"You can," Sophie said, shifting her gaze to somewhere beyond Annette. A faraway look glazed her eyes and a long moment passed before she spoke again. "It happened to me. Malcom and I met in France while he was on a school trip. We were both very young—but somehow we knew. Over the course of only two days, we fell in love. After he returned home, I came here to see if what we had was real. We were married not long afterwards, and our love lasted a lifetime. I stayed on this ranch and made a life with him that was filled with bliss." She stopped and turned to Annette. "Could you live in Canada?"

"I don't know," Annette answered truthfully. "I haven't been asked. I attended university with very different dreams in mind and have applied for work in Paris."

Sophie nodded her head sagely. "Life has a way of changing our plans," she said. "Sometimes it is for the better, and sometimes for the worse. We have little say in the matter when our hearts are involved." She leaned forward and patted Annette's hand. "You must do what is right for you and everything else will fall into place."

"Thank you. You're an inspiration to me, Sophie."

Annette thought of the older woman's words all day as she worked side by side with her sister, Sandra, and Sophie. They fed the crowds outside, and helped out wherever they could. Perhaps it didn't bear thinking about, considering Jeff hadn't asked her for anything permanent. Maybe, to him, their relationship was a summer romance and nothing more. Honestly, he didn't seem like that sort of man, but she'd been wrong before.

As the time drew closer for their date, she became nervous. It felt like ages since she'd dressed as she loved to do. What would Jeff think of it? Perhaps he was used to women in jeans and would find her style frivolous or self-absorbed. Still, she knew she was not the same woman who had boarded the plane in Paris only a week ago.

By five o'clock, Sophie and Gabrielle shooed her away from helping any further. She went quickly upstairs to shower and change. With a towel wrapped around her head, and a fuzzy red bathrobe tied at her waist, she fingered the lilac dress in the closet. Jeff thought her beautiful, she reminded herself. Surely he would like this. Yet, she was worried.

Carefully she applied a light shimmering shadow to her lids, a glossy lipstick, and mascara to enhance her almond-shaped eyes. She took extra time with her mane of glossy hair and then slipped into the dress.

It was as flattering as she'd remembered. Pale lilac tulle overlaid a mid-length, A-line skirt that cinched around her small waist. It was cut in a halter-neck style, leaving the delicate curve of her shoulders bare. The most dramatic effect was where the tulle came up under her throat and tied at the nape of her neck in a trailing bow with a sheer tulle back. It was so feminine and pretty. She slipped on the matching heels and twirled in front of the mirror. Perfect. A pair of dangly pearl earrings, a spritz of perfume, and she was ready. Would he like it?

Someone tapped on her door and then opened it a crack. "Jeff is downstairs," Gabrielle whispered, sticking her head inside. "And he is one hot looking man tonight." Her mouth fell open at the sight of Annette standing in her lilac dress and she whistled. "You are going to knock him dead," she exclaimed. "I feel like I should stand at the top of the stairs and announce you."

Annette giggled and swept past her. The deep timbre of Jeff's voice floated up to her and her heart caught in her throat as she tapped down the old wooden stairs in her stilettoes. The voices stopped.

As she came into view, she saw Jeff waiting for her. He

wore all black. From the button-up shirt, straining across his broad muscled chest and shoulders, to the matte black jacket, to the narrow fit of his black jeans, he was the most handsome man Annette had ever seen. His usual dusty, black hat had been changed for a new one and the silver belt buckle at his waist shone in the lamplight. He looked serious and a bit nervous.

However, it was his reaction to her that made her heart thrill. He yanked off his hat and tossed it to one side, ran a hand through his curly hair and stepped toward her.

"I'm almost afraid to touch you…" he said in a voice that cracked. "*Tu es très, très belle,*" he announced in a perfect French accent. He took her by the hand and twirled her around to admire every angle. "I don't know how I deserve to be with such a wonderful woman as you." His thumb drew a circle on her palm and his dark eyes gazed into her own.

"You spoke French," she said, feeling pleased he'd made the effort.

"Your sister was kind enough to school me. Shall we go?"

He grabbed his hat and held out his arm. She took it, feeling like the most beautiful woman in the world. Although Jeff's truck sat waiting, he paraded her past it. It was quiet outside. Everyone who had come to work had since gone home. They walked silently along the path past the piles of lumber, the skeleton of a barn that was taking shape with every passing hour, and the hopes and dreams of the new and improved Triple T Ranch.

They came to the corral where Pearl stood with her head lifted, ears perked, and eyes fixed on the distant mountains. He whistled and she trotted to them. Reaching into his pocket, Jeff brought out a carrot and gave the treat to the mare who crunched it happily.

"Do you always walk around with garden vegetables on hand?" she asked, a smile lurking at the corners of her mouth.

"Only for special occasions," he said. "I just thought she should be here." He took Annette by the hands and turned her to face him. "I want to thank you for coming to Canada, for what you've done for Sophie, for me—and for Jessica," he said, looking deep into her eyes. She started to open her mouth to say that it had been her pleasure, but he touched the tip of his finger to her lips.

"Most of all I want to say that I love you. I think I fell in love with you the first time you tried to get into the saddle and took a leap of faith that flattened me into the dirt. You're wonderful. You're beautiful in the midst of a storm, battling a fire, or dressed like a princess..." He took a breath. Her heart felt as though it might leap right out of her chest. Could this be happening? It was like a fantasy.

"We've only known one another a week and maybe I shouldn't be saying this, but I can't help myself." He lifted her hands and kissed them in turn. "You have a life in France, and a possible job that you trained hard for and would love. I'd never try to stop you from following your dreams, but...if you ever, I mean ever wanted to trade it in for a life in the wilds of Canada with a man who loves you from the depths of his heart, then I am here..." His voice broke and he cleared his throat. "I'm asking you to marry me."

She looked into his face and realized she wanted to wake up beside him every day. She wanted to go for rides with him on her dear Pearl. She wanted to feel the pine-scented winds that blew down from the mountains on her face and stand beside him through good times and bad. She already loved Canada, but most of all she loved him.

"We've only known one another a week," she started off by repeating his words. "Yet in that time my world has been turned upside-down." She took his hands and placed them on her waist. "It's so much better than I ever could have imagined. I believe it was destiny that brought us together. Love knows no bounds of time or space. I love you, Jeff… and yes, I would stay and build my life with you here happily."

With a cry that was very nearly a sob, Jeff pulled her to him and found her mouth in a kiss that sealed their love for a lifetime.

Epilogue

They were married in September, beneath the red and orange leaves of maples that grew in profusion along the south side of Sophie's back yard. It was a clear, crisp autumn day and the scene had been set with baskets of sunflowers and a bower woven from red willow branches threaded with white roses.

Although Andrew, Gabby's husband, was changing in the room next door, Gabrielle and Annette dressed together in the tiny room with the slanted ceiling she'd slept in over the last few months as she and Jeff grew to love one another even more. It was cramped with the two of them together, but they wouldn't have it any other way.

Annette hadn't seen her sister in the months following their holiday and it had been a tearful reunion when she had picked up Gabrielle and Andrew at the airport the day before. She thought back to that blissful moment.

"We 'ave so much to talk about," Annette had said, squeezing her sister tight before kissing her brother-in-law on the cheeks in *les bisous*, the French way. "And I can't wait for you to see my dress."

"Designer?" Gabrielle teased.

Annette laughed. "Uh, no. Those days are done and good riddance to them. I still love pretty clothes, but they aren't as important to me now. I want to tell you that I start work at a prestigious art gallery in Calgary after Jeff and I return from our honeymoon."

"Oh! That's wonderful," Gabrielle's eyes widened with pleasure.

"Congratulations!" Andrew exclaimed. "You're going to have the best of both worlds. I'm so happy for you."

"*Merci beaucoup*. Tell me what 'as been 'appening in Paris?"

"We have some news for you too," said Andrew with a loving look at his wife. He still wore his cowboy hat on the streets of Paris, and tipped it back on his head now, but had adopted the language and customs as his own. The wine shop was doing well, and their marriage was a union that brought them both much joy. Annette was happy to see it.

She looked at them now, and at her sister who was positively radiant with happiness. "No?" she said, angling her head and looking from one to the other. They stopped beside her vehicle in the airport parking lot, and she looked at them in shock. "Really?"

"Yes!" Gabrielle chortled, patting her flat stomach. "We're almost four months along although you'd never know it. The baby is due at the end of February—Aunt Annette." She beamed.

Annette hugged and kissed them both again.

"This is brilliant news," she exclaimed. "It's almost hard to contain so much happiness."

She came back to the present with a sigh and looked

past her sister to the new red barn out Sophie's window. Cars and trucks were parked in an orderly fashion. Guests were making their way in laughing groups to the chairs that had been arranged earlier in the day by Jeff and Jayke. All of their neighbours had been invited to the festivities and more than two hundred people were expected to attend. Good thing the sky was cloudless and bright, otherwise they'd have been trudging through the sand of a training arena to be wed.

Still, she thought with a little flip of her head, that would have been okay too. As long as her beloved Jeff was the groom, she would have married him in a swamp. Walking to the closet, she slid her dress off the hanger and stepped into the rustling folds. Gabrielle helped pull it into place and used the satin ribbons to lace it together at the back.

She surveyed herself in the full-length mirror with satisfaction. It didn't matter to her if the whole world thought her plain and her sister beautiful, as long as one man believed her to be the most gorgeous woman on the face of the earth. Jeff knew her soul.

She adjusted the thick, lacy off-the-shoulder straps and admired the tight bodice and full A-line skirt covered in floral lace. It was exactly what she had always envisioned for herself—just not on a cattle ranch in the Rocky Mountains' foothills. That part was better than she could have dreamed.

Her long auburn hair shone in the sunlight like liquid fire. She had decided to leave it loose and only added some elegant diamonds, that Jeff had bought her, to her throat and ears. Gabrielle appeared in the mirror beside her, and she stepped aside. Her sister was gorgeous, as usual, in a form-fitted ruby-red dress with a full skirt. It was, perhaps, a little tighter than intended around the middle, but no one would ever guess her precious secret.

"Come here," Gabrielle said, and Annette moved back into the mirror's reflection. The two women stared at themselves. "Talk about something good coming out of something bad," she continued. "You are a living testament to the saying."

"It's true. Now, I want to get married."

Holding up their skirts, they swished downstairs. Annette's parents were waiting in the living room to walk her down an aisle strewn with fall leaves and flowers. Strains of violin music echoed through the house. When the music changed, Gabrielle winked at Annette. She was ready to lead them down the aisle as her matron of honour.

"Are you ready, my love?" asked her father, holding out his arm. He was resplendent in a dark suit and red tie. He kissed his daughters' cheeks four times and blinked hard.

"I am." She gave her other arm to her mother, looking lovely in a gold brocade dress suit. Her golden hair was pulled into a chic chignon and her lovely face, so like Gabrielle's, was wreathed in smiles.

With a final kiss for the bride, Gabrielle took her bouquet of white roses and led the way out the back door.

They followed, walking between rows and rows of familiar faces who stood to smile and wish the happy couple well. But Annette only had eyes for Jeff.

He waited for her in a black suit with his black hat. His teeth flashed white in his usual dark stubble and his eyes promised her the love she'd always dreamed of having. Even as she slowly exited the house he was stretching out his hands. 'Come to me, my love and let us begin a lifetime of happiness,' he mouthed.

And she did.

With Love From Paris

Years later, Jeff led the way through a grove of poplars on a frosty morning in December. He rode his horse, Champ, while Annette brought up the rear on Pearl. Their seven-year-old twins, Anna and Jessica, rode between them on ponies. The snow was powdery and sparkled in the noonday sun. The horses' breath puffed in white clouds as they trudged along, watching for the tracks of wild animals.

"I'm cold Daddy," Jessica's pinched little voice came from behind the heavy red scarf muffled around her neck. Her cheeks peeked out too, rosy with cold.

"What do you say we stop for a while and build a fire?" Jeff asked. "I think Mum and I might just have some cocoa and sandwiches in our saddlebags."

More by Helen Row Toews

vinci-books.com/theawakening

Can one troubled teen save a magical realm on the brink of darkness?

Kayden Bramley is having the worst year of his life. New town, new school, and now he's stuck caring for his sick grandmother. But when a mysterious stranger reveals that Kayden is the last hope for an endangered magical land, his grandmother confirms the shocking truth. Armed with his Runestaff and newfound courage, Kayden embarks on a perilous quest to claim his heritage and defend a land under siege.

Turn the page for a free preview…

The Awakening: Chapter One

A storm was brewing, but it was no mere tempest. Edged in purple, the boiling black clouds swirled ominously over Respiele's lair. Durgot knew it signalled the beginning of war, and the end of life as he knew it in his beloved land of Erinbourne. Unless, somehow, it could be stopped.

A sigh escaped his lips as he bent over the old wooden table in his home within the mountain portal, scrawling ancient script onto a thick sheet of yellowed paper:

> *Alainea is alive, yet I fear she is gravely ill and unable to heed the summons. Despite these ominous tidings, I leave at once for the Southern Portal of our realm to secure aid from the boy. The Gemstone of Power will be restored to our King.*
>
> *We shall not fail. Preserve all faith.*
>
> *DF*

He considered the assurances he had written. The

words sounded far more confident than he felt. What sort of boy was this Kayden? Could he be convinced as to the urgency of their quest, or of the part he was destined to play in it?

And, though Kayden had Alainea's eyes, would her genes run strong enough within the young man to fit him for this task? Could he withstand the hardships that lay ahead? At this point, he was the only hope they had.

Erinbourne was in peril.

Stroking his beard in agitation, Durgot blew on the page to dry the ink, rolled it tightly, and reached for his cloak and travelling bag that hung from a hook in his warm kitchen. He then grasped the runestaff that was never far from his hand and shut the door soundlessly behind him, before descending the long flight of stairs down to the ground. There was little light, as thick woolen clouds had obscured the semblance of a moon, but he knew the trails within the hollowed-out center of the mountain where he lived and had no need of it.

He came at last to his north door, an impenetrable sheet of marble fitted into the rock that led to Erinbourne. Digging a hand deep into his coat pocket, he withdrew a large, ornate key, turned it in the lock, and pulled.

The massive door swung back. Durgot caught it before it opened too far and leaned in expectantly. A huge, hulking figure waited for him in darkness. Its eyes, gleaming like flaming embers, the only sign of its presence within the cavern.

"Ah, my old friend." Durgot breathed into the still night air. "Thank you for coming. I am off straightaway to the other side. Deliver this missive to the Resistance and waste no time in your return." He placed the scroll into the creature's paw.

"If the boy returns with me, he will most certainly need your aid," Durgot said. "We shall, I hope, meet you here three nights hence."

As the creature turned to leave, the moon skidded into view, illuminating the long, gleaming spines that covered its body before it melted into the inky darkness of the cave and disappeared.

With a sigh, Durgot leaned back away from the entrance, and pushed the door into place. Locking it, he shifted his pack, took up his runestaff, and retraced his steps back along the path to the south side of his mountain home, where he opened an identical door with another, elaborately fashioned key.

This door had not been unlocked in many, many years and protested with a squeal as he tugged it wide. Durgot stopped, willing the sound to cease, and hoping no one was there to have heard the loud screech of the ancient hinges.

He knew the enemy was actively searching for him and the portal that had been laid into the rocky edge of Durgot's mountain since time began. They desired access to the hidden world outside their own in order to find the Gem of Power.

However, as he listened, Durgot heard nothing amiss. He slipped through the doorway, pulled it shut, and locked it behind him. There was still a lengthy distance to cover before reaching the last great portal between his realm and the one where he would find the boy.

Allowing himself to make use of the wavering light provided by the image of a sickle moon on his runestaff, Durgot navigated the steep, rocky steps down to the Enchanted River and crossed to the other side of it using the magic of his staff. He moved briskly across the bridge he had created, not looking at the dark waves licking the wood beneath his feet. Tugging his cloak tighter against the chill, he picked his way along a roughly hewn passageway carved into the solid rock. Condensation from the river had made the channel slippery and treacherous, and the footing was poor. Though slow, each step he took led him deeper into the recesses of the rock and closer to his goal.

Later, he emerged into a small, circular chamber which marked the entrance to Kayden's world. Durgot paused to gather himself. Much was riding upon this first meeting and time was running out.

Was the lad too young to understand?

Lifting his runestaff, Durgot turned it until he could see the engraved image of a mountain. Concentrating on the carving, he watched as it began to emit a shimmering light near his hand. He knew the moment to strike was near. The staff, used in this way, was the only means to open the portal, but he had not done it in many years. Durgot moved closer to the wall, traced his fingers along the rock, searching for the cleverly concealed niche that released the gateway between their worlds.

There it was.

He drew back and with all his strength, struck the niche with his staff. A hollow sound reverberated in the room and then, in a shard of silver light, a crevice split open along the rock face. It grew and widened, snapping and crackling with energy until Durgot stepped through the blazing Southern Portal, and in the sudden breeze, gathered his billowing cloak around him.

Behind him, the great portal slammed shut as though it had never been there at all.

Durgot fixed his gaze on the twinkling lights of a farmhouse through the distant trees ahead.

"We shall soon see," he said.

The Awakening: Chapter Two

The school day had been awful. Kayden kicked gravel along the driveway as he hashed it over in his mind, wishing for the hundredth time it was Friday instead of Thursday, and that Emerson High was closed for the weekend.

Tenth grade would have been a piece of cake back home in Toronto. Here, it was torture. His thoughts drifted back to how good life had been such a short time ago when school let out for the summer in the city. If only he could just go back.

He spotted his father repairing a corral. After climbing a few rungs of the nearest fence Kayden hollered, "Mom called to say she has to work late!"

His dad straightened, vaguely waving a hammer in acknowledgement before turning back to the broken wood rails. Work was all either of Kayden's parents had done since he and his family arrived on his grandparents' ranch two months ago, to save it from ruin. It was another one of the changes that had made life so horrible.

Kayden glared at the Rocky Mountains, glowing in the

last moments of evening light. *I hate it here*, he thought, trudging along a well-worn cow path past the corrals. He used to love spending summers on his grandparents' ranch, but all that changed when he was forced to live here, for good. First Gramps had died several years earlier, and then, just before summer started; Gran had a stroke. The ranch wasn't the same without them. Every day he worried about her and whether she'd recover enough to return home.

Another part of his frustration was thanks to the harassment he was getting at his new school. His first day there couldn't have gone worse. Tripping over a chair in the lunchroom, and spilling chocolate milk on Dillon, the biggest bully of all time, just as the boy was trying to impress a girl, was not cool. Dillon had made Kayden's life miserable ever since.

Back home in Toronto, Kayden had always been a bit of a loner, but he'd had one good friend at least. Now, he had no one.

He'd been active in sports too and played a lot of baseball before they moved. He was their best pitcher and a respected member of the team. *Would that ever happen again?* He swatted at weeds that flourished next to the fence line.

Then, to top it all off, he'd just gone on his first date *ever*, with the prettiest girl in the school, before they'd sold their house and moved.

Yet, these feelings of resentment and anger were emotions he couldn't share; there was enough of a burden for his parents, without him adding to it.

Pausing at the tree line, Kayden swiveled around to consider his father's childhood home. The ranch, nestled in the Rocky Mountain foothills, had always been a great place to visit when Gran was around.

It was a nice enough setting: a large, white, two-story

house with a sprawling veranda, an old red barn set near the road, and various other smaller sheds where livestock sheltered during the harsh Canadian winter. It was pretty, and who could complain about the beauty of the Rockies? They were gorgeous neighbours.

Still, scenery wasn't the problem.

Sighing, he spun around and marched along a path through a thick bluff of poplars. He frowned from beneath the auburn hair that fell in an untidy tangle across his face and gave his head a practiced flick. Haircuts, along with many other aspects of the life he'd always known, had fallen by the wayside since his family had left their life out east.

Around a bend, he emerged into a small clearing. The peace and solitude of the place had drawn him ever since stumbling upon it. Since then, he'd spent many hours reading, or just sitting and thinking upon a vast boulder at its center, a remnant left behind from the last great ice age.

Yet, something felt different today. The air was strange —it seemed darker and heavier as he pressed forward. He glanced toward the stone and froze. Someone was perched on top of it.

Kayden took a step back.

"Do not depart. I have been waiting for you," the shadowy figure said.

Kayden remained fixed in place as the person continued in clipped tones, "Be assured I mean you no harm, young sir. Please step forward, that I may articulate without fear of curious ears."

As Kayden continued to stand, feeling shocked, the unknown person gave a long, drawn-out sigh, before the voice floated across to Kayden once more. "I simply wish to speak to you without raising my voice. Can you come closer?"

Kayden found his feet carrying him toward the speaker, whether compelled by curiosity or some other strange force, he wasn't sure. As he drew level with the rock, he noted with further surprise that this was quite an odd-looking person. It was an elderly man with long, grey, unkempt hair and an equally untidy beard, who sat staring towards the faraway peaks with a long, intricately carved stick held tight in his hand.

He was dressed strangely, in a long coat of pale blue that trailed down over the rock and flapped slightly in the breeze. Trousers of the same material ballooned out from beneath the coat and hung in folds around his ankles giving him the appearance of a boy trying to wear his father's clothes, while a wide-brimmed, navy-blue hat balanced atop his head.

Although an unusual figure, he seemed harmless enough until he fixed Kayden with a piercing gaze from bright amber eyes set in a lined face.

Kayden wilted under this scrutiny as though his very thoughts were being measured. Unconsciously, he straightened his shoulders and stared back.

"This is private property," he said with indignation. "What do you think you're doing here?"

"I know well the current keeper of this land," the man said, an unexpected smile forming across his face. He tilted his head to one side and slid from the stone, belying his advanced years. "I perceive a similar intrepid tendency. This is good."

The man who dropped to earth before him could not have topped four feet. Kayden stood a head and shoulders taller than the stranger, but still felt oddly humbled, as though he were in the presence of someone significant.

"Allow me to introduce myself, young Kayden. I am

Durgot Flandish, Keeper of the Southern Portal, and your servant as in times of old." He bowed low.

Resuming his scrutiny of Kayden, he continued, "Time constraints will not allow reminiscences here, but yes, I knew both of your grandparents many years ago, and have been truly grieved at your grandmother's current misfortune. However, the present time calls for expeditious action and, as her descendant, you must answer the call in her stead."

"The call?" Kayden repeated, shaking his head as if to clear his mind of this strange scene that played out before him. "And how do you know my name?"

"You shall have answers," Durgot said, and then waved his arm dismissively, "but we are short on time and there is much to relay."

Kayden sensed the seriousness of the situation—whatever it was.

"Alainea, I mean, your grandmother is unwell?" It was more of a statement rather than a question. After Kayden's nod of affirmation Durgot continued, "Then you must secure the Emerald without her aid."

Kayden, overcoming his initial shock, looked for a means to escape, and began to edge away. "Well, nice meeting you and all, but I should be heading home now. Don't wanna be late for supper," he mumbled.

"My dear boy! You cannot simply walk away. We are relying on you. There is no one but you to fulfill the quest." Durgot took a steadying breath. "I realize I have not properly explained my presence here. Allow me to apologize and rectify this error on my part."

Durgot stared at the mountainous skyline now dimming in the gathering dusk.

"I will be as brief as possible. In any case, it is unwise to reveal too much. I hail from the land of Erinbourne," he said, with a nod towards the distant peak, "a hidden, parallel world to your own—another dimension if you will—found by passing through the very core of that mountain. Only once, in an exceptional circumstance, was the boundary between our two worlds breached, allowing your grandfather to pass through to Erinbourne. But that is another story involving your grandmother and the great dragon, Dranich, who died in battle. It shall be told another day.

"My presence here marks the second time this portal has been opened willingly since our worlds began. I have come for a gem of great power, the Emerald to be exact, and for the one who possesses it. The Emerald belongs to the Erinbournians and must be located. It was concealed in this foreign land, by the one to whom it was entrusted long ago."

Durgot stretched his lips into a slow smile. "Namely, your grandmother."

"My Gran?" Kayden shook his head to clear it and felt ready to bolt. "My grandmother had a stroke three months ago and can't even talk." A sudden vision of Kayden's many visits to this farm over the years popped into his mind. Gran was a sweet old lady, quietly living out her uneventful life as she continued to raise cattle and farm the land after Grandad's death. "You can't mean Gran or me," he said, backing away. "I'm leaving."

Durgot raised his staff. The night closed in as though a blanket had been thrown over the meadow, shutting out all light and air. Kayden felt panic rising from the pit of his stomach. He stopped and took a deep, shuddering breath.

"If you do not find the Gemstone of Power, our enemies will," came quiet words from the darkness.

Kayden tried to calm himself in the sudden gloom. Was it the stick this crazy guy was holding that darkened the clearing? It was like he'd switched off the sun. Squinting, Kayden could make out a faint glow from where he knew Durgot stood. *How did he do that?*

"What enemies and why is it my job to find your stone?" Kayden asked, playing for time as he looked around him in the darkness, straining to spot something, anything familiar, so he could see the path to get home.

"I realize our meeting here must seem quite extraordinary to you, even frightening, but you need not fear me," Durgot said. "I ask only that you lend me your ear. Charles, your grandfather, also assisted us once, long ago."

Kayden felt as though he only understood about half the words this man was using, but his tone was reassuring. Relaxing a little, he turned back to listen. As he did so, Durgot lowered his staff. The heaviness lifted and Kayden could distinguish his surroundings once more.

"The circumstances during that time were unusual to be sure," Durgot said. "Charles was not meant to be in Erinbourne, but once there, he demonstrated an astonishing ability to be close to the Gems of Power without succumbing to their...inherent power. He also showed an uncommon courage."

"However, it is your relationship to Alainea that I am most interested in," he said. "She is one of the Garde, an ancient race of people who live within the mountains. We safeguard the border between our lands. I am also a Garde. It is the way of our people that, as a sign of heritage and an indication of gift, only the first child of every second generation may be born with tawny eyes."

"You do have Alainea's eyes, do you not?" Durgot

asked, but Kayden could tell the man knew it already. "You are one of us, young Kayden, whether you have known it or want it to not be so, and as such are endowed with your grandmother's same ability, meaning several things, but mainly that her runestaff and the Emerald will respond only to..."

Kayden interrupted him. "Are you crazy? On drugs or something? My grandmother didn't come from inside some mountain! She always told us she came from, *the old country.* That means Europe, or England or something. I'm not sure what kind of trick you're trying to pull here, but I think I'd know if she came from some other world."

Kayden scowled at the little man, crossing and uncrossing his arms.

"I shall not say more of that now," Durgot said in a soothing voice. He glanced up at the last rays of sunset. "You must return to your home. No more of your time shall be taken, young Kayden, but somewhere, deep within yourself, you must feel that what I say is true. Dwell upon it lad, and then you must locate the gem."

"Are you *still* going on about that rock of yours? I've never heard Gran talk about it, or whatever that other thing is that you said was hers. And I can't ask her now." He flicked hair out of his eyes and said, more to himself than Durgot, "I have enough trouble without all this crap."

"Alainea held it in trust for us," Durgot said softly. "There has been no need of the Emerald in my land since the time of your grandparents' departure. It was best kept out of the reach of some who would seek to misuse its power. Hence, the gem has been hidden somewhere on this farm for...time passes differently here, but it must be for about sixty of your years. Once found, the Emerald must be taken through the portal, carried safely across Erinbourne, and delivered into the hands of King—"

"And how's that *my* job?" Kayden interrupted.

"Naturally, that is a simplified description," Durgot continued, as though he hadn't heard what Kayden said. "It is not a journey without risk. But…" Durgot stretched out a hand and grasped Kayden's arm, stopping his restless movements. "If you choose *not* to help us, there will be danger for you here as well. The presence of a Gemstone can be sensed, which means enemies are not long behind me in their search for it."

Durgot sighed heavily and dropped his hand away as Kayden stared at him in disbelief, "I will give you one last piece of information, by which you may know I speak the truth. Your grandmother will have her runestaff here on your farm."

Kayden threw his hands wide. "Her what?"

"It is a walking stick like my own," Durgot said, waving the sturdy pole in Kayden's face. "It will be in plain sight among her effects since it has no special significance to anyone in this place. Find it and you will see the runes, or carvings, etched into the wood, similar to the one I carry. Hold her runestaff in your hand and it will respond to you as the true Garde you are."

Kayden leaned in to inspect Durgot's staff. It was about the length of a broom handle, but sturdier. Symbols were engraved deep into the polished wood from top to bottom, but Kayden could make out only three in the dusky light: a crescent moon and a shining sun flanked the elaborately carved letters DF at the top.

"By this," Durgot said, "you may understand of what I speak, for Alainea's runestaff bears the initials AI. In Erinbourne her name was Alainea Ilstyne."

With that, the odd little fellow turned away, and Kayden knew the conversation was over. Durgot melted into the shadows. "I shall return to this place a final time, two days hence. If you accept the quest, I shall expect your presence. If not, then all is lost."

Kayden turned like an automaton and began retracing his steps back to the farmhouse in the gathering darkness, his mind racing.

Had his grandfather really helped save some other world sixty years ago? Was his grandmother honestly from some alternate dimension? Through a mountain portal? *That's crazy!*

It sounded like an excerpt from one of the books he'd read recently; a fantastic tale told by some irrational little man, certainly not real life—especially his.

"One last thing I should have told you," called a distant voice from the shadows. "The final reason you are uniquely suited for this task. Alainea's father is brother to the King of Erinbourne. You, my dear boy, are next in line to the throne."

Grab your copy…
vinci-books.com/theawakening